Elanora stepped into the street, breathing a sigh of relief at having escaped Mr. Atwater, even if she hadn't come away unscathed.

His words still rang in her ears, a death knell pealing *December twenty-fourth*. Christmas Eve. After which, she'd have two weeks to vacate the property unless... unless what? There was treasure hidden in her garden? A chest of gold doubloons in her attic? A knight in shining armor who would ride to her rescue, sweep her off her feet, cover her debt and they would live at Heartsease happily-ever-after? That's not how the world worked. It was...

Oof! She ran right into a solid wall of...man. Her gaze went up and up to broad shoulders, chocolate eyes and dark hair. The wall smiled. Recognition fluttered in the pit of her stomach. She *knew* this wall of man. It might have been years, but she'd recognize those eyes anywhere.

She whispered his name in disbelieving surprise. "Tristan. You've come home."

Author Note

This Christmas story was inspired by aspects of Dickens's Christmas stories. Everyone knows *A Christmas Carol* (1843), but did you know that Dickens wrote five Christmas stories after that, many of which continued to feature ghosts and the supernatural? One of my favorites is his 1851 essay, "What Christmas is as We Grow Older." The essay encourages us to understand how our perceptions of Christmas change over time, and to welcome the Christmases that were as opposed to mourning what never was or what can never be again. This is the theme I adopted in *The Captain Who Saved Christmas*. The story explores the nostalgia and the sadness of Christmases past, and the choices we can make for Christmases present and future. This requires Elanora and Tristan to revisit who they once were and who they are now. They have to get to know each other again, and in some ways get to know each other for the first time beyond the associations of the past. This requires no small amount of trust on both their parts. Tristan is determined to restore Elanora's faith in the magic of Christmas, and Elanora discovers that anything is possible when we lead with love during the holidays.

Research note: I did take liberties with the concept of a Christmas fair in the fictional village of Hemsford. Many Christmas fairs were primarily on the Continent and not in England itself at that time. As the industrial revolution progressed and department stores became more accessible, traveling fairs declined, but that decline would not be felt for forty or so more years.

BRONWYN SCOTT

The Captain
Who Saved Christmas

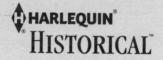

ISBN-13: 978-1-335-59570-6

The Captain Who Saved Christmas

Copyright © 2023 by Nikki Poppen

Recycling programs
for this product may
not exist in your area.

For questions and comments about the quality of this book,
please contact us at CustomerService@Harlequin.com.

Harlequin Enterprises ULC
22 Adelaide St. West, 41st Floor
Toronto, Ontario M5H 4E3, Canada
www.Harlequin.com

Printed in U.S.A.

Bronwyn Scott is a communications instructor at Pierce College and the proud mother of three wonderful children—one boy and two girls. When she's not teaching or writing, she enjoys playing the piano, traveling—especially to Florence, Italy—and studying history and foreign languages. Readers can stay in touch via Facebook at Facebook.com/bronwynwrites, or on her blog, bronwynswriting.blogspot.com. She loves to hear from readers.

Books by Bronwyn Scott

Harlequin Historical

The Art of Catching a Duke
The Captain Who Saved Christmas

Daring Rogues

Miss Claiborne's Illicit Attraction
His Inherited Duchess

The Peveretts of Haberstock Hall

Lord Tresham's Tempting Rival
Saving Her Mysterious Soldier
Miss Peverett's Secret Scandal
The Bluestocking's Whirlwind Liaison
"Dr Peverett's Christmas Miracle"
in *Under the Mistletoe*

The Rebellious Sisterhood

Portrait of a Forbidden Love
Revealing the True Miss Stansfield
A Wager to Tempt the Runaway

Visit the Author Profile page
at Harlequin.com for more titles.

For Cheryl H., who was
looking for her Christmas spirit.

Chapter One

Monday November 16, 1846, Sussex, England

For Elanora Grisham, the Christmas season was, without a doubt, the most awful time of the year, a time when the ghosts of the past pressed so near she could feel them as they brushed by and hear their whispers in her ear; a time of year when coin was much harder to come by than those unrelenting spectral visitations.

While the little village of Hemsford made merry and the merchants stocked their shelves with once-a-year delicacies, *she* would spend the next eight weeks scrambling behind the scenes to make ends meet, smiling outwardly and going through the motions born of upholding tradition so that no one guessed at the turmoil beneath the surface or the tragedy that would fall come the New Year. She would not fail those who relied on the beneficence of the Grishams. They would have peace one last year, even if that peace was at her expense; even if such peace was temporary and would not extend past

Christmas. It was all she could afford, all she had left to give them.

Elanora laid aside her pen and sat back from the writing desk. She took a moment to remove her spectacles and rub the bridge of her nose. As awful as Christmas usually was, this one would be worse. It would be the first without her brother, Teddy, and it would be the last at Heartsease, home to five generations of Grishams, but not a generation more, because somehow in the last generation, the Grishams had failed. She still hadn't worked out how or when. Had it simply been one act? Had it been Teddy's fault for mortgaging Heartsease to pay for some cargo only to have it sink to the bottom of the sea and him along with it? Or had it been a series of acts beginning with the end of the wars in 1815 when her father had made a too-late investment in an ammunitions factory. That had been the first big loss, although she'd always believed the Grishams had sailed through that until she was informed otherwise. Perhaps she'd been wrong. She was used to being wrong. Since her parents' deaths, she discovered she'd been wrong about a great many things: money, love, the magic of Christmas; illusions all.

Elanora put her spectacles back on. Christmas money wasn't going to materialise out of thin air. She was going to have to hunt for it. Sweet heavens, when had Christmas gotten so expensive? Even with careful planning and setting aside a little bit throughout the year, she was still short. Christmas was costing her 3 percent more than last year and 3 percent more than she'd budgeted for. She added the column once more and sighed. Economies would have to be made. Again.

She'd become quite proficient at that. But making economies assumed there were places to cut to begin with. Elanora scanned the list, searching for a few more luxuries that could be cast aside and found none. Where would those economies come from? Nowhere that she could see, unless she considered halving the amount given to the charities and the Boxing Day bonuses. *No*, she told herself firmly. She would not consider it, not when she knew how much people counted on those little mercies, and not when it might very well be the last time it was within her power to provide them.

A little voice in her head mocked, Might *be the last time? You know with certainty that it is. Nothing short of a financial miracle can change that. Heartsease is lost. There will be no coming back from this.*

There was only moving forward from it as best she could.

Elanora sat up a bit straighter. There was no use moping over what could not be changed. She needed to focus on the present. If there was no money to wring from the Christmas account to balance itself, then the money and economies would have to come from somewhere else. She reached for the estate's main ledger and turned to the back pages where she recorded savings. The solution became painfully obvious as she stared at the small amount written there.

She could use the money she'd set aside for Teddy's headstone. It had probably been hopelessly fanciful, after all. The amount wasn't enough for a headstone yet. She had months of saving still to reach that goal, but what she did have would balance the Christmas budget and bring joy to the people she and Teddy cared for. Teddy wasn't even in the cemetery. He'd been lost at sea along with the last hopes for the Grisham fortune. It was she who had needed it—not so much as a headstone but as a touchstone, a marker, a reminder, of the last of what her life had been, before it was diminished entirely. It would have been a place to go, a place where she could have done her remembering. Although maybe it was best not to remember. Wasn't that why she resented the ghosts? Because they weren't really ghosts? Because they were memories, reminders of what once had been? Good Lord, the ghosts were not treading lightly today.

She ran the sums one more time to check her numbers. Moving the funds would work. The dead could wait. It was the living who couldn't. The living needed their traditions and bonuses and figgy puddings. Speaking of puddings, it seemed she'd solved the financial problem in the nick of time. Elanora's ears picked up the brisk clip of the housekeeper Mrs Thornton's shoes on the hardwoods in the hall, prompt as always for their weekly meetings.

Elanora rose to meet her, finding a smile and tucking away all signs of distress. No one must know about the troubles until the last. She would not have anyone worried on her behalf. 'Mrs Thornton, please come in.' She gestured to the pair of faded rose chintz chairs set before the little fire. Mrs Thornton took her usual seat on the left, 'the housekeeper's chair,' they had dubbed it. It looked no different than the chair on the right, but Mrs Thornton had sat in *that* chair for years, serving Elanora's mother, and prior to Mrs Thornton's tenure, it had been the seat of the housekeepers gone before.

A maid came in with a tea tray and left. Elanora poured and made small talk with Mrs Thornton as was their custom before getting to business. It was the way her mother had approached these weekly meetings, and Elanora had kept the practice after her death. She listened to Mrs Thornton share a new receipt for getting stains out of table linen, the latest news of Mrs Thornton's daughter, who lived in the next village over and was expecting her second child, and the cost of groceries, which provided Mrs Thornton with the perfect segue to discuss the matters of the house.

'Stir-Up Sunday is this week,' Mrs Thornton mentioned, reaching for a seed cake. 'Cook will be wanting to buy ingredients for puddings when she goes to market and she'll want to start setting aside things for the Christmas food baskets.'

Elanora smiled politely at each request as if she wasn't madly adding up the sums in her mind. 'Of course, Mrs Thornton. Tell Cook to make her lists and I'll have funds available for her when she goes to market on Wednesday.' Which meant she'd have to go to the bank tomorrow to make the withdrawal. It was not an errand she was looking forward to for numerous reasons.

Mrs Thornton cleared her throat and asked somewhat tentatively, 'The staff want to know if the Christmas pantomime will go ahead this year.' There was a certain gentleness to the enquiry that had Elanora on alert. The panto was a long-standing tradition at Heartsease. The doors of the great house were opened to the village for an evening of food and entertainment. It was a much looked forward to festivity and a very expensive one. Did Mrs Thornton guess there were financial problems? Panic flickered in Elanora's stomach. If Mrs Thornton knew, who else might? She'd tried to be discreet, to not let on.

Elanora folded her hands in her lap and fixed Mrs Thornton with a calm stare. 'Why wouldn't it go on as usual?'

'On account of your brother, miss,' Mrs Thornton offered softly.

Ah. Teddy. She could keep her secret awhile longer. The panic receded only to be replaced by that too-familiar sense of loss. 'It's a kind thought, Mrs Thornton, but Teddy's been dead for six months and we've satisfied our mourning obligations. He loved the Christmas panto. He'd not want it set aside for something that cannot be changed. Please tell the staff to make the usual preparations.' She would not deny them the Christmas treat, especially if it was to be the last.

Mrs Thornton smiled with relief. 'Thank you, miss. Everyone will be delighted to hear it.'

Elanora rose, suddenly desperate to escape the room, the memories. It was all too much. If this was any indicator of how the rest of the season would be, she wasn't going to last. But she had to. People were counting on her even if they didn't realise it. 'If that's all, Mrs Thornton? I'll be in the garden until luncheon.'

There was solace in the garden. And peace, and life, even in the winter when it lay hidden beneath the ground, invisible. Elanora shut the wall door behind her and breathed a sigh of relief, her escape complete. *Mostly complete.* Ghosts, unlike neighbours and servants, were not respecters of walls. She had no doubt that eventually a few would follow her out. But for now, she had the garden to herself.

This had always been her place, the one spot where she could go at Heartsease that was entirely hers. Her mother especially had believed that everyone needed a spot to call their own that wasn't merely a bedroom, but a place where one could create and express themselves. For her father and Teddy it had been the stables and curating a string of the best horseflesh in Sussex. For her and her mother, it had been the garden, where they both found quiet solace from the busyness of Heartsease in the planting and growing of things. Elanora loved nothing more than to help something grow, to feel dirt beneath her fingers, to watch the brilliant shades of flowers come together in the baskets and borders she planted.

She strolled the little paths of her walled garden, her secret garden; no one was allowed here but her. Not that anyone ever attempted to come in these days. There was no one left who cared enough. A little smile teased her mouth against her better judgement. Once, though, it had been quite the game to keep Teddy and his best friend, Tristan Lennox, from her garden. She wouldn't have minded Tristan visiting the garden but she had to put up a protest on principle. It would never have done to admit having a crush on her brother's friend, not when a five-year age difference separated them. She'd been smart enough to know at fifteen that nothing could come of such an infatuation except incessant teasing and rejection.

Elanora stopped her perambulations to check the roses. They were her pride and she'd carefully put them up for the winter two weeks ago, pulling their leaves and tying the canes. She hoped she would be allowed to take a few cuttings with her when she left and she would leave strict instructions for whoever owned Heartsease next about their care. 'You'll be fine,' she reassured the roses. Somehow, she'd be fine, too. She would retire to the cottage on the edge of the property and start her roses anew in a garden that could definitely benefit from her attentions. In time, the hurt of leaving Heartsease would cease to cut so deeply; in time, she'd make a new life, and the people who depended on her would find others to depend on. Perhaps that would be a relief, although at present it felt more like worry. 'For everything there is a season,' Elanora murmured to her roses. She just wished this season wasn't one of them.

Captain Tristan Lennox halted his horse atop a rise that afforded a view of Hemsford village. Mid-November in Sussex was the absolute best time of the year, a bridge between autumn and winter; the last of the autumn leaves littered the ground in a carpet of gold, while dark branches stretched to the wintry sky, eager to don a mantle of snow—*if* Sussex should be so blessed. He drew a deep breath full of clean, cold, fresh air and satisfaction. If there was anything he loved more than frosty Sussex afternoons in November, it was a Sussex country Christmas in December. He would be home for Christmas for the first time in ten years, thanks to a strong sense of wanderlust and the rigours of a British army that was spread across an expansive empire that kept a man thousands of miles from home.

As a result of that absence, however, he'd seen some interesting Christmases abroad, but none of them matched Christmas at home. From the traditions leading up to Christmas, to the church bells at midnight and the mummers' plays on Boxing Day, he loved it all. It was a time of hope and remembrance, which made it admittedly bittersweet and complicated. And still, he revelled in it because behind the complexities, there was joy.

This year would be no exception. His best friend, Theodore Grisham, had passed away unexpectedly in the spring. He would need to pay his respects, to mourn the loss of Teddy even as he celebrated Teddy's favourite season without him. Just as two other families would be celebrating the season without their beloved sons. He patted his saddlebags, thinking of the two visits he'd need to make. Two Sussex boys in his unit had died and he'd promised to deliver their effects. There would be tears on those visits, but there would also be the quiet joy that came with celebrating a life. He would see to it. Soon. Within the week. But these first moments were time for his own homecoming.

Tristan raised a practiced eye to the grey sky, the old tremor of childhood excitement flickering as the child within him wondered: Would it snow this year? It was cold enough. The more practical adult within him thought it unlikely, although there were still weeks until Christmas, time for the cold to settle in. But this part of Sussex was close to the sea, which meant there was moisture for snow but often not the chilly temperatures needed to turn that moisture to ice. Still, one could hope. The skies also told him it was getting dark. He needed to hurry if he wanted to make it home before he lost the light. He kicked his horse into a jog down the rise and towards the fork in the road. He remembered this fork well, despite not having travelled it for a decade. Left to Heartsease, right to Brentham Woods. For a moment Tristan hesitated, tempted for old times' sake to take the left-hand path. How often in the past had he arrived at this exact point and done just that—seeking out the easy laughter and cosy comforts of Heartsease over the focused industry and rigid schedules of Brentham?

But not tonight. Caution asserted itself. Teddy wouldn't be there. Heartsease would be different with all of them gone, all except Elanora. For all things there was a season, and tonight was not a season for sadness or what-ifs and might-have-beens but for joy over what was. Tonight was for Brentham, for homecoming. His trunks would have arrived yesterday and his family would be expecting him.

He gave a nod to the left fork as if to say, *Not now, but soon.* He turned his horse to the right. Towards Brentham Woods. Towards home.

Home. It was the right choice. Tristan reined in his horse, taking a moment to savour the sight before him.

It was exactly how he remembered it. Brentham glowed in the dusk, a jewel shining in the quiet of the night, the lamps lit and radiating light out into the evening through his mother's lace curtains. The peaceful image was something of a misnomer. Inside, the house would be an efficient bustle of activity as the evening meal was prepared: pots clanking purposefully in the kitchens, his mother's china discreetly clinking as the table was set with a full complement of goblets and silver— his mother insisted upon it. Every night a celebration, she'd say—and even though dinner wouldn't be served until seven on the dot, his father insisted on promptness. His brother would be finishing the day's paperwork, because Julien insisted that a man who did not vigorously schedule every hour of his day from eight until five was not tapping his full faculties. And maybe, just maybe, amid all the efficiency, they were on the lookout for him.

If the Grishams were the embodiment of comfort and cosiness, the Lennoxes epitomised industry. 'Waste not, want not' was their motto when it came to time. Time, like money, in the Lennox opinion, could be spent, invested, and made, and heaven forbid both time and money were wasted. A Lennox must be accountable for how each pound was spent as surely as they must be accountable for how each minute, each hour of the day, was passed. To waste time glancing out the window to see if he'd arrived, especially when they already knew he *would* arrive, was decidedly un-Lennox-like. Tristan chuckled to himself and urged Vitalis forward into the drive. It didn't mean he wasn't loved. Tristan knew empirically that he was.

His mother loved him enough to write endlessly newsy letters while he was abroad so that in some ways it felt as if he wasn't half a world away from the neighbourhood and people of his boyhood. His father loved him enough to purchase a commission that had allowed him to follow his dreams of travel while teaching myriad lessons in leadership, self-sufficiency, and responsible living. Of course, there was the underlying assumption that he'd return home and bring those lessons to bear for the betterment of the family business: investment banking.

That last remained to be seen. Tristan might be out of the army but he wasn't sure the wanderlust was driven out of him even after ten years of travel. There was always some place new to go, something new to see, or was it simply that what he was searching for he hadn't found yet and it was still out there? Somewhere. If he looked long enough, hard enough, he'd find it. Still, it would be good to be home for a while, but that didn't mean he was ready to stay; nor did it mean he was ready to join his brother and father in their ambitious, industrious pursuit of wealth. Making one's own money was part of his father's sense of self-sufficiency. While Tristan wasn't sure a career in investing was for him, he could at least appreciate the attitude—unlike others in Hemsford who found the pursuit of self-made wealth a rather foreign concept for a man who fashioned himself a gentleman. In their opinion, a real gentleman didn't make money. The neighbourhood preferred the easy leisure professed by Richard Grisham, which went far in explaining why it had always been the Grishams who ruled Hemsford Society when he was growing up.

In the drive, Tristan dismounted and gave the strong bay a pat on the neck as a groom ran up. 'Captain Lennox, welcome home, sir.'

Tristan stared for a moment, the groom familiar and yet unfamiliar. He felt he ought to know this man. 'Joey, is that you?'

The groom tugged a forelock. 'Yes, sir. It's Joe now, though. I'm the head groom for your father's string.'

Father had a string now? That was news and a relatively new occurrence given there'd been no mention of it in the last letter he'd received back in April.

'I'm not surprised.' Tristan extended a hand to shake. 'You were always ambitious and my father likes that. Besides, you were also damn good with the horses. Take good care of this one. This is Vitalis and he's carried me a long way.'

'I will, Captain. I will see to him personally.' Joe nodded towards the house. 'They'll be happy to see you.'

As if on cue, the front door opened and his family poured out, his mother running towards him, arms open, ready to envelop him; his father and brother following at a statelier pace but their greeting no less affectionate after his mother had her way. There were embraces all around, after which his mother linked her arm through his and led him into the house. 'You're taller than I remember.' She laughed up at him. 'Broader, too.'

'Ten years will do that.' Tristan laughed with her and put an arm about his mother, letting the initial euphoria of homecoming wash over him. Lord, it felt so good to be home, the wanderlust in him temporarily quiet at last. God willing it would stay that way long enough for him to make up for lost time.

Chapter Two

The years fell away. By the time Tristan changed for dinner, he felt as if he'd never left. By some magic, he'd been seamlessly reincorporated into the home. His room was as he remembered it: dark blue counterpane on the bed, the sturdy oak furniture of his boyhood dusted and polished, his personal effects arranged on their surfaces. His trunks had been unpacked on his behalf when they'd arrived yesterday. His bureau was already filled with his linen and shirts. His razor was laid out, his jackets and trousers in the wardrobe, pressed and ready for wear.

Looking at his room it was hard to believe he'd been away for ten years. And in some ways—nonphysical ways—perhaps he hadn't truly been absent, Tristan reflected as he tied his cravat. There'd been pages of letters over the years. The Lennoxes were copious letter-writers, as industrious in their writing as they were in their other pursuits. After all, industry required detail.

His father and brother had written about the estate

and about their latest business ventures, inviting Tristan to invest with them. And he had, throwing in his army pay to help them raise their stake. He'd done it primarily to help his brother get a start in business rather than with an eye towards acquiring any great wealth. Whatever he'd made on an investment, he'd rolled over into his brother's next venture. Still, it had been pleasant to learn his brother had a good head for business and the investments had paid a little.

His mother had slipped her pages in with his father's. It was through her that he'd stayed abreast of neighbourhood news. She'd been the one to break the news to him in her flowery script of Anne Grisham's death.

The guiding light of our quiet corner of Sussex has been extinguished.

And a few years later she'd sent news of Richard's passing.

The loss of the Grishams has left a gaping hole in our little society.

A hole it seemed the Lennoxes had graciously moved to fill. In the letters that followed the deaths of both Anne and Richard, his mother had shared that his father had been elected to Richard's position as master of the hunt and then appointed as magistrate. His mother was now president of the local garden club, a position that Anne Grisham had held indisputably for years. By Sussex standards, the Lennox star was at last in ascendancy after years of being a family of only mid-dling importance—something that had galled Tristan's father. 'Simply because we weren't born and raised here for centuries,' his father would grouse. The Lennoxes had moved to Hemsford when Tristan was ten, but the Grishams had already been here for five generations, as had many others. In this part of the world, everyone knew everyone and always had. Roots were important to Hemsford. People seldom left but when they did, they always came back. They always stayed. Could that ever be him? What would it take to make the idea of staying in one place appealing?

Tristan took a final look in the mirror and gave his cravat one last tug. His brother's valet had offered his services but Tristan had declined. He'd spent his adult life dressing himself. There was no reason to change that. It was rather interesting, though, that his brother had. Proof, Tristan supposed, that not everything had stayed the same. Satisfied that he'd pass muster, Tristan headed downstairs for supper with his family.

Cook had outdone herself, making all his favourites: roasted beef with baby potatoes accompanied by a rich red wine favoured by his father because he had it on recommendation from the Duke of Cowden, a man his father both revered and resented; and for dessert, there was an apple pie with fresh cream.

As the pie was served, his father asked the question Tristan had been braced all night to hear. 'What are your plans now that you're out of the army?' Even a ten-year absence did not excuse idleness. A Lennox must always be doing something.

Julien broke in before Tristan could answer, perhaps thinking he was coming to his rescue with a timely intervention. 'I was hoping, Tristan, that you might consider working with me. My business ventures require more time than I have on my own to oversee them adequately, and I'm thinking of getting into real estate. But I'd need a partner for that.' He smiled broadly. 'We have a lot to talk about, brother. Perhaps tomorrow?'

Tristan nodded, thankful for the reprieve even if he wasn't sure he could accept such a generous offer long-term. He had plans for post-military life, but they were not as settled literally or figuratively as his father would prefer, and he didn't want to say anything about them until he had the letter in hand confirming everything. 'I could find time tomorrow. I do have a few calls to pay of my own to families of boys in the regiment.' Out of the corner of his eye he saw his father nod approvingly at the proposed activity. Tristan hid a smile. Heaven forbid he come home and lie abed for a morning. Tristan glanced towards his mother. 'I would also like to call at Heartsease and pay my respects to Elanora.'

His mother gave a soft, sad smile. 'Absolutely. You must go, although I think you will find her much changed.'

Tristan mistook her meaning. 'I am sure I will. Ten years is a long time.' Elanora had been fifteen when he'd left, a coltish young girl who'd been leaning towards tallness with long blond hair always in a tangle. She'd been precocious and energetic like the rest of her family, and also uniquely herself—a girl who liked animals, especially horses, and had a fascination for words. She quieted only when she was in her garden, out of respect, she'd said, for her plants.

His mother shook her head. 'I meant changed beyond the passage of time. Heartsease, too, is not as it once was.' Tristan paused, reorganising his thoughts at his mother's words. Ten years for a young girl would be an especially long time, a time in which she'd move into adolescence, then from adolescence to a come-out, to courtship and marriage and motherhood. For a girl of Elanora's background—wealthy, the promise of good looks and a genteel upbringing—she would have come out in London and here at home. She would have been courted by the best of Sussex and barons' sons in London. The girl he'd known would be, *should* be, married by now with a toddler at her skirts, and yet he could not recall his mother mentioning such an occasion in her letters. It was not something his mother would have left out, yet it seemed in the past few years, mentions of the Grishams had become less frequent in her letters.

'Is there no one with her?' Tristan asked, taking a swallow of wine.

'No, she's quite alone,' his mother said quietly while his father shook his head.

'It's a sad business what's happened there. So much tragedy in so short a time. First Anne, and then Richard just a couple years later.' His father had been the best of friends with Richard Grisham. 'We tried to help them when Richard died. We offered guidance with the estate and the finances, but Teddy was stubborn and now Elanora continues in that vein, much, I fear, to her detriment. It's hard to say what goes on there now. She is not seen out much.'

That last didn't sound like the Elanora he knew, although the stubbornness did. It ran in the family. For Teddy stubbornness had been akin to fearlessness. There was nothing he wouldn't attempt. Once his mind was made up, it was impossible to dissuade him. It was something Tristan had alternately admired and worried over in his friend. He'd learned early in their friendship how to play the diplomat and move Teddy away from true danger. It was a skill that had stood him in good stead in the army. Reckless men could be found at all levels of society. He finished his wine, guilt digging a little harder at him. If he had been here, could he have stopped Teddy from going with that last cargo? Would Teddy be here now, waiting for him at Heartsease if he'd come home instead of extending his tour of duty?

'I think Elanora is struggling,' his father began but a look passed between his father and his mother full of unspoken words as his mother moved to intervene.

'Not now, Cameron. Our son is home. Tonight is for happier things.' With her usual deftness, his mother moved the conversation on to other topics. He would have to wait and see for himself what had happened at Heartsease, but his concern was awakened along with a sense of urgency. He'd send a note first thing in the morning, asking to call. He was starting to regret not having taken the other turn at the fork in the road. He did not care for the air of foreboding that seemed to hover at his shoulders, casting a slight pall over his homecoming.

* * *

Elanora could not bring herself to like banks. They seemed to her nothing more than hospitals for the financially ailing. Even a financier's vocabulary carried a tinge of the macabre to it. Mortgage, after all, meant the death pledge and had its roots in old French and Latin; a pledge, Teddy had explained, laughing at her fears over the mortgage on Heartsease, that was either ended or declared 'dead' once the payment was satisfied or if the person paying could no longer make the payments. 'That will not be us, though, Ellie,' he'd said. 'We'll have money left over once I'm back with the cargo.'

But Teddy had, for once in his charmed life, been both wrong and unlucky. Neither he nor the cargo had come back, leaving her to tackle the taciturn Mr Atwater, who stared at her from behind the polished surface of his desk at the Atwater and Schofield Banking Company with a combination of pity, remorse, and disgust. He did not respect her. He'd made it clear on several occasions that women should not be handling the family finances—never mind that there was no one else to do it—and that somehow, because she was a woman, this whole mess was her fault even though she'd not signed the mortgage, nor invested in the doomed cargo or gone to sea with it. But she *had* been the one to turn down his nephew Elias Bathurst's proposal last spring on the heels of Teddy's death. That had not endeared her to him. It had, instead, added fuel to the long-smouldering Bathurst-Grisham feud instigated years ago between Teddy and Elias over a dispute at the swimming hole.

So far, the visit today had gone relatively well. She'd

asked for the Christmas funds, and he'd handed them over with less complaint than usual. Her hopes were rising that she might get out of the bank without discussing the loan. She rose, trying not to look rushed, when what she really wanted to do was run for the door with her reticule full of pound notes. 'Thank you for your time today, Mr Atwater. I hope you have a pleasant afternoon.'

He rose partway from his chair and gestured back to the one she'd just vacated. Her hopes sank. 'If you please, Miss Grisham, there is one more item I wish to discuss with you.'

She tried for deflection and a smile. 'I do hope you've tied up your roses, Mr Atwater. They should be prepared for winter by now.' Mr Atwater's roses were his pride and joy. Last spring people had come from miles to view his latest grafting project. If she could engage him in a discussion of horticulture, perhaps he'd forget the loan.

'Yes, Miss Grisham, I've tied up the roses. But that's not what I wish to talk about. There is the delicate issue of your mortgage.'

Elanora sat back down, her hands discreetly curling into the fabric of her reticule for strength. 'What is it you'd like to discuss?'

'The due date is fast approaching. The twenty-fourth of December. I wanted to be sure that you were aware of that and of the consequences that will follow if the loan is not paid. If the bank does not have its seven thousand pounds by then, there is no choice but to foreclose on the property, given that you've already missed the last two payments. Do you understand what that means?'

It meant the same thing it had meant the first time the details had been gone over with her after Teddy's death in April, and the same thing it had meant when she'd missed the first payment in September. It had not changed. It meant she would lose her family home. It meant she'd spend the rest of her days in a cottage tucked away and forgotten. But Mr Atwater would not appreciate that clapback answer. He dealt in money not in emotions, and whatever emotions he might have invested in her situation likely favoured his nephew. 'Yes, I am aware.' She forced a polite smile. 'If that is all, I have other errands to attend to.'

Mr Atwater's solemn mien hardened into impatience over this polite waiting game that they both knew would only end one way. 'Is there any chance you will be paying the loan back in full?'

Elanora pulled on her gloves with a brisk efficiency to hide her agitation and the fear the blunt question engendered. She would not let him see how much the prospect of the future unnerved her. She met his gaze evenly, trying to keep a bit of a snap out of her tone, trying to be professional. He could be impatient and get away with it. If she tried the same, it would be labelled a woman's hysterics. 'No, there is not. If there was, I would have paid it already.' She certainly wouldn't have missed two payments if she'd had the funds.

Some of the hardness left him. 'I *am* sorry, Miss Grisham. Your father was a well-respected man. Out of courtesy for his memory, the bank has already delayed in foreclosing in the hopes that something might materialise.' That she might marry, might find a husband who would carry the mortgage for her, do business with Mr Atwater instead of making Mr Atwater do business with her; that she might reconsider his nephew now that her straits were more dire. 'May I enquire, Miss Grisham, where you will go? Are there any relatives who might take you in?'

'No, there is no one.' She hated being forced to say it out loud. She rose once more before he could remind her that there was indeed someone who would rescue her. His nephew was still keen to wed. 'Now, really, I must go, Mr Atwater.' If she lingered, he would persist, saying things like 'Truly? There is no great-aunt? No distant cousins?' to which her answer would still be no, and to which he might be indiscreet enough to push his nephew's suit once more on Elias's behalf. Worst of all, she feared if she stayed too long she risked running into Elias himself, who made it a rather regular habit to call on his uncle there.

Elanora stepped into the street, breathing a sigh of relief at having escaped Mr Atwater and an encounter with Elias Bathurst, even if she hadn't come away unscathed.

Mr Atwater's words still rang in her ears, a death-knell pealing: *December twenty-fourth.* Christmas Eve. After which, she'd have two weeks to vacate the property unless…unless what? There was treasure hidden in her garden? A chest of gold doubloons in her attic? A knight in shining armour who would ride to her rescue, sweep her off her feet, cover her debt and they would live at Heartsease happily ever after? That was not how the world worked. It was—

Oof! She ran right into a solid wall of…man. Her gaze went up and up to broad shoulders, chocolate eyes, and dark hair. The wall smiled. Recognition fluttered in the pit of her stomach. She *knew* this wall of man. It might have been years, but she'd recognise those eyes anywhere. She whispered his name in disbelieving surprise. 'Tristan. You've come home.'

Chapter Three

She saw her own disbelief mirrored momentarily in those chocolate-dark eyes as he, too, struggled for recognition. The worried thought flitted through her mind: Had she changed so much that she was beyond identification? Then came a slow smile as the remembrance came to him, the rich timbre of his voice rolling over a single word, 'Elanora?' His smile broadened. 'How wonderful it is to see you, even if I did almost plough you down in the street. My pardon for that. My thoughts were elsewhere.'

Elanora laughed, something she'd not expected to do so soon after leaving Mr Atwater, and found herself answering his smile with one of her own. Then again, Tristan always could make her smile even over the littlest of things. Joy, delight, happiness—those things seemed to follow Tristan wherever he went, which had always struck her as ironic given that his name meant sadness. 'As were mine. My thoughts were not on the street. We are perhaps both to blame.' Goodness, but he was taller than she remembered, and even more dashing than she recalled, but those recollections were years old and based on a gangly adolescent with a quick smile. She was very much aware this was a man who stood before her now.

Tristan's gaze flicked briefly to the window behind her with its gold etched lettering. 'You've been banking. I hope it went well.' Panic fluttered at his words. She had to remind herself he couldn't possibly know. The remark was simply polite conversation only.

She gave another smile. 'It went as best it could. It is fair to say expectations were met.'

Tristan's smile faded and the conversation turned sombre. 'Yes, of course. El, I was sorry to hear about Teddy. My mother wrote with the news.' He touched her gloved hand briefly. Even through the kid leather she felt the warm comfort of him. How long had it been since anyone had touched her? Offered her genuine sympathy that wasn't accompanied by a gossipy probe into her circumstances? But Tristan had always been genuine, even with the tag-along little sister of his best friend. That sincerity had been the source of her infatuation when she was younger. Apparently, it still was, if the racing of her pulse was an indicator.

'Thank you, Tristan,' she said softly. The temptation threatened to say more, to lay out all the troubles she kept so well hidden from others. But that was hardly fair to Tristan, and the street was not the place to dissemble. Besides, what could he do about any of it? He'd been gone for years and she'd never been one to play the damsel in distress. She firmly believed if there was any saving to be done, it ought to be by herself.

He squeezed her hand, his voice low and private. 'I sent a note to Heartsease this morning. It probably just missed you. But now I can ask you in person. I want to call at the house and officially pay my respects.'

Elanora dropped her eyes, real embarrassment creeping into her cheeks. She was regretting her decision to spend the grave marker savings on Christmas. 'That's kind. But I should tell you there's no headstone to see, and of course, there's no body. It's just a cross in the ground.' There should be more, she scolded herself. Teddy deserved more.

'It doesn't matter, El. I want to come and walk there with you, grieve with you as I would have if I'd been here.' Tristan's gaze drew hers up. 'May I come tomorrow?'

She should say no. She should not let him see what Heartsease and her life had become. He would see too much; there was risk that he'd read between the lines of what she'd hidden so well from so many. And yet, she could think of nothing she wanted more than to have time with him. She withdrew her hand, conscious that their conversation was running overlong for a chance meeting on the street; conscious that he'd called her El, his long-time nickname for her when everyone else had called her Ellie, and that it still pleased her as much as it ever had. In that brief glow of pleasantness she was rash; she did not think about her answer, only that she would see him again, and have a moment like this again. 'Yes, please come.'

'Until tomorrow, then.' He stepped back, favouring her with a twinkling smile.

What a difference a smile could make. She lived on that smile and its wave of happiness the rest of the day, temporary though it would be. Happiness didn't last; that was one more illusion she'd learned to accept. But while it did, she let it buoy her spirits as she made a few purchases in town, trying to enjoy shopping instead of focusing on the money leaving her purse. She used to love to shop when coin had never been a concern. In those days, she could shop to her heart's content. Now that joy had become one of her most dreaded chores; a task, no longer a pleasure. That smile carried her home, where she gave Cook the funds for the Christmas pudding and the food baskets. It followed her into the garden when she checked on the roses. It accompanied the piano she played after dinner that night instead of spending another hour with the books that wouldn't be balanced despite her best efforts, and it tucked her in that night, sending her to sleep with a pleasant memory from the day instead of the dread instilled by Mr Atwater.

Tristan was home and somehow that made everything seem just a bit brighter for the time being. The voice in her head was quick to remind her that such brightness, such happiness, was ephemeral. It belonged only to the moment. It would not last. Life had taught her that. It had also taught her that such ephemera was a poor emotional investment.

Tristan arrived promptly at eleven, head bare, hair windblown, just the way he liked it. To feel the wind was to feel alive. The day was crisp and fine, the perfect day for a ride. Both he and Vitalis had enjoyed a gallop in the meadows that preceded the drive at Heartsease. Vitalis's breath emerged as a puff of steam in the cold air as Tristan slowed him to a trot, taking in the rambling house that had been at the core of his childhood as much as his own home.

At a distance, Heartsease was still the home of his memories, constant and unchanged by the march of time, but up close the comfortable estate wore the past decade with less élan than one might have hoped. Nature was having its way with Heartsease, slowly but insistently creeping towards the house, starting with lawns that were once trimmed and pristine but were now long and ragged, filled with leaves shed from the old oaks that lined the drive. The oaks themselves were still resplendent, boasting the remainder of their crimson leaves against the crisp blue sky, but showing no signs of their usual careful pruning—something that would not have been tolerated in Anne Grisham's day. Nor, he would have thought, in Elanora's.

Tristan trotted down the drive, the house coming into fuller view along with the fountain that crowned the drive: Aphrodite at Rest, which had given the estate its name. Here, too, nature had begun to encroach. The fountain stood, clogged with leaves. Ivy ran wild up the west corner, and the white shutters framing the windows were greying, in need of a good whitewash. No groom rushed out to take the reins as he swung off Vitalis. He led Vitalis towards the stable block, the anxiety he'd felt at supper the other night upon hearing his mother's news regarding Heartsease returning in force. At least on the outside, things had indeed changed at Heartsease. The place had once been an immaculate garden of an estate and his own heart sank at the sight of it.

'Halloo,' Tristan called out, looking into the dim interior of the stable, his gaze noting that here, order and tidiness still held sway. The main aisle was swept and a few horse heads popped over the stall doors, but the rest of the massive stable was quiet. The great Grisham string was gone. Dear Lord, what had happened here? But he knew. It was all too much for one person to manage, even if there was an enormous crew of workers, which there didn't appear to be. Elanora couldn't possibly handle overseeing groundskeeping, stable upkeep, and the house on her own. Nor perhaps was there a need to. One person couldn't ride twenty horses. The vast world of Heartsease had shrunk. Perhaps it was no surprise that the staff and services had, too.

An older man shuffled out from the tack room. 'Master Tristan!' The man's eyes brightened with delight. 'Miss Elanora said you'd be by today.'

Tristan grinned at the sight of the familiar face. Old Mackey had already been old when he and Teddy had been running underfoot at the stables. But age had not dimmed the man's appreciation of good horseflesh. 'This is a fine fellow.' Old Mackey ran a hand down the length of Vitalis's neck, crooning nonsense to the gelding. 'I'll take good care of him, Captain.' The old man's smile dimmed. 'It's not how it used to be, is it?' His sharp gaze followed Tristan's. 'It was just too big for Miss Elanora. It broke her heart, but it was the practical choice,' he conceded, clearing his throat. 'It's good of you to call on her. She could do with some company these days. We all could. This place is too quiet. It never used to be with you and young Mr Theodore about, and Mr Grisham heading the hunt club. Those were the days, weren't they? But everyone is gone now.'

'You're still here.' Tristan tried to cheer the old man. 'And the stables look good. You do yourself proud.' Even if the stables were empty, the part of the stable that remained in use was as pristine as ever. Mackey's space may have shrunk but he'd not lowered his standards.

The sound of a horse in the stable yard drew Tristan's attention. Old Mackey nodded towards the arrival. 'That will be Miss Elanora now. She rode out to try and meet you.' He took the reins and led Vitalis away.

Tristan strode outside as Elanora brought her horse to a halt. She was dressed in blue today, a good colour that brought out the colour of her eyes and the gold of her hair, hair that was as windblown as his, as if she'd ridden hard and fast. Perhaps she had. She and all the Grishams had always erred on the side of neck or nothing when it came to riding. 'Wait, let me help.' He quickened his step to hold the horse's head as she dismounted, all quick, fluid grace. As usual, he recalled. *That* hadn't changed even though the quick girl he'd known had become a stunning woman whose youthful agility had transformed into graceful athleticism.

Elanora Grisham was a woman a man would look twice at when she entered a ballroom, or any room, for that matter. Even if that man was himself. The honesty of that admission was still a bit surprising to him. He'd not expected to notice Elanora in *that* way. Yet, yesterday in the street there'd been no mistaking that he *had* looked twice before that realisation had set in. That reaction was still there today, although he was better braced for it. Today he'd only looked once and found it deuced difficult to look away.

'I missed you on the road,' Elanora said brightly, smoothing down the blue skirts of her riding habit. 'You must have come cross country.' She was breathless, confirming his assumption was correct. She *had* ridden hard. Had she enjoyed it as much as he? But he didn't think it was that simple. His suspicions suggested that unlike him, she'd not been out for a pleasure gallop.

'I couldn't resist the meadows with this weather,' Tristan confessed, studying her more closely, trying to guess the purpose behind her morning ride. Her cheeks were flushed and her gaze was nervous in the way of someone who was trying to pretend everything was normal. But if everything had been normal, she would have responded with 'Me, too.'

Instead, she said, 'Have you seen Old Mackey?' Her tone was too bright as she probed for information. Ah. She wanted to know how long he had been here and how much he had seen, or perhaps been told. Old Mackey wasn't known for his discretion. It confirmed Tristan's suspicions. She'd not wanted him to see the stables, to see how things had deteriorated. Had she ridden out to meet him in the hopes of directing him away from the estate altogether? It was possible to access the little chapel and cemetery without coming to the house first. Perhaps that had been her hope.

He smiled to ease her obvious discomfort. 'Who is this pretty girl?' He turned his attention to her horse. 'Surely, this can't be Marian?' Marian had been a high-spirited six-year-old mare when he'd left, a birthday present to Elanora from her father.

'It is.' That brought an honest smile to Elanora's face, and Tristan couldn't help but remark the transformation, the way her eyes lit and her expression softened. Elanora Grisham lived up to the promise of her beauty when she smiled. The coltish girl he'd known had become an attractive woman with warm blue eyes and an even warmer smile that evinced the innate kindness and gentleness that had always been a part of her. No one loved caring for others, from plants to horses, to puppies and people, like Elanora Grisham. Growing up, she'd made a habit of taking in strays and finding them homes. The stable had been as full of her abandoned kittens and pups as it had been of Richard Grisham's fine hunters.

Talking about the horse was safe ground and they chatted about Marian as they untacked her and brushed her down. Even at sixteen, Marian was in good shape and still quite obviously Elanora's pride. 'She could clear three six with ease at the hunt,' Elanora boasted with another wide smile as they took her inside to her stall. 'No one could touch her, not even Aramis.'

She'd said too much and the comfort they'd established with small talk dissipated. Aramis had been Teddy's horse. At the mention of his name, a dark, nearly black, horse with a greying muzzle poked his head out over the stall door with a wicker. Out of instinct, Tristan petted the long nose and fished a sugar cube out of his pocket. 'Hey, old boy, you're still here, too. What a pleasant surprise.' But the emotion at the sight of his friend's horse choked his throat and he swallowed hard. He'd not counted on this reaction. Aramis and Teddy had been inseparable and untouchable, a true pairing of horse and rider if ever there was one. He had summers full of memories of crashing about the countryside with Aramis and Teddy. The pair had been fearless.

'Who else is still here?' Tristan asked softly.

'A driving horse to pull the gig and a couple of my father's favourites.' Elanora cleared her throat as if the emotion of the moment had caught her, too. 'The others have been sold. Your father bought several of them but these were too old. He didn't want them. No one did.' Something cracked in Tristan's heart. The grand Grisham string had been reduced to a handful of misfits. It didn't seem right.

'I didn't know,' Tristan said quietly, pieces coming together. So this was where his father had acquired the string Joe referred to. He'd not had time to tour the Brentham Woods stables yet. He would take a closer look tonight.

'I am grateful, of course. The horses needed a home, and with your father heading the hunt club now, it made sense.' She forced a smile. 'Besides, I don't think Aramis would have left.' She gave a soft laugh. 'I think he's still waiting for Teddy.'

Tristan nodded. 'It wouldn't surprise me. Horses are loyal like that to the people they loved, and he loved Teddy. There was nothing quite like them. Except maybe you and Marian.'

She smiled at him. 'And you and Saint.'

He chuckled. 'Saint was a mediocre horse at best.' But he'd loved him. Saint had been the first horse that had really belonged to him. What Saint had lacked in bloodlines he'd made up for in heart. One could learn a lot about love from a horse. Perhaps that was why he liked working with them so much.

'You elevated him.' She smiled at Tristan and it buoyed his spirits, a reminder that reminiscing needn't be sad. 'Shall we go see Teddy?'

She led him out to the path that wound down to the little stone chapel and the family cemetery that was too full. But there was a sense of peace in strolling beneath the autumn leaves with her. Perhaps it was because she was a connection to Teddy, the only other person who could fully understand all Teddy had been and what Teddy's friendship had meant to him. At the cemetery, he held open the iron gate and let her pass through ahead of him. Here, someone was winning the battle against nature. The cemetery was well cared for, the grass clipped, weeds and leaves absent from the headstones. He slid a gaze in Elanora's direction. Of course it was her. She was spending her time here. With her family. 'Teddy's over there.' She led him past the marble stones marking her parents' graves with their names carefully, expertly, etched to a plain white wooden cross.

At the sight of the graves, Tristan's grief rose on her behalf. The girl he'd known had lost so much in so short a time and it had changed the woman who stood beside him now. Beneath her striking beauty, this woman was guarded in her expression, more subdued than the tomboy who'd begged to come along on adventures with him and Teddy. He'd not minded. He'd rather liked not being the youngest, liked the role of being an older brother. Liked having an ally when Teddy's fearlessness was out of control. Sometimes it took the two of them working together to rein him in. He and Elanora had become an unlikely team, united in their common purpose of managing Teddy.

They were still managing Teddy, albeit in a different way, a fact driven home by the sight of his friend's grave, and his own grief hit him anew. How was it possible that Teddy was gone? He'd been so full of life, larger than that life. How was it possible that death held any power over such a person? 'He was the best friend I ever had,' Tristan offered solemnly. 'He was selfless, fearless, he made every day an adventure.' Sometimes too much of an adventure. Could they have reined him in together one more time if he'd been here to help Elanora?

'He did,' she averred with a sigh. 'Thank you for those words, for coming here and sharing with me.' She paused, searching for words of her own. 'When Teddy died, there was no one who really understood who he'd been.' For a moment her gaze met his and he dared to read between the lines. Teddy had been fearless, yes, but that fearlessness had to be carefully managed behind the scenes. It was something they'd never spoken of but implicitly acknowledged. 'But you do. I knew you would.' Her cheeks flushed as her gaze went back to the wooden cross. 'I'm sorry it's not more.'

'There's no need to apologise,' Tristan quickly absolved, but his worry and guilt grew exponentially. The desolate quality of the stables, the state of the front lawns and drive, and the lack of a proper grave for Teddy all led to certain concerning conclusions. It wasn't just grief that had changed Heartsease. Other factors played a part, too. He thought about her visit to the bank. Had that been for reasons beyond regular business?

He'd thought nothing of it at the time, but now, seeing it coupled with the state of Heartsease, he had to wonder if there was more. What sort of a situation had Teddy left her with? How deeply had the loss of that cargo affected her? Losing cargo was no small thing. If there were financial problems, he would find a way to convince her to let him help. He would make up for not being here.

Seeing her among the graves of her family tore at his heart. What chance did one woman stand if she was alone in the world?

I will see her cared for before I go, Tristan vowed silently to the white cross. *No matter how much she resists. I promise you, old friend.*

He couldn't save Teddy, he was too late for that, but he could help Elanora. By doing so, perhaps he could square with his conscience for failing Teddy, for not being here when Teddy needed him. He would not fail Elanora. After all, it was what Teddy would have wanted.

Despite the blue skies, a cold wind blew through the cemetery. Elanora shivered and Tristan took the opportunity to focus on the living. 'Perhaps we might go inside for a cup of tea and good long conversation. You can catch me up on all that has happened.' He offered a friendly smile, tucking her arm through his, knowing full well the gesture gave her no chance to protest. She was going to have to let him into the house whether she wanted to or not, and perhaps, more importantly, let him into her thoughts. She needed help but she was too proud to ask for it, or perhaps too scared. A woman alone could be vulnerable even among well-intentioned friends. If he knew what she was up against, he could find a way to offer help without her having to ask for it. If the army had taught him anything, it was that one did not rush in blindly to combat a foe; one had to understand the ground first.

Chapter Four

He was on her ground now, but that made her far more nervous than it should have. By rights, her home ground should have given her the advantage. Tristan was the one who'd been gone for ten years. But instead of protecting her, her home exposed her. As they sat in the drawing room of Heartsease, settling themselves with Cook's tea tray, Elanora saw the space as Tristan might see it: the faded carpet and curtains, the worn furniture that had not been updated since he'd left.

'Cook still makes the best gingerbread men,' Tristan complimented, reaching for another one. 'How have things been, El? Truly? You needn't hide it from me.'

There was nothing *to* hide. He'd seen it all. Her reckless invitation to come to Heartsease had left her revealed after spending the past six months inventing excuses to keep people away. The shambles had been easier to hide when Teddy was alive. In the years between their father's death and his, the shambles had mostly been internal. There'd been no outer signs of the financial turmoil lurking beneath the surface at Hearts-ease. Even when Teddy discovered the financial rot after their father's passing, he'd bent all their resources to-wards keeping up appearances to see that Heartsease gave no clue to the world the Grishams were struggling.

But since April, without Teddy, the dam holding back signs of misfortune had burst. It was as if nature had known Elanora was on her own now, that she hadn't the funds to fight back, to keep up those appearances Teddy had been so good at managing. Wasn't this the fear she'd had about Tristan's visit? Nothing had es-caped his notice. She'd seen his eyes tracking the state of the stables and no doubt he'd noticed when he'd rid-den up that the lawn wasn't the verdant landscape it had once been. She'd hoped to prevent that by meeting him on the road and redirecting his route. She'd failed and now here he was, making her pay the price for his company with his probing.

'My father says you're being stubborn. Is that true?' he asked point-blank when she didn't answer.

'Respectfully, I think your father confuses my pref-erence for privacy with what he claims is obstinance,' Elanora corrected.

'Heartsease and the Grishams were never terribly private places or people in the past,' Tristan prompted, and she heard the question beneath it: *What has changed so that you require privacy now?* Privacy meant secrets, which meant she did have something to hide, after all.

'You've been gone a long time, Tristan.' She smiled to soften the reminder that one didn't simply drop back in and expect things to be as they once were. It was the only defence she had.

Tristan leaned back against the sofa and crossed a long leg over one knee, undaunted with the rebuke. 'Then catch me up. My mother wrote long, newsy letters but even so I find there are still some surprises, not the least being that you are not swarmed with beaux or married by now.' And she might have been if she and Teddy hadn't decided to use her dowry for other purposes. Perhaps it was for the best. She didn't want to be married for her money. Without a dowry it became obvious what the source of interest in her was.

'Are you suggesting that I am on the shelf?' It was a bold statement for him to make but there were worse topics to address. 'One could say the same for you. Thirty is quite an advanced age,' she teased gently, hoping to deflect the conversation away from herself.

Tristan laughed. 'But *I* was in the army, moving about the world. Hardly ideal conditions for starting a marriage with no home, no roots, to offer.' Elanora would wager such practical considerations would matter less to the woman who managed to capture Tristan's attentions. It would be enough for that woman to have him all to herself no matter where in the world they went. Even she would be tempted to leave Hemsford if it were for him, and that was saying something given that she had never had any desire to leave Hemsford, to leave her home. She might have been more surprised by the realisation if it had any teeth to it. But it was only a mere hypothetical reckoning at the moment. She was infatuated with Tristan. But not he with her. That had never been the case growing up and there was no reason for it to be the case now. He'd called today because he was a friend of the family's, nothing more, and she was all that was left of that family. Still, the question lingered longer than she'd have liked in her mind: What *would* she do for Tristan? How far would she go? It was a question that would never require an answer.

He took a swallow of tea, the teacup looking ridiculously dainty in his hands. 'So there are no swains in the wings waiting to sweep you off your feet?' He persisted with the conversation.

'None that I would allow.' Elanora poured another cup of tea to give her hands something to do. Her attempt at deflection had failed and she tried to make light of her answer.

'That you would *allow*?' Tristan queried. 'Hmm. I think my father may have been right. You *are* being stubborn.'

She fixed him with a stare. If gentle redirection didn't move him, perhaps blunt honesty would. 'I did not want their brand of vulpine pity.' There'd been the crafty, sly few who'd seen opportunity for themselves after Teddy had died. A woman alone and an estate for the plucking seemed to them easy game. Of course, a discreet hint or two about having no dowry combined with a cold shoulder from her had sent them on their way. Most of them, at least, had been dissuaded. It had taken a bit more to put off Elias Bathurst, especially when it was clear that his uncle had been indiscreet and mentioned the mortgage to him.

'I don't offer pity, El. I offer help. It's what a friend

does,' he countered smoothly. 'It's clear you need some. Friends *and* help,' he clarified. 'Between the two of us, we can have the estate back to its usual looks by Christmas.' He smiled broadly, no doubt expecting the offer to be met with delight and even relief.

It was on the tip of her tongue to snap out that there was no point in it, that all the work would be for naught, that there was no money to *bring* the estate back to its usual looks, even with the best of intentions, but that would be giving away too much. He assumed she was simply overwhelmed. Perhaps it was best if he kept believing that since it would protect other more dangerous truths. Instead, she said, 'You were Teddy's friend, not mine. I was just a tag-along nuisance.'

Tristan spread his hands on his knees. 'I disagree, but if you want to couch it that way, then allow me to help out of respect for Teddy. He wouldn't want you struggling alone if I could do something about it, if I could help you find your feet in these early months as you adjust. Will you allow me to hire some men? I can have them here the day after tomorrow.'

His eagerness raised alarm within her. She could absolutely not permit that kindness. She couldn't afford it, literally. 'That's not necessary. I can manage, Tristan.' She couldn't pay those workers, but yet again, she could not say that out loud without giving away too much. It seemed all things these days led towards the debt and the impending disaster of December twenty-fourth.

'But you don't *have to* manage alone. That's the point.' Agitation rose in Tristan's voice, exasperation evident. She was trying his patience. 'I've never understood how you can offer so much help to those around you and yet you accept no help for yourself, even when you need it.' He arched a brow. 'Often to your detriment although you haven't seemed to learn that lesson.' He fixed her with a stern look that made her feel ten again. 'I remember a girl who insisted she could cross the old creek bridge on her own even though her brother and I warned her otherwise. We had to jump in and save her when she fell in over her head.'

Elanora felt her cheeks heat at the memory. 'I would have swum to shore myself. I was doing fine. It was you and Teddy who panicked.'

'We had good reason. The creek was roaring that day.' Tristan didn't back down. 'And yet, I don't think the woman before me has learned the lesson that pride goeth before a fall, quite literally in some cases.'

'Other things go before a fall, too,' she snapped. His scold raised her temper. It was an idealistic reproach from a man who knew nothing of what she'd endured these past years. If he knew anything, he'd know she no longer had any pride left to her. She had only the protection of privacy, of keeping her own counsel and whatever defence a sharp tongue could offer her. She set down her teacup and answered his stare with a hard gaze of her own. 'Things like love.' Something she'd been raised to believe was selfless, but in reality was perhaps the most selfish thing of all. She waited, wanting to shock him, wanting him to argue with her.

Once, Tristan would have risen to the bait but this man merely arched a dark brow to signal his debate. 'Do you care to explain?'

'My father died of a broken heart. He chose his grief over Teddy and me, and over Heartsease.' She'd barely gotten the words out before the old anger rose as hot and strong as ever. Five years had not diminished it. 'He simply didn't want to go on without my mother, and so he didn't. He rode out one day on his favourite horse, sat down under his favourite tree, went to sleep, and never woke up. He left us without any preparation, without any goodbyes.' He'd left them with no words of wisdom or words of warning that Heartsease was foundering. She and Teddy had been ill equipped to deal with the revelations that followed their father's death.

'I am sorry, El. Your parents were a stunning couple. Everyone adored them. About your father... I didn't know.'

No one did. Everyone thought Richard Grisham died of a heart ailment and that was true as far as it went. Only she and Teddy suspected that ailment wasn't a physical condition but an emotional one. She gave him a sharp smile, turning her anger in his direction instead of at the ghost of her father. A living target was so much better.

'How could you know? That is *my* point, Tristan. You cannot walk in here after being gone for so long and start fixing things. My parents are dead. Teddy is dead. Things are different now. You can't pull me out of this roaring creek. You know *nothing*. You can fix *nothing*.'

It was much too late for that. Even so, she could not allow it. To let someone else fix her problems would be to relinquish her own autonomy, to be under an obligation she could never repay. Even if that person was Tristan—or perhaps *especially* if that person was Tristan. It would be as mortifying now as it had been when he'd pulled her out of the creek at ten, just as unaware of her infatuation with him then as he was now.

Elanora rose, some of the anger leaving her now that it had been spent. 'Thank you for coming. I will not take up any more of your time.' She didn't dare. The longer Tristan was here, the more he saw, and the more tempting it became to want to transfer her burdens to his shoulders. But they were no longer children, no longer playing at adventures. This was real life, with real consequences. The things they did and said were no longer limited to the roles they played in childhood games, left behind when the game was finished. These things, these choices, these words, would follow them always.

He studied her for a long moment with those dark eyes of his and she thought he might call her bluff. Instead, he rose and offered her a nod. 'Perhaps it is me who should not take up any more of *your* time. Thank you for *allowing* me to drop by.' There was a wry emphasis on *allowing* as he deliberately borrowed her word, the word she used to set and maintain her boundaries, as a reminder to herself that she was in charge. But in this moment, she hated the word. To maintain those boundaries, she'd treated a friend shabbily, gone even so far as to denounce their friendship.

As soon as the sound of his boot heels faded and the front door shut behind him, Elanora sank to her chair, admonishment for her behaviour reeling and ready in her mind. Teddy would be ashamed of her for treating his friend, *their* friend, in such a manner. Tristan had always been welcome at Heartsease. She'd told him as much yesterday in the street. But she'd not honoured that welcome today. Yet, what else could she have done? She would not burden Tristan with her troubles when there was nothing he could do about them. Even if there was something he could do, she'd meant it when she'd said she didn't want pity, didn't want to be in anyone's debt any more than she already was.

Pity created obligation; to accept pity was to surrender her independence, to owe a man for the rest of her life a debt that would never be paid in full. Elias Bathurst with his ill-timed proposal a week after Teddy's death had made that abundantly clear. He'd been happy to pay for a lifetime of her gratitude in exchange for the estate.

With you on my arm, no door will be shut to me, and our children could aspire to marriages in the peerage. Between the Bathurst money and the Grisham name, I will be unstoppable. I might even earn a knighthood. You will thank me for making you a lady.

He'd viewed her as nothing but a stepping stone to his aspirations of greatness, a tool to be used to overcome his own social deficiencies. Elias Bathurst had discovered that money didn't unlock all the necessary doors when one had a disagreeable personality. And of course, the mention of children made it clear just how he intended to enjoy her. She'd refused him politely but that had not been enough. Elias had pressed his suit to the point she'd felt it necessary to press her knee to his groin with just as much force. He'd left shortly after that.

Elias Bathurst was one more thing she didn't want

Tristan to know about. It would only stir old bad blood. She'd managed Elias and she'd managed Mr Atwater, letting the banker know that her finances were to be kept just as confidentially as the next client's. He'd had no right to share the details of the mortgage with his nephew even if she was a woman. Should he be indiscreet again, she, too, might be indiscreet and share Elias's botched proposal in a way that would see him excluded from the certain social circles he valued. That was all settled now. The last thing she wanted was Tristan planting Elias a facer in defence of her honour. It would call the wrong sort of attention to her.

Attention was something she'd been very good at avoiding since Teddy died. Privacy and independence were her watchwords these days, the last two luxuries she could still afford, and yet the price for them had been quite high today. It had meant driving off Tristan. After such a set down, Tristan would have no reason or desire to return to Heartsease. Which was what she'd intended, and what she ought to want. But if that was what she wanted, why did she feel as if she'd just lost her last friend?

Tristan did not think he'd ever been delivered such a blunt dismissal as the one Elanora had given him today. He swirled his after-dinner brandy in a cut-crystal glass, studying the play of light from the fire in his brother's study, as his mind revisited the day. Elanora had not been able to get rid of him fast enough, which seemed odd given that she'd invited him out. Why invite him at all if she hadn't wanted to see him?

'You saw Elanora today, didn't you? How was your visit?' Julien asked, reading his mind, setting out the ledgers on his desk that he wanted to share.

'Illuminating,' Tristan replied absently. The visit had been revealing as much for what it had not shown him as for what it had, much of which had been out of character for the girl he remembered. His mother had warned him, but still, the change had been saddening. There'd been moments when he'd had glimpses of the girl she'd been. They'd been there in the woman who'd met him in the street yesterday, taken by the surprise of his sudden reappearance, and in the woman who'd smiled while talking of her aging horse. But they were glimpses only.

This new young woman had a cold loveliness to her, sharp eyed and even sharper tongued, both of which masked a beautiful smile and an even more beautiful soul. Even so, she had only been moderately successful in hiding those attributes just as she'd been only moderately successful in hiding the tragedy at Heartsease that went beyond the cemetery. Truth, like nature, would out. He knew her. She might be able to fool others but she could not entirely fool him. 'I think the trouble at Heartsease goes beyond grief.' He voiced the hypothesis he'd been formulating since he'd ridden away, Elanora's dismissal ringing in his ears.

That got Julien's attention. He moved around the desk and took the club chair across from him. 'What kind of trouble?'

'She's overwhelmed and unwilling to take help. I cannot fathom why. I don't think it's just sheer stubbornness. Instead, I think the stubbornness is a cover for something else. She didn't want me to see Heartsease. She rode out to catch me on the road and redirect me to the cemetery without going by the house or the stable, I am sure of it.' He slid his brother a look. 'Father bought most of the Grisham string.'

'Just recently, after Teddy died. There was no time for any letter to reach you,' Julien explained. 'It was both the practical and neighbourly gesture to make. Father is in charge of the hunt club now. Why reinvent a good string when one already existed and was in need of a new home? It relieved her of a great financial burden. Keeping horses is an expensive proposition even in the country. They require quite a support staff.'

Yes, they did. It wasn't just the expense of hay and shoes. Horses required grooms and trainers, and in turn, *they* required wages. Tristan thought about Old Mackey, running the remnants of the stable on his own. 'She has only the one groom.' That was more indicative of other concerns than just a sign of someone who was overwhelmed with the changes brought on by a death in the family, particularly a male death, especially when contrasted with the large, active grooming staff here at Brentham Woods, all of whom were necessary to keep the horses fit. 'It wasn't only the stables,' he mused out loud. If it had been, he could have understood it as an outcome of having fewer horses to care for. 'There weren't any gardening staff. The lawns do not look as if they've been trimmed regularly.' Something Anne Grisham would not have allowed. He paused, thinking about the other things he'd noticed. 'Have you seen Heartsease of late?' he asked Julien.

'No,' Julien confessed. 'I haven't been over since May when we picked up the horses. We wanted to give her time to grieve in peace and she made it clear she was not interested in company.' *Since May.* Once, the Grishams and the Lennoxes had not gone a day without seeing one another.

'The house has not been kept up and the staff has been diminished.' Not enough gardeners to take care of the lawns. Probably not enough people to keep up the house, either. Now that he thought of it, he'd not noticed maids dusting and cleaning. There'd only been the reference to Cook and Mrs Thornton, and he'd only seen the one maid who'd brought the tea tray. He'd assumed there were others. Perhaps he ought not have. 'The absence of staff prompts other questions. Why would she let so many go if there was work to be done? Work she could not do on her own?'

'Finances?' Julien asked. Money was always his brother's first answer. In this case, finances was also Tristan's one. His mind went again to the impact of the lost cargo.

'Money's never been a problem before at Heartsease, and there would have been the money from selling the string.' Surely, that would have offset the cargo losses. But he remembered also the reference Elanora had made about her father not preparing them. Not preparing them for what? Were there indeed financial difficulties that went beyond a single cargo? He recalled how she'd dismissed his offer to hire help. It was either because she didn't need the help or she couldn't afford it. It now seemed more likely that the latter was true. The staff was gone, perhaps for financial reasons, and the estate had suffered because of that. A lack of funds meant a lack of staff, and a lack of staff left work undone.

Julien gave him a look of intrigue as he took a slow swallow from his own glass. 'Did she say anything today about how Teddy had left things? She would not discuss it with us back in May.'

'No.'

He recalled her words. *You know nothing.* That was fast becoming more than angry rhetoric. There was clearly something he did not know, something she didn't want him to know. He'd gone out to Heartsease, perhaps looking for personal closure to his grief, but the visit created more questions than it had answered.

Julien nodded towards the desk with its ledgers. 'On a happier note, are you ready to see how much money I made you while you were out seeing the world?' His brother smiled. 'You might be surprised to know that you've become a wealthy man.'

'Really?' Tristan returned the smile, noting how excited his brother was to have this discussion. For his brother's sake, he tried to redirect his thoughts away from Elanora and Heartsease. One thing was certain: she'd meant to drive him off today with her unnatural aloofness. The girl he'd known couldn't have changed so much. He couldn't possibly let her get away with it. Elanora Grisham was in trouble and he was a soldier.

He did not run from trouble; he ran towards it. 'Well.'
He followed his brother to the desk. 'What have you
stirred up while I've been gone?'

Chapter Five

'Stir up, we beseech thee, O Lord, the wills of thy faithful people.' Reverend Thompson intoned the familiar words from the Book of Common Prayer, standing, as he did each year, in the centre of Heartsease's large kitchen, surrounded by the Heartsease tenants and staff. As well as the memories and ghosts he couldn't see, but Elanora could feel. They were gathered around her as assuredly as the tenants and their children and nearly as physical in their presence. One of the tenants' children, a little girl, tugged impatiently on her mother's hand, whispering a question about how much longer it would be before they could make their wishes?

Elanora remembered that feeling, of being eager to stir the pudding, to mix in the charms, to make her wishes for the year. In some ways, Stir-Up Sunday had been as exciting as Christmas itself. There'd been food and drink laid out for everyone and a silver penny for each of the children, distributed by her father with a smile and a winking reminder not to spend it all on candy, knowing full well they probably would. How she'd loved this Sunday before Advent and, oh, what she wouldn't give to have those days back, to have her father swinging her up in his arms and putting her on his shoulders in order to keep her out of trouble as the vicar opened the ceremonies.

Today there were no shoulders to climb on, to rely on, not even Teddy's like there had been in the years since her father's death. Even Teddy had deserted her, joining forces with the ghosts. Now everyone was looking to her to kick off the Christmas festivities and traditions. She could not disappoint them, not when it would be both the first and last time she'd oversee the festivities as mistress of Heartsease—a position that was never supposed to have been hers. The mistress should have been her mother, or eventually Teddy's wife. But fate had been cruel and now it was up to her. She would do her best.

Elanora studied the faces gathered in the big kitchen of Heartsease: Old Mackey, Cook, Mrs Thornton, the remaining housemaids, Reverend Thompson and his wife, the tenant farmers and their families who took great pride in coming up to the big house and celebrating with the master's household. She tied on an apron and cast a surreptitious look about the kitchen. Heartsease had done its best. It almost looked like old times. Cook had laid out the usual fare: ham, breads, ginger biscuits, heaping bowls of mashed potatoes and green beans. Between the sacrifice of Teddy's tombstone and Cook's hard work, the largesse of Heartsease had not been compromised. Cook, in her usual way, had spared nothing. No one would go hungry today as they worked on the pudding, and there would be baskets filled with the remainder going home with families today. The kitchen itself was spotless, ready for the making of pudding. No one would guess what it had taken to put out this spread, to make sure that if one didn't look too closely one wouldn't see the chinks in Heartsease's armour. Teddy had been a good teacher in that regard. She'd learned a lot about managing impressions from watching him.

Elanora made sure everyone had a cup of something: brandy, eggnog, cider, warm milk spiced with cinnamon for the children, in order to drink the celebratory toast her father had offered annually. She gave the signal, raising her mug along with her voice. She swept the room with a wide smile. 'To another year of health and wealth spent with those we love both here and above.' It was a lie, of course. She knew already they wouldn't be together next year. Heartsease would have a new owner. Wealth would be a dubious concept.

Do not think on it, the voice of Christmas Present whispered. *Be in the moment. All we have is now. Have you learned nothing from Teddy? Nothing is guaranteed but this moment.*

And it, like so much, was fleeting. Yet, she was unable to let go of the losses of the past, and the uncertainty of the future cast a pall over her enjoyment of the day.

Everyone cheered and drank; one of the tenants offered a reciprocal toast to the Grisham generosity, which she accepted with the graciousness her father and Teddy had always shown. Cook took over after that, moving everyone to different stations to chop nuts, grind almonds, and the other sundry chores needed to assemble the pudding. There was laughter and singing and eating as people moved about the kitchen, conversations rising and falling as people caught up with one another. A decent harvest was in, the hard work of the autumn behind them. This was a time of celebration, of planning, the farmer's schedule not unlike the planning and waiting in the season of Advent.

For them, the world was still a certain place. Elanora moved from group to group, listening to them talk about next year's crops and which fields would be left fallow. She'd let them have that certainty awhile longer. Perhaps it wouldn't be so bad for them, though. Whoever the new owner was might come to amicable terms and they could all stay. Change might be minimal for them. It wouldn't go as well for the staff. The new owners would bring their people. The remaining staff would likely be out of work. Especially if that new owner was Elias Bathurst, who would turn them out just to spite her.

Elanora bit her lip and turned away for a moment to hide her anguish at the thought. The new owner could very well be him. Heartsease would go to auction and he would buy it there, a consolation prize for her rejection.

The temptation of the practical whispered wickedly in her mind: *He would still marry you, even now, even after your knee in his baubles. He would make you beg for the sake of his insufferable pride, but he'd do it. He needs the Grisham name as much as he needs the house. Marry him and you need not ever leave your home. This is the easy answer. Perhaps you should rethink—*

A knock sounded on the kitchen door, interrupting her thoughts. Elanora excused herself to answer it, wiping her hands on her apron. 'Tristan?' His name came out as a question. He was the last person she'd expected to see on the kitchen step, especially given the way she'd treated him.

He smiled broadly as if she'd not rudely dismissed him a few days prior. 'I hear there's quite a stir up going on here today.' His gaze rested on her, brown eyes twinkling, giving him an entirely too boyish, too appealing, of an air, and her pulse, caught off guard, skipped as it once had of old. Never mind she was well past the age for girlish infatuations, but no one had seen fit to tell those infatuations that. 'I thought I might drop by and join the fun, if you don't mind?'

'I don't mind at all.' She was momentarily flustered. She'd not expected to see him; she'd not been ready to have his windblown, bare-headed good looks happen to her all over again. He moved to step inside but she remembered herself and what she needed to do. She placed a hand on the arm of his greatcoat, her body too conscious of the casual touch that should have meant nothing but instead burned her hand through the thick fabric. 'Wait, Tristan.' She stepped outside with him and shut the door behind them, the noise of the kitchen fading. 'I need to say something before you go in.' Some of the merriment disappeared from his eyes and she thought perhaps he was braced for another set down. 'I owe you an apology for the other day. I behaved abominably towards you.'

He shook his head and she saw his gaze relax. 'You don't need to apologise for anything. You were right. Things have happened here that I know about only from a distance through whatever mention might have been made in a letter from home. I was, perhaps, a bit heavy handed with my comments without fully understanding the situation. *I* apologise for that and for any insinuation I might have made that suggested you were not capable. It seems we have to learn one another anew. We are no longer the children we once were.'

No, certainly not, Elanora thought.

Childlike was not the descriptor that came to mind when she thought of Tristan. He had shoulders like Atlas, and the confidence of Zeus radiated from every pore, every word. Her summertime playmate had become a commander of men.

Be careful, caution whispered. *He's led companies of men. He is used to giving orders, to having his way. How will one lone woman resist all that? Especially one who has been infatuated with him for over a decade? Your fantasies and his best intentions will have every secret out of you in no time.*

As if to prove it, Tristan's dark eyes fixed on her sternly. 'That does not change my desire to help you, nor does it change your need to perhaps bend your iron spine a bit and accept that help.'

'It's not that I'm opposed to middle ground.' Elanora smiled. 'It's that I *am* opposed to having no ground of my own at all. There are so few things a woman can count on, but she must have that at least.' Fewer ties meant more ground of her own, less ground to be pulled out from under her. More ties meant dependence, ground ceded to others. Marriage ceded all the ground, made her the property of another, took her rights and obliviated them. Taking help from others was only a lesser form of that. It created obligation; it gave ownership of her to others. She'd owe those she was obliged to as assuredly as she owed the bank.

Tristan nodded solemnly as if he could read the depths of her mind. 'It's good to see not everything has changed, then. You're still fiercely independent. I would never seek to undermine you, El. You know that.'

She did know that. 'It's not you I worry about, Tristan. It's the legal system, society, and all the things you and I cannot control.'

'But those worries are not for today, El.' He offered a gentle grin. 'There are to be no worries on Stir-Up Sunday.' He gave a nod towards the door. 'Now, might I have a cup of the Heartsease brandy? I do remember your father had the best brandy for miles and it was served liberally at the stir up.'

'Was? It still *is*. Come in and see.' She laughed, letting her worries go for the first time that day, letting the memory cheer her instead of drag her down. She had made peace with Tristan and she felt lighter than she had in days. Perhaps she could and *should* set those worries aside for a few hours at least and enjoy the day she'd taken such efforts to prepare.

Christmas Present whispered again, *If it's to be the last, make it the best.*

Inside, the stirring had begun. Groups had formed at the various pudding pans and Tristan's arrival was greeted with great enthusiasm as he took off his coat and rolled up his shirtsleeves. He went straight to the station known as the children's station, where Cook always had a pudding the children could stir. Pudding needed an inordinate amount of stirring and it was good to have a large family or group of friends to help with it. One person couldn't stir the pudding up alone. For a moment Elanora bit her lip and firmly thrust the reminder away that next year she'd not have a Christmas pudding. She'd be alone, no one to stir with. A pudding would be nigh on impossible.

But not today.

Today she had Tristan in her kitchen, looking irresistible as he worked with the children.

She watched as Tristan lifted one of the smaller children up on a chair and helped them to stir the thick mixture with a big wooden spoon. 'Do you know how many ingredients are in the pudding?' he asked.

'Thirteen!' the child proudly announced, using both hands on the spoon while the adults laughed.

'And do you know why?' Tristan prompted the group of children at large.

They gave the question some thought, one of them shouting, 'To make it delicious?'

Tristan chuckled. 'I thought the same thing when I was your age, but Reverend Thompson taught me that each ingredient stands for Jesus and the twelve disciples.'

Reverend Thompson joined the group, laughing. 'I am glad my lessons stuck, Captain.'

The child stirring began to tire. 'Did you make your wish?' Tristan asked. The child nodded. 'Very good, then your job is done. Go get a ginger biscuit from Cook.' He lifted another child onto the chair and winked at Reverend Thompson as he asked the children, 'Did you know we stir east to west to remember the journey of the three kings to visit Baby Jesus?'

It was hard to look away from Tristan and the children as Elanora moved about the kitchen, encouraging people to eat and drink, her own Christmas spirits lifting at the sight of Tristan at the children's station. He was a natural with them, easy-going and friendly, treating them as equals, never talking down to them or lecturing.

'I don't imagine he'll remain a bachelor for long now that he's home and his military days are behind him,' Mrs Thompson said slyly, helping herself to another slice of ham. 'He'll make a splendid husband.'

And a splendid father came Elanora's unbidden thought.

It was the thought of a woman who'd once dreamed of a family and home of her own that would be like the one she'd grown up in, full of laughter and love. But that was before...before she'd realised that love exacted its own price, that happiness was a fleeting condition, that security was not guaranteed. 'I'm sure he would,' Elanora agreed politely with Mrs Thompson and moved on quickly, but not before she could see the wheels moving in Mrs Thompson's mind, thinking of all the girls that might be sent in Tristan Lennox's direction, girls much younger than her twenty-five years. She ought not be jealous but a certain covetousness made its own stab, a reminder that she could lose Tristan again, that his presence in her life was, like all else, temporary. It seemed she was doomed to lose him either to his own wanderlust or to another woman. She should know by now all the best things in life were fleeting, even the best of men.

'Elanora.' Tristan beckoned her over to him. 'I think the pudding is ready for the charms. What do you think?' She peered into the pan, aware the children watched her expectantly. The charms had always been her favourite part.

'I think so,' she agreed, taking a small cloth bag from the pocket of her apron. She opened the drawstring and handed out the charms. 'Here's a wishbone for good luck, a thimble for frugality, a ring for hopes of marriage.' The children wrinkled their noses at that but she was acutely aware of Tristan standing beside her in shirtsleeves, forearms muscled and exposed, the sight of them sending a little thrill through her. Who'd have thought a man's forearms would evoke such a reaction? She blamed it on Mrs Thompson's words. She reached into the bag for the last charm, a little tin anchor. 'For safe harbour,' she said, closing her eyes briefly for a wish of her own, a safe harbour of her own. She'd been at sea for so long. She opened them and smiled brightly. 'Are we forgetting anything?' she asked the children with feigned innocence.

'The pennies!' they clamoured.

'Oh, yes, the pennies!' Elanora exclaimed, taking out a second pouch. 'A penny for each of you since you've been such good helpers, and one penny for the pudding for wealth.' The children's eyes lit as she dropped a penny into each of their hands. In the moment, their joy became her joy. It felt good to give. These pennies could not save her, could not make a difference in the debts she faced. But they would make a difference to the children. For some, that penny would buy an experience they'd remember, perhaps the experience of walking into the mercantile and purchasing a favourite candy or a small toy. That experience would give them a sense of responsibility, of agency and independence. For others, their sense of responsibility might come through saving their penny. Still other children might contribute their penny to the family and experience responsibility that way. All were valuable lessons.

Charms mixed, Cook came over to wrap the pudding and prepare it for steaming and storing. Outside, the sun was going down and families began to gather their children. Elanora excused herself from Tristan's side to help prepare baskets to send home, aware that Tristan's gaze followed her even as the men took him into their circle around the brandy cask for a final drink.

Questions whirled in her head as she tried to ignore the attentions of his gaze. What did he see when he looked at her? What was he learning anew? She supposed she ought to be flattered. Isn't this what she'd dreamed of as a young, infatuated adolescent? Of catching Tristan's eye? But now the idea of catching Tristan's eye was fraught with underlying worry as well. To draw his attention was to draw his scrutiny and perhaps his questions, questions that she didn't want to answer. She

wondered what might she inadvertently reveal? What
was she going to regret? What was she going to wish
she'd kept better hidden? It might all be fancy, the moment of light-heartedness with the children playing with
her thoughts; he might not be interested in her at all.

Of course, the biggest question was why did she
care at all? What Tristan thought or didn't think could
change nothing. Her path was cast. Her choices were
made. This little interlude, these daydreams that fran-
chised old girlish fantasies, was a pleasant diversion,
nothing more. Elanora hazarded a glance in his direction, letting her eyes meet his. He raised a mug to her,
his open smile lighting his face, and she smiled back.
How could she not? His goodwill and cheer were infectious. In that moment she knew why she cared. She
wanted this from Tristan—his openness, his friendship,
a piece of the good old times. If he knew the truth, the
whole truth, she would have only his pity. It was inevitable because her situation was indeed pitiful. She
didn't want his pity any more than she wanted him to
try and solve her problems. All she wanted were these
moments, this pleasantness and the fantasy of hope it
allowed. Thank goodness that was all she wanted because that was all she could have. This was the way in
which wishes came true for her in these days.

Chapter Six

'**D**id you make a wish?' Tristan came up beside her in the kitchen doorway as the last of the guests departed Heartsease, heading off into the night content and happy. He was rolling down his shirtsleeves, retiring his forearms from view much to her disappointment.

Goodness, she had to get this attraction in hand! It was not well done of her. She wasn't a fifteen-year-old girl with a crush on her brother's best friend and stars in her eyes when it came to the mystery of what a man was. She was a twenty-five-year-old woman who'd solved that mystery with rather disappointing ease only to learn that men were, after all, exceedingly fallible creatures; her brother and father, both imperfect, as well as the men who'd called after her brother's death, each with their own unique flaws and agendas. But when Tristan was around, she conveniently forgot all that. 'Well?' He nudged her with his elbow. 'Did you make a wish or not?'

'Yes, and because I know you'll ask, it's already

come true.' She sighed and leaned against the doorjamb, pleasantly weary now that the day was done. At
least one of her wishes had come true. Tristan grinned
at her sauciness and she was struck by how easy it was
to be with him; to joke with him, to unburden herself
as she'd done at the graves, knowing that he would understand the messages beneath the words and that she
could reciprocate in kind by reading the secret histories
behind his words. They'd not had to say much in the
graveyard in order to connect, to understand all that lay
between them, all that went beyond words.

'I'm glad.' His eyes twinkled like polished onyx,
fixed on her, the attention warming and unnerving all
at once.

'What is it?' She raised a self-conscious hand to her
cheek, fighting the urge to squirm beneath the intensity of his scrutiny.

'You're happy. Making others happy pleases you,'
he said simply. 'You're beautiful when you smile.' The
words made her flush. She'd not been expecting that.
After all the years of wanting to be seen by Tristan,
dreaming of it, she was ill prepared for such a moment. This had not been one of the thoughts she'd considered he'd have when she'd watched him at the keg
with the men.

'Tristan, are you flirting with me?' she scolded teas-
ingly once she'd recovered her wits.

'Maybe. Or maybe I'm simply offering a sincere
compliment.' His eyes darkened to the shade of a night
sky, that midnight gaze lingering on her face, his tone
solemn as he reached for her hand and laced his fin-

gers through hers. 'Your parents and Teddy would be proud of you. You gave the people of Heartsease a day worthy of the Grisham legacy.'

The words touched her but she'd not done it alone. 'You helped.' She smiled softly at him, wondering if he felt it, too, that something more than honouring the dead was binding them in this moment. Or was it just the remnants of a day filled with tradition and happy memories playing tricks on her? 'You were marvellous with the children.' He'd been marvellous with her, too, whether he realised it or not. He'd helped her find the joy in a day she'd been dreading. 'I enjoyed today.'

He made a playful frown. 'You didn't think you would? You always liked Stir-Up Sunday.' Did she imagine that those dark eyes lingered not just on her face but also on her lips?

Her skin prickled with awareness of him, of how close they stood in the narrow doorway, of the spicy, winter scent of him mingled with the homey smells of Christmas food. It was hard to keep up an ordinary conversation when her mind wasn't exactly focused on words. 'I always liked the stir up because of the people I was with. Now those people are gone.' The love and security she'd associated with them was gone, too.

'Not all of them. I'm here.' He paused before continuing, a little furrow forming at his brow. 'Teddy would want you to be happy, El. He would not want you to give up joy.'

'But perhaps *I* do.' She managed a weak smile.

'You don't mean that.' Tristan raised their joined hands between them, his own gaze studying them, palms together, fingers laced. His hand was much larger than hers. 'You were made for joy, El,' he said quietly.

Sometimes she wished she weren't. 'Joy can hurt. There can be pain underneath it, beneath the remembering even if it is in remembering the good times.' She sighed, allowing herself the luxury of staring into the dark depths of his eyes. 'I wonder if I had felt joy a little less that everything now might not hurt as much.' She'd been so happy, surrounded by so much *good* growing up that to lose it all seemed to her indecently cruel. Perhaps if she had been more temperate, she might have managed to save a little of it.

'We have to fight for joy as much as we have to fight for anything else, I think. The world is quick to take it from us if we don't guard it.'

He touched her cheek, his fingers warm as they made a gentle cup of her jaw, his gaze tender. A tremor or yearning swept through her on the waves of a single wild thought: *He is going to kiss me.*

The moment stretched between them, one heartbeat, then two. Tristan licked his lips, his body moved infinitesimally towards her, and then something shifted in his eyes. He stepped away with a clearing of his throat. 'I must be off. Mother will have supper waiting although I can't imagine eating another bite after the feast laid out here today.' He reached for his coat and the moment was gone, but not entirely.

Even after she'd watched Tristan ride away, the potential of that moment remained, hot and vivid in her mind, of the way his eyes had lingered, the way his body had leaned in. She had *not* imagined it. He had nearly kissed her. Why had he stopped? Or maybe more importantly, why had he started? Of their own volition, her fingers went to her lips. Perhaps neither answer mattered. Perhaps all that mattered was that he almost had. She could live on that moment for a long time without harm, a lovely limbo of potential that could exist apart from reality. She smiled a little to herself as she went back inside to help with the cleaning up.

Tristan had almost kissed her.

Good Lord, he'd almost kissed Elanora! What had he been thinking? Not even galloping Vitalis across the dusky fields could drive those two thoughts from Tristan's mind, followed by other thoughts like what would Teddy think if he were alive? On the front end of it, a man didn't kiss his best friend's sister without permission and there were consequences on the back end, consequences that Tristan was in no position to contemplate.

He'd not come home to stay. His priorities on this visit were clear. He'd come home for Christmas, to see his family, to pay his respects, to transition into the next stage of his life, which involved *more* travels, not fewer. He'd not come home to fall for a childhood friend or to entertain the thought of settling down in one spot forever. Yet, the novel question he'd posed to himself that first night—*what would it take to stay?*—seemed less novel tonight, the answer more tangible than rhetorical.

Elanora was the kind of woman a man would stay for. She was kind and giving. She cared for people and was filled with the gift of genuine compassion. That compassion lit up any room she was in; it was the source of her true beauty. He wondered how many men looked beyond her pretty face, though? None of those who had called upon her after Teddy's death, from her account. A stab of envy pricked at the thought of other men courting Elanora. But that envy came from an irrational place. He *wasn't* courting Elanora. Wanting to steal a kiss in the doorway wasn't *courting*. What it was was getting caught up in a moment. Homecoming, Christmases, memories, and seeing an old friend had all conspired to create a rather perfect storm of longing.

He put Vitalis over a low stone fence and they came down on the other side in a satisfying thud of hooves on turf. In hindsight, he was *glad* he hadn't kissed her. He'd promised himself he'd see her cared for, her problems managed, before he left. Beyond that he could offer her nothing more and she was not a woman a man kissed unless he *could* offer more. Yes, it was best, he thought as Vitalis's hooves thrummed beneath him, that the kiss hadn't happened. Logically, he'd been right to step away, although physically his body was not presently in agreement with him. He pushed Vitalis to greater speed, the ride requiring more attention from his body in the hopes that the exertion would dispel his lingering arousal. He could not show up at his mother's dinner table in his current state.

But no matter how hard he rode Vitalis, he could not dislodge the other reality. He wanted to see her again. Soon. But in a manner that didn't constitute courting. He would not create an illusion for either of them. By the time he reached Brentham Woods, he had an idea.

He'd send a note inviting her to go with him to call on the families of his two fallen soldiers. She would be the ideal companion for the undertaking. She knew what loss felt like; she would not offer them empty platitudes.

Tristan swung off Vitalis and handed him over to Joe, satisfied with the plan, his mind organising the details. He'd send the note right away. He'd call for her at ten and they could ride out together, weather permitting. If the weather did not permit, he'd bring the carriage. Either way, he'd get to enjoy her company while carrying out his duties and perhaps he'd be able to probe more deeply into her situation. It was a good solution all around, as long as he didn't try to kiss her again. He had no fairy-tale ending to offer her or anyone at the moment.

Chapter Seven

Tristan looked like a young girl's fairy tale come true the next morning as he rode down the drive on Vitalis, dressed in the scarlet coat and gold braid of a cavalry officer. Elanora had not seen him in uniform since the day he'd left Hemsford all those years ago. He'd looked handsome then to her fifteen-year-old eyes. He still did. The sight of those broad shoulders in scarlet wool set her pulse to racing against her will and she couldn't help but smile as she gestured to the weather. 'We are favoured,' she called out. 'We get to ride today.'

The prospect of riding with Tristan brought her more satisfaction than she dared admit. She'd been unduly excited last night to receive the unlooked-for invitation to join him. She'd awakened anxiously this morning to check the weather, her anticipation rising at the sight of dry skies.

Excitement. Joyful anticipation.

These were not adjectives she'd used recently to describe her days. But despite the sombre motive for the

outing—to visit the families of Tristan's fallen soldiers—
she was looking forward to it.

Tristan brought Vitalis to a halt, his gaze resting on
her for an odd lingering moment not unlike the moment last night on the kitchen steps. An all-too-familiar
warmth awoke in her belly. Would there be other such
moments today? Did she want there to be? Would they
end differently? Did she want them to? What would a
different ending mean? Could it mean anything? She
already knew the answer to that last question. It was
ridiculous of her to play this hopeful game of what-if.

'Do I pass inspection?' she teased, suddenly self-
conscious in the violet wool riding habit. Perhaps she
should have worn the blue, but he'd already seen her in
that and she admitted privately that part of her wanted
to look her best, especially after yesterday. 'I've got
lunch in my saddlebags and a blanket for picnicking,
if that helps.'

'Well, then, in that case, you pass,' Tristan laughed.
'We'll go to the Thomsfords first. We can cut across
fields most of the way.' She knew what those fields
meant: they could gallop and jump, and her already
high spirits soared.

Whatever oddness she'd sensed in him disappeared
as they set the horses to a lively canter in the fields,
leaving the road behind. These were the fields of their
youth and they knew the bridle trails and paths by heart.
At a low stone fence, Tristan flashed a look she recognised too easily. 'Shall we jump or go around?'

She laughed over her shoulder. 'Do you really have
to ask?' She gave Marian's flanks a smart kick and

within three strides they were over it, Tristan and Vitalis coming down alongside them. Oh, this felt good! The wind in her face, Marian sure and steady beneath her, the day spreading out before her with possibility. There would be no worries today, just riding, and racing, and perhaps the indulgence of old times.

They covered the ground to the Thomsfords quickly, and all too soon had to return to the road. They found the home of Sergeant Thomsford's family easily, a farmhouse just off the main thoroughfare. Tristan helped her dismount and then retrieved a box from his saddlebags. He tugged at his jacket and put on his helmet for the formal visit even though he'd take it off again when they entered the house. 'Are you sure you don't want me to wait outside?' she offered one last time.

He gave her a brief smile of assurance. 'I think your company will be most welcome. Sergeant Thomsford's mother and sister will appreciate your presence.' He lowered his voice as they walked to the door. 'I am hoping with you here, there might be a time when you could draw the women off by themselves so I could have a word alone with Sergeant Thomsford's father. Before he died, Sergeant Thomsford mentioned he was concerned about the family's finances without the support of his pay. Apparently, he'd been sending some of it back for his brother's schooling.'

Their knock was answered by Thomsford's father, who leaned heavily on a cane and ushered them into the front parlour, where the sergeant's mother, sister, and younger brother sat solemnly waiting. Tristan made the introductions and presented Thomsford's mother with the box. 'May these items bring you comfort, ma'am, as your son brought comfort to a great many in his company. He was and is sorely missed.'

Thomsford's mother wiped at her eyes with a lacy handkerchief and Tristan sat beside her, keeping a hold of her hand as if it were the most natural thing in the world. He was good at this: talking with people, offering comfort, drawing them out, Elanora realised as she took a seat next to the sister.

'Your brother talked about you often.' Tristan directed the comment towards young Robbie, who Elanora guessed must have been about twelve. 'How is school? Your brother enjoyed hearing about your studies. He said you excelled in Latin.'

'Very well, Captain,' Robbie began, at first startled at being made part of the conversation and then relaxing as Tristan drew him out with questions and told stories of the boy's brother that made him smile. There were assurances, too, that his brother had loved him very much and had been proud of him.

Elanora took note of how Tristan moved the conversation to each family member in turn, encouraging their own stories and remembrances with his prompts, even as he made personal enquiries to ascertain how they were doing now that Derick Thomsford was gone from them. These conversations were not unlike the conversation he'd shared with her at Teddy's grave, conversations that provided a chance to share. The sister shared that she'd delayed her engagement in the wake of her brother's death, and Mrs Thomsford mentioned that it was difficult to afford Robbie's school. They weren't planning on sending him in the winter until they could sort out their finances. That earned her a scolding look from Mr Thomsford, and Elanora sensed it was time to separate the group so that Tristan could have that talk.

When Mrs Thomsford asked if she'd like to see her son's room, Elanora took the opportunity to include the sister and young Robbie in the group and followed Mrs Thomsford upstairs. Tristan threw her a covert look of thanks as she passed him.

When she returned to the sitting room twenty minutes later, it was clear some accord had been reached and that a burden had been lifted from the father's shoulders. They took their leave after that amid thankyous from the family, but to Elanora's eye, Tristan seemed distant as they rode out, as if some part of the meeting had left him displeased.

'What is it?' She waited until the house was out of sight, slowing Marian to a trot before letting the mare fall into step beside Vitalis on the quiet lane.

'They shouldn't thank me. I've done them no favours. Their son died a year ago and I'm just now visiting them.'

She furrowed her brow. 'You wrote to them immediately when their son died, and you've come as soon as you could. You've been home less than a week. I don't think anyone expected more.'

'I could have come sooner. They've been struggling for a year. I could have prevented that if I'd known, if I'd been here.' He fixed her with a sharp stare that penetrated along with his words as he made his confession. 'I could have come home last autumn, just weeks after the measles outbreak passed. But I chose to extend my tour in the Caribbean for another year. I *could* have been here. Not just for them, but for Teddy.'

For a moment she was struck by the import of those words. She let herself imagine how different things could have been last autumn. Teddy hadn't left yet on the fateful voyage. There was a message beneath even that, too, and Tristan slowly gave voice to it. 'If I had come home then like I should have, Teddy would still be alive.'

That assumption was more myth than reality and as much as it might be nice to believe it, she could not let Tristan bear that cross. 'We can't know that, Tristan. Not even you can stop ships from sinking.'

'But I could have stopped him from going.' There was a lot of history behind that premise. How many times had she watched Tristan talk Teddy off the metaphoric edge of stubbornness gone too far, that point where obstinance became unreasonable recklessness? Too many to count.

'I did try to talk him out of it,' Elanora admitted. She'd not talked to anyone about the last days she'd seen her brother alive. She'd begged him not to go even as he packed his trunks. He might have died six months ago, but he'd left her almost a year ago, right after Christmas, in fact, for a journey he'd not come back from. His decision to go had been as reckless and irrational as the investment itself.

'So his moods did not improve?' Tristan asked after a long silence. This was also something that was never discussed, something she long thought only Tristan and she noticed, or named. Where everyone else saw Teddy's dynamic personality, his tenacity and energy for life, Tristan saw something deeper, darker. He saw the manic quality of those moods, the extreme highs, the desperate lows, and how quickly those moods could shift. Her parents had dismissed them as adolescent caprices. Others had encouraged Teddy's wildness as part of sowing his oats. But Tristan had understood it was more than that.

She shook her head. 'You are not responsible for him.'

Tristan gave her a sharp look. 'Neither are you.' But that did little to mitigate the constant guilt that was with her every day, and she suspected that Tristan felt the same. Surely, she could have done something? Said something that would have made a difference? But what? Did the answer matter now that Teddy was gone?

She spied a tree in the middle of a meadow and took the opportunity to move away from the awkwardness and hurt of the conversation. 'Why don't we picnic over there? Race you.'

Tristan kicked Vitalis into a canter and let her get away with the ploy. He recognised the signs of a ruse when he saw them. Elanora was trying hard not to talk about her brother. Still, he'd learned enough for now to fill in more of what had transpired at Heartsease even if it was not exactly uplifting. It awoke the protector's spirit in him. He didn't like the thought of Elanora there alone trying to reason with Teddy in moments of mania, and yet that's what she'd done for five years after her father had passed.

'Tell me about Barbados,' she asked as they laid out the picnic. He took the other end of the old quilt and helped her spread it on the ground beneath the oak, indulging her with tales of the Caribbean.

'Barbados is, to my eye, one of the loveliest places on the planet.' He stretched out on the blanket, watching her unpack the saddlebag lunch, his appetite rousing from the morning's exertions. It was a delicious collection of leftovers from yesterday's stir up. There were thick pieces of bread and savoury slices of ham, a jug of cider and a bag of ginger cookies. 'The water is a brilliant turquoise in some places, a deep blue in others, the sand is white and it's warm year-round. Everything is warm, the water, the air, the sand. There's no fog, no damp. It's unlike anywhere I've ever been.' He smiled. One could not help but smile when talking about Barbados.

'I'm glad you got to see such a place. You always did want to travel and now you have.' She smiled back, tempting him to ask the question that had recently flared in his mind.

'Would you like to see such a place someday?' Deep inside him, he wanted her to say yes, wanted to discover that among the many things they had in common, there was this, too, this desire to wander the ends of the earth.

She shook her head and that flicker of hope died inside him. 'I can't imagine leaving Sussex, not even for a Season in London.' She stacked slices of ham on her bread. 'Perhaps it's best that Mama got sick the year I was supposed to make my debut. I don't think Marian or I would have done well in the city. This is where we belong.' She cocked her head sideways. 'Is this where you belong? Do you think you'll stay?' She laughed. 'Has your father already asked what your plans are?'

'The first night, in fact.' He laughed with her, even as he knew he was glossing over the first part of her question by only answering the second half. Despite his disappointment, it felt good to be known like this. He'd had friends in his company and he'd been friends with the other officers, but it wasn't the same. They didn't know his past, his family, his home. Elanora did and there was something intangibly wonderful about that, a connection neither of them could have with any other, a connection that could not be duplicated.

The voice in his head began to whisper: *Is it a connection worth staying for?*

Or perhaps in her case, would it be a connection worth leaving for? What would she say to the life he *could* offer?

He turned thoughtful. 'I do have plans, but I am waiting on word before anything is official. Until then, you'll have to keep it a secret.' He'd not meant to tell anyone, not even Julien, but this was Elanora. He trusted her implicitly. 'The army would like me to supply the cavalry with horses. I would travel on occasion to the Continent and the breadth of England gathering the finest horseflesh for the army. There would be a training component as well for part of the year, probably in London at Horseguards since no other place has the space.'

'It sounds perfect for you.' Elanora smiled but he sensed sadness beneath it.

'But?' he prompted.

'It means I'll be losing you again. You were meant to travel but I was meant to be here. I *want* to be here.' It was true as far as it went but Tristan didn't think it went far enough to explain the sadness he saw in her eyes. It was gone in the next moment as she reached for the ginger snaps. 'Time for dessert.' She smiled, broad and wide, the sadness veiled.

It was a dazzling smile, as dazzling as the woman who wore it. She'd been stunning this morning, waiting for him at the end of the driveway in her violet habit, her blond hair in a sophisticated twist beneath a little hat. He'd had to look twice to make sure it was her. He was still getting used yet to seeing this grown-up version of Elanora, of his response to her, this lovely woman she'd become. The urge to kiss her, to taste all that loveliness, had returned in force today, proving his yearning yesterday had not been the isolated magic of a carefully wrought moment. It would have made things simpler if it had been. It also would have made this conversation on the picnic blanket less dangerous, less tempting, especially given what he knew now: that she saw her life *here*. And he wasn't sure that he did.

But he'd not imagined her loveliness or her compassion. Both had been in evidence at the Thomsfords today; the way she'd listened, the way she'd intuitively known what he needed. She'd been a partner during that visit, perhaps in large part because she knew what grief felt like, the emotions it stirred up, and what people needed because she'd needed those things herself so very recently. But she'd had no one to care for her.

'Thank you for helping at the Thomsfords'.' He

filched another ginger snap from the bag. 'You were very good with the women.'

'I took my cue from you. You set the tone. I am only sorry that you've had to become so proficient in such discussions.' Elanora pushed a loose curl behind her ear. 'Did you have the conversation you needed with Mr Thomsford?'

Tristan nodded. 'I arranged for young Robbie to be able to attend school and I assured him that his daughter need not delay her engagement on account of concern about her dowry.'

Elanora was quiet for a long while, a slow smile taking her face as understanding dawned. 'You're a generous man, Tristan Lennox.'

'So was Derick Thomsford,' Tristan answered solemnly. 'He would have done it if it had been within his power to do. More importantly, Mr Thomsford saw the wisdom of accepting those gifts. Mr Thomsford is a proud man, too. But he recognised when his pride became a detriment for his family. There might be a moral to that story in there for others,' he said pointedly and without any attempt at subtlety.

If she saw his parallel, she said nothing and carried on with the conversation. 'What of the other family we're to visit? What should I know about them?'

Well, Tristan reasoned as he told her about the Prinks family, *Rome wasn't built in a day.*

He'd not expected to conquer all of Elanora's obstacles in a single outing. He was just beginning the siege. Sieges took time and he had time. The army would not require anything of him until the New Year. That gave him five weeks from yesterday, the entirety of the Christmas holiday, to solve her problems so that when he left, she would be taken care of. It was what Teddy would have wanted and it was what he'd promised himself he'd see done. If only she were as easy to care for as the Thomsfords had been. If only she didn't come with other, unexpected temptations. Helping Elanora was becoming more complicated than he'd anticipated. It had stirred up emotions and questions he'd not thought to feel or to ask.

Chapter Eight

It was as if Stir-Up Sunday had set off a flurry of Christmas preparations—which of course it had. The village of Hemsford had turned to Christmas overnight. At least it seemed that way to Tristan's eye as he walked the High Street, taking in the festively draped bow windows of the shops. Some were draped in red and green fabrics while others sported fresh evergreens and holly as backdrops for artfully arranged displays of once-a-year specialities.

Tristan paused with the crowd before the dressmaker's window who were oohing and ahhing over the exquisite red velvet dress on display with its low-cut bodice and puffed sleeves dripping with snow-white lace meant to reach to a lady's elbow and the edge of a long white silk glove. The skirt itself was luxuriously full. Tristan couldn't imagine how many yards of fabric had gone into the skirt alone, but even to a man's eye, the gown was a thing of beauty. His first thoughts went immediately to Elanora. She would swoon over it. She'd always had an eye for pretty things; a tomboy who'd liked arranging the flowers of her garden as much as she'd liked getting her hands dirty planting the seeds. Her bouquets had adorned every mantel and tabletop Heartsease had to spare in the springs and summers. Which was why the current condition of Heartsease was something of a mystery to him.

Tristan eased himself away from the crowd and continued his walk, mulling over the puzzle. Elanora loved her home. How could she have let it fall into disrepair? There had to be a reason. Perhaps more than one and maybe he wasn't being fair. It had barely been six months since Teddy died. Perhaps she simply hadn't had the willpower to face the task of running Heartsease alone? Perhaps she didn't know how? Teddy would have borne the brunt of the inheritance and its responsibilities after their father's death. Although, Tristan reasoned, one would have thought Teddy had learned a bit more about preparation from his father's own mistakes. Then again, Tristan thought wryly, Teddy thought himself untouchable, immortal.

Even so, a lack of energy? A lack of willpower and fortitude didn't sound at all like Elanora, a girl who had never been able to sit still, who was always out of doors with her garden and her horses.

But what do you know? came the reminder. *Ten years changes people. Time alone changes people, and she's had grief and loss to deal with on top of that. She is not a fifteen-year-old hoyden any more than you are a boy barely twenty. You've changed, too*, his conscience scolded. *You've both seen death too much.*

But some things haven't changed, he answered himself, his feet stopping in front of the baker's window with its bright arrangement of carefully iced ginger cookies enticing passers-by. They gave him an idea. Surely, Elanora's sweet tooth was one thing that hadn't changed. She'd enjoyed the ginger snaps at their picnic as much as he had. Neither had her fierceness changed. Elanora had never been a shrinking violet, and she'd not been one yesterday. She'd ridden with her trademark fire and confidence, taking the stone fences in the meadows with ease. And she'd shown plenty of spark with him, arguing with him, challenging him. Elanora was just as fierce as she'd always been.

Because she's defending something. You remember how ferocious she was about her garden when you and Teddy tried to sneak in that one summer.

Oh, he *did* remember. She'd strung up a tripwire, which had dumped a bucket of dirt on their heads that had turned to mud when they tried to wash it out. What was she defending now? Herself? Her home? But from what? And why would she feel she had to defend it from him? Hopefully, iced ginger biscuits would help him get some answers.

He pushed open the bakery door, setting the bell to tinkling as the pleasant smell of baking bread wafted over him. 'I'll take a dozen of the iced ginger biscuits.' He smiled at the young woman behind the counter and she smiled back, giving a coy toss of her dark curls as she boxed up the treats.

Tristan thanked her, careful to be nothing more than polite. He'd had his share of experience being a new bachelor in towns and knew the kind of attention one could attract without even trying. He didn't want anyone getting the impression that coming home was synonymous with looking for a wife. He'd have to be very clear with his mother on the subject. Apparently, Julien had a close call with her matchmaking efforts a few years back.

Tristan appreciated the caution. Forewarned was forearmed. No wife for him, not yet, at least. He wasn't opposed to marriage; in fact, the idea of a partner appealed to him greatly. His parents' marriage, the Grishams' marriage, had shown him the potential of what marriage could be with the right partner. It had also shown him the great responsibility both parties shouldered. To expect a good partner, he had to be a good partner. He still had plenty to sort out for himself before he was ready for that, starting with whether or not he was even going to stay in Hemsford, which was why his rather sudden and growing feelings for Elanora posed such a conundrum. He didn't dare care for her in that way and not be able to stay.

If the offer from the army came through—and there was no reason to think it wouldn't—staying was unlikely. If he were to marry now, his wife would either need to travel with him or be left behind for long stretches of time, which in his mind defeated the purpose of marriage in the first place. How did two people build a relationship when they weren't together?

He tucked the box under his arm and headed for the livery where he'd left Vitalis. If Elanora wouldn't come to town, then he'd bring a bit of town to her. He hoped perhaps a sweet treat would soften her up when she realised what he meant to do. He was going to get his answers and Heartsease was going to get the help it needed one way or another.

It was the noise that finally got to her; the sound of something thumping periodically against the side of the house. The first time, she'd not paid it any attention. She'd been too absorbed in weeding the beds in her garden to care overmuch. Weeding was a good task to occupy one's hands so that one's thoughts could wander without disaster.

Today her thoughts insisted on revisiting every moment of her outing with Tristan. She should not allow it. Nothing good could come from it. She was just feeding an old girlish infatuation. Even worse, she was feeding new fantasies; not fantasies where Tristan had now returned and could fix all her problems—she'd never been the sort to want that kind of a fantasy—but a fantasy where Tristan returned and saw her for herself, not as the sister of his best friend, nor the orphaned sister of his best friend, or a woman in want of a man simply to make her life easier, but just as herself.

That was what had made the picnic so intoxicating. There'd been moments when the fantasy had been near enough to touch; when they rode and raced and laughed into the wind just the two of them, nothing between them—not Teddy, not the past, just them, as they were now. But how could he see just her when there was so much to see past? The grief and the loss were just the two aspects he knew about. If he knew about the money, about the debt and the mortgage, it would be even harder for him to see just her and not her problems. Even if he did manage to see her, what did it matter? He was planning to leave again. Which was all for the better. He wouldn't be here to see her move to the cottage, to see her lose Heartsease. If she could just keep it hidden from him until after Christmas, her secret would be safe.

There came the thud again and the muffled sound of wood against wood followed by a pounding, of a hammer and a nail. Elanora set aside her hoe and pulled off her work gloves. She strode out of the garden, following the sounds around to the front of the house. Her gaze arrested on a man atop a ladder fixing a loose shutter. Not just any man, and not just fixing. It was Tristan and he'd been whitewashing the shutters. For a moment her heart was in her throat as she gauged the distance between him and the ground. 'Tristan! Get down from there at once!' she called up. She wasn't sure what sort of condition that ladder was in and she did not want to have to explain to the Lennoxes why their son had fallen.

'What are you doing?' she scolded as Tristan climbed nimbly down the ladder.

'I am cleaning your shutters. That one needed a bit of extra attention.' He gave her a grin, brandishing the hammer. 'I was wondering how long it would be before you noticed.'

'I was in the garden.' She gave the front of the house a longer look. He'd been here awhile. All the second-storey windows had been done except the one she'd caught him on. 'It looks good,' she admitted. The upper shutters looked clean and sharp against the bricks and she felt a wave of embarrassment sweep her over the state he'd found them in. 'But you didn't need to,' she added.

'Yes, I did. You wouldn't let me hire any men for you, so I did it myself. One doesn't need any great skill for whitewashing. He nodded towards the lower windows. 'If you feed me lunch, I'll finish these afterwards. You'll be hosting the Christmas panto in a few weeks. We must have Heartsease looking its best.' *We.* Did he have any idea he'd said that? Or any idea how the simple word affected her? How much she wanted that to be true? To have a partner, to not be alone. But she was too much of a burden now for any decent man. Only adventurers like Elias Bathurst would have her now, men who couldn't get land and respectability any other way. Even if Tristan was a possibility, she would not drag down a friend into her debts.

'I can do them. I am sure you have better things to do with your time.' She tried to argue but Tristan was intractable.

'If you want, you can help,' he countered. 'But I am staying and finishing the job.' He was already striding around back to the kitchen door. 'Are you coming, Elanora?' he called over his shoulder. 'I've brought you a treat from town. Iced biscuits from Manning's,' he teased her.

She shook her head and laughed. 'I hate how easily you can persuade me.'

Tristan held the door for her. 'I think it's more the case that you know quality when you see it.'

Inside, the kitchen was warm and it was clear that Cook had been more aware of the goings-on outside than Elanora had been. Lunch was already laid out on the long worktable, and a big pot of ham and potato soup bubbled on the stove, filling the kitchen with the rich aroma of hot food on a wintry day. Cook had taken herself off for a cup of tea with Mrs Thornton, leaving the kitchen to them. 'Don't let Cook see that box from Manning's or she'll be jealous,' Elanora warned laughingly, but her breath caught as Tristan raised the lid. 'Oh, they're too lovely to eat.' She furrowed her brow and counted. 'There's a dozen here. Who is going to eat that many?'

'Us?' Tristan chuckled. 'You know you can't eat just one and neither can I.' He passed her an iced biscuit. 'Shall we start with an appetiser before the soup?' They allowed themselves one biscuit as they ladled soup into bowls and cut slices of Cook's dark, crusty bread.

'These are so good,' Elanora exclaimed with a sigh, brushing the last of the crumbs from her hands. 'I don't know what I did to earn such a treat, but I'm glad I did. Thank you, Tristan. It's been a long time since I've had an indulgence.'

'I'm glad you enjoyed it. It's my way of saying thank you for making the visits with me, and I suppose it's my way of sweetening you up to answer my questions.'

Elanora braced as Tristan paused to take a spoonful of soup. 'What questions?'

'Questions about Heartsease. You're right. I know nothing. But I'd like to, and I know that something isn't right here. You wouldn't let me hire men to clean the place up. That's not like you. You love your home. So I thought about it and concluded that perhaps money was tight. That would explain why there weren't already enough staff around to do the usual maintenance. Am I right?'

She tried to brazen it out. 'One person doesn't need the size of staff we had here.' Tristan shook his head, not fooled.

'But the house itself does, Elanora. One person living here or twenty, the gardens and the grounds still need staff.' Tristan sliced himself another piece of bread. 'I will not be put off today, Elanora. I want the truth. There should be that at least between friends. How bad was the hit from the lost cargo?'

'Not so bad that we can't do Christmas right at Heartsease if that's what you're asking. I was waiting until spring to do any major cleanup and repairs.' Not a lie exactly. She was waiting until spring, with the understanding that Heartsease's new owners would see to those repairs. They would no longer be her responsibility.

Tristan held out the box of biscuits as a peace offering. 'Don't get prickly on me, Elanora. I meant no insult. I am merely trying to figure out how things stand.' Tristan took a biscuit for himself. 'You have to admit how things look. I met you coming out of the bank, the Grisham string is gone, the house needs a few touches, the last investment didn't pay, and you're essentially alone here at the head of what looks to be a faltering enterprise.' He held up a hand to ward off her protest. 'I do not mean to hurt your feelings. I am only telling you how it looked to me. All those signs pointed straight to money problems. Tell me I'm wrong and I'll let the subject be. Or take the help I offer and we'll have you on your feet in no time.'

This was what she didn't want. 'I don't want you to throw money at me as if I were the Thomsfords.' And because she was feeling a bit raw, she added, 'Besides, it wouldn't be enough.'

Tristan refused to be insulted. 'Why do you say that?'

'You can't support all of Sussex on a captain's pay.' She was somewhat amazed that he could afford to pay for a boy's schooling and a dowry. But perhaps he'd been saving. She wasn't sure what a soldier spent his money on, and he wasn't supporting a family, so maybe he had a little set aside or perhaps his parents had helped. Still, it wouldn't make a dent in what she owed the bank or what it would take to run Heartsease as it was meant to be run. Hers were both short-term and long-term money problems. A man could spend a small fortune trying to redeem Heartsease. She'd never realised before what it took to run an estate year in and year out.

'You show me yours and I'll show you mine,' Tristan parried. 'I'll show you my books if you show me yours. Do we have a deal?'

She shook her head. One glance at the books and he'd know that he'd been right about most of his suppositions except the last one—that the lost cargo was a financial anomaly, a one-time setback that, given time, she'd eventually recover from. He would see what it was really costing her to put up one last Christmas of generous giving even though her heart wasn't in it. He might even see that the joy of Christmas had been lost to her, buried with her brother at the bottom of the ocean, next to a pile of debt. 'Tristan, you don't have to solve my problems.'

'Fair enough. But perhaps I could at least advise you and you could do me the favour of letting me do some work around the place while I wait to hear about the contract with the army? It would give me something to do and you know how my father is about idleness.' Tristan gave his eyes a playful roll.

She felt her resolve weakening. She probably shouldn't agree to even that much, but the prospect of having a partner, of having someone come alongside her and work on a project for just a short time, was an unlooked-for present. One she could manage. It wouldn't last. He would leave. This was temporary, and temporary, for once, worked in her favour. She could let this brief time together feed her soul as long as her soul understood from the start this would end. She would have something beautiful to take into the bleak future with her, something to hold against the dreary existence that would come. Such an arrangement would be safe enough as long as he stopped prying. 'I have conditions of my own. No more money talk, though, Tristan. I do need help around here and it would be nice to clean a few things up for Christmas.' Even if only to keep others off the scent of her demise. She'd been banking on entertaining at night to hide the problems at Heartsease. 'If I can admit to needing the assistance, can you promise not to bring up money again?'

Tristan grinned. 'Admitting you have a problem is a big step for someone as stubborn as you are. I'll take that deal.'

So would she. She could have Tristan for a while longer and Heartsease would benefit, too, while still protecting her secrets. For a little while, she could have it all for a short time, one last time. There would be a price for that, though. Tristan would be furious when he found out she'd hidden the mortgage from him, and he *would* find out eventually, but by then it would be too late for him to feel obligated to do anything about it. She had no illusions about that. But for now, she would allow herself this one last gift: Tristan's company.

Chapter Nine

Tristan's company became a fixture at Heartsease immediately. The next morning he'd arrived early, prepared to trim the ivy on the west corner before Elanora had even eaten breakfast. If he'd been ten minutes earlier, she'd still have been in her nightclothes. Then he set about tackling the lawns that ran along the drive, raking up the leaves in enormous piles, a process that took the rest of the week, even with Elanora helping him.

'I don't believe I've ever seen this many leaves all in one place. I think we finally got them all,' she laughed, leaning on her rake as she surveyed the lawn, feeling a sense of accomplishment. She flexed her hands inside the big work gloves where they gripped the rake handle. Her hands could believe it. Even with the protection of gloves, she felt the effects of the yard work. Still, it had felt good to work outside this week. She'd spent too much time indoors for her tastes these past few months, but running the estate as best she could demanded it; yet one more sacrifice she'd been required to make since Teddy's death.

'There were a few times when I never thought we'd get all the leaves raked.' Or parts of the lawn trimmed into submission, or the oak trees pruned. That last was a relief for her. The trees should have been pruned every few years, but she could not recall her father or Teddy having had it done. The oaks had become dangerous with limbs that were too long and too thin, making them candidates for breaking under the weight of snowfall or strong winds. Tristan had been a proverbial workhorse, labouring from the moment he arrived until the end of the day. And even then, he made a point of visiting Old Mackey in the stables and helping with tack or cleaning the stalls.

'You are inexhaustible.' She smiled in Tristan's direction. Despite the cold, he'd shed his coat and rolled up the sleeves of his work shirt, offering her another glimpse of those forearms she so admired. She'd been doing far too much admiring this week. Not content to admire him through the window, she'd bundled up and come out to work alongside him. All for embarrassingly selfish reasons: to be near him, to talk to him, to listen to the stories of his travels as they worked. And all of it a dangerous sign of how deeply her infatuation was running these days. Each look, each touch, only strengthened it.

The more she got to know Tristan, the more she wanted to know the fascinating man he'd become. He was not merely a man who enjoyed his travels, but a man of compassion, of determination, of empathy.

These were rare qualities in a society that said a gentleman must live a life of indolence and leisure in order to earn that moniker. Tristan was a man who wanted to contribute to building a better world. Where he saw needs, he sought to find solutions, like he had for the Thomsfords.

In theory, it was an admirable trait. In practice, though, it worried her because it made her a target for his goodwill. He would look at her and see someone in need of fixing. She wanted to be seen as more than that. This week had proven it on both accounts. It had also raised the reminder that Tristan would leave, something she liked to conveniently forget. When he spoke of his travels, of the blue waters of the Caribbean, the warm sun of the South Pacific, the spicy scents of India, his face came alive. How could such a man ever be happy making a life in Hemsford? How long would it take for Hemsford to become too small? The place she loved would be nothing more than a cage for him.

He came to stand beside her, taking the rake from her and setting it aside. 'We got it done sooner than I planned. I didn't expect to have a partner.' He gave her a boyish grin. 'Now I wonder what I will do next week. Maybe clean out your attic or repair fences if the weather cooperates. You're smiling. I see the prospect of such chores pleases you.'

In actuality, it was the promise of his company that pleased her. She need not give up her fantasies just yet. Oh, how pathetic and desperate she'd become! Apart from her infatuation, she'd not realised how alone she was, how starved for company she was. She sighed and let her gaze wander up the drive, taking in the newly cleaned lawn, the whitewashed shutters, and the trimmed ivy. Her lip gave an unexpected and embarrassing tremble she couldn't hide in time.

'What is it, El? Did I miss a spot?' Tristan teased but his dark eyes were concerned.

She pulled off her gloves and swiped at the tears stinging in her eyes. 'It's just that the house looks good. It looks like it should and I am ashamed that I let it fall into disrepair.' But what choice had she had? There'd been no money to keep staff on and so many other things had demanded her immediate attention in the months since Teddy died. There'd been papers to file, bills to pay, creditors to stave off until she could organise her funds and carefully dole them out. All of that had taken time.

'It wasn't serious disrepair, El, just surface level. It wasn't anything that scrubbing and trimming couldn't fix.' Tristan reached for her hand, a friendly gesture only, but that didn't stop it from sending a warm ripple of awareness up the length of her arm. 'I'm glad you let me fix it. Even more, I'm glad you came outside and helped me fix it. We've always made a good team, El.' He looked at the house and then back at her. 'There's one more thing we should do, though.' He kept a hold of her hand and tugged her towards the drive. 'We need to fix the fountain.'

The fountain was messy business. Elanora cleaned the piles of matted, soggy leaves out of the wide basin, while Tristan crawled underneath to repair the hydraulics, getting wet and muddy for his efforts. But those efforts were rewarded when the fountain gave a cough and water spurted forth in a rush before settling into a steady stream. 'We did it!' Elanora cheered, her throat tightening at the sight of the fountain that was the symbol of Heartsease, flowing again. She'd not realised how much the fountain had meant to her, how much she'd missed it until now.

Her parents had loved that fountain, had loved telling the story of how it had come from a villa in Italy, making a courageous journey across the Continent. The fountain had always been a symbol of love and hope at Heartsease, and when it had gone silent, it had seemed that hope and love had gone silent in her as well. All had been lost. But now... Oh, she dared not spend time on fanciful notions. Hope was still lost. That had not changed. Still, it meant something to have the fountain for a little while longer. Joy began to surge in her heart as she stood listening to the fountain. Joy was temporary, she cautioned. Joy would not last. But for the moment it filled her, lifted her up, and she soared on its wings, a reckless Icarus. Without thinking, she threw her arms about Tristan and hugged him close as she whispered, 'Thank you.' It was a thank-you for more than he knew: for the house, for his company, for bringing happiness to her life even if only for a short time, and to her great joy, he hugged her back, his arms tight about her.

She would have liked to stay that way for a long time: wrapped in his arms, warm, safe, and listening to the fountain, her head lying against his chest. But to want such a thing, to encourage such an action, was dangerous. It took her thoughts in perilous directions of what might be if... *If* he was to stay in Hemsford. *If* she wasn't burdened by a debt she would not willingly pass on to a husband she loved. *If* she could be sure this happiness would last beyond the moment, that it wasn't an illusion. Too many *ifs*. Too many obstacles. She could not make him happy and she would not make him pay for hers. But a certain thought began to form, born of a taste for passion and the reality that she'd never marry—something she'd known long before this: What if there was a middle ground? What if they understood he would leave and that she expected nothing more from him? It was a dangerous thought, a wicked thought, sparked by those moments on the steps, on the picnic blanket, when there seemed to be something more than friendship between them: to have him for one night. Would he give her that? Would she allow herself that? Of course she would. This was a natural evolution of the deal she'd already cut herself—that she could have a moment's happiness with Tristan because she knew it would end; she did not overestimate the moment could ever mean more beyond the now. This was merely taking it one natural step further. Whatever happened between them or didn't happen between them, their time together would be short. Might as well make the most of it. She could not control what happened after, but she could control the present.

He looked down at her with a broad smile and she tipped her head up, her heart leaping, still locked in its own fantasies, imagining for a moment that he might kiss her, as he almost had on the kitchen steps. 'I'm sorry,' he chuckled, 'I fear I've got you dirty. I'm filthy.'

'I don't mind.' She cleared her throat and reluctantly stepped back, the power of the fantasy deflating with reality. She brushed at the front of her garden coat. 'Having the fountain fixed is worth a bit of dirt.'

'I have an idea.' Tristan grinned. 'We've got so much done here, why don't we go into the village tomorrow and take in the Christmas fair while the weather's good? The town looks like a Christmas village, the shop windows are decorated, and the baker has outdone himself with biscuits this year. The ones I brought are just the start. There's the most stunning gown in the dressmaker's window, you simply must see it to believe it. My poor man's view description will not do it justice,' Tristan joked.

His enthusiasm was infectious, dangerously so, making her feel reckless. As a rule, she'd limited her time in town after Teddy's death. Out of sight was out of mind. People were less apt to talk about her if she wasn't there to remind them with her presence. She couldn't bear people speculating about her, no matter how well meaning they were. But with Tristan staring down at her, his dark eyes glinting with fun and mirth, she was tempted to break her self-imposed rules.

But what if Mr Atwater says something indiscreet? He's done it once. What if Elias Bathurst is in town?

Her conscience gently prompted her with reminders of the risks she would take if she was to brave visiting the town. The wrong word from the wrong person in front of Tristan, and her secrets would be exposed.

'El? Don't you think the Christmas market would be fun? You used to love it.' Tristan seemed genuinely perplexed by her lack of reaction; sadness lurked in the depths of his dark eyes. His enthusiasm quieted. 'What has happened to your Christmas spirit, El? The girl I knew couldn't wait for the market and didn't dread Stir-Up Sunday. Things and people *do* change, I understand. But tell me that hasn't. One should never outgrow Christmas.' He reached a hand out to tuck an errant strand of hair behind her ear, a soft, gentle gesture that matched his gaze. 'Come to the market, El, and let me show you what Christmas can be again.'

She wanted that more than anything, to feel alive again, to feel free again. She'd had a taste of that leaping fences earlier that week and a taste had only made her hungry for more, only made her realise how much she'd been missing. Her heart lurched at Tristan's words, launching a rebellion against the dictates of her mind, a rebellion against six months of grief that never wanted to end. Suddenly, it became more difficult to explain why she couldn't go than to simply say, 'Yes, all right, then. I'll go to the market with you tomorrow.'

Tristan grinned. 'It will be fun, El. I promise.' He paused, his grin turning wry. 'It will be like *new* times. We'll make new memories.' That was what she was afraid of. That she *would* have fun, that she *would* make new memories. Old ones she could deal with. They couldn't be changed. But new ones had the power to change everything. She wasn't sure she was ready for that, for opening herself up to the possibility of new hurt. But perhaps, she reasoned with herself, if she was very careful, she could handle it.

Tristan managed to make it back to Brentham Woods with enough time to wash up and get himself together before supper, something that was not as easily done as he would have thought. That hug at the fountain had produced physical and mental effects that insisted on lingering. Not even a brisk gallop on Vitalis had dislodged them. The feel of Elanora in his arms, the sight of her smile when the fountain gurgled to life, the all-encompassing joy when she'd lifted her face to his. The sight had done strange things to him, leaving him both aroused and contemplative. Had he *ever* made another person as happy as he'd made her in that moment? If he had, they'd certainly never expressed it the way she had.

He'd hugged her back, caught up in the feel of her, in the celebration of the moment, looking at all they'd accomplished. This had been a good week, one that he'd thoroughly enjoyed, working outdoors, seeing the house reflect his efforts, and hers. He was honest enough to know that her company had made a difference. When he'd first thought up the plan to simply do the chores at Heartsease himself, he'd hoped to at least see her at lunch. But he'd gotten more than lunch. Working with her had given him an opportunity not only to reinitiate their friendship, but also to build it anew in the empty space left by so many years apart.

In some ways for him, reclaiming Heartsease was analogous to reclaiming her, to waking her up. Her reticence to attend the market had touched something deep within him. Loss had stolen a part of herself along with her family. He would not let loss keep her. One did not let a friend slip away like that.

Is that what she is to you? Is that why you roused to her today as you've roused to her all week? Why there'd been that moment when she'd smiled up at you and you almost kissed her—and not for the first time? One of these days almost *will become in truth. And what then? Will you stay for her? Will you give her one night, perhaps two, and leave her? Could the two of you live with that?*

Could his honour live with that? It was, admittedly, not a traditionally honourable thought. Gentlemen did not engage in one-night affairs with gently bred young women. And yet, was it honourable to *not* give her this? To deny *them* this? It did not feel honourable to walk away from their passion.

The questions whispered the provocative thoughts that required him to acknowledge he enjoyed her company beyond the confines of his pledge to help her. Things had progressed, at least in his mind, far beyond the need to help her, the need to grieve the loss of Teddy. He *wanted* to ride with her; he *wanted* to take her to the market. For a man who had arrived in Hemsford certain that his travelling days were not behind him, a man who made sure to never encourage matrimonial intentions, these were distracting realisations indeed, especially when they centred around Elanora Grisham, a woman who could not be taken lightly.

Chapter Ten

A light frost had fallen in the night, the thin, icy layer covering the meadows until they sparkled like fields of diamonds beneath the afternoon sun. Tristan could not have asked for better weather in which to enjoy the Christmas market or to make the drive over to Heartsease in his father's curricle.

He'd taken the time that morning to brush the carriage horses—two matched browns with sleek, dark coats and black manes and three white socks apiece—until their coats looked like silk. Determined to make the outing as festive as possible, he tacked them up with bells on their harnesses. They snorted and stamped, setting the harnesses to jingling as Tristan tucked an old plaid red wool blanket beneath the seat. He wouldn't need it; he'd be plenty warm in his greatcoat of Petersham wool. But Elanora may find it comforting, especially on the drive back this evening when temperatures would be much colder than they were right now.

She was ready for him when he arrived at Heartsease. She stood on the front step, dressed in a long black wool cloak, a plum woollen day dress peeping from beneath. Even from a distance, he could see her face light up at the sound of the jingle bells.

She gave a delighted clap of her hands as he tooled the curricle around the fountain, which, thankfully, was still working after his efforts yesterday. He hopped down, the skirts of his greatcoat flapping about his boot tops. 'My lady, your carriage awaits.' He swept her a playful bow and she laughed, taking his hand and stepping on the wheel rim to reach the bench.

'This is wonderful.' She settled on the bench and he leapt up by her side, picking up the reins again. 'This is a splendid surprise, Tristan. You must have worked for hours on their coats. They gleam so!' Whatever time it had taken to groom them had been worth it to put that smile on her face and to get their day off to a good start. The crisp air put colour into her cheeks and he couldn't help but show off a bit, getting the horses to lift their knees as the village came into sight.

'What a whip you've become,' Elanora laughed as he pulled into the livery. He was glad he'd reserved a place ahead of time. The village was busy, full of people who had travelled over from neighbouring areas.

He swung her down, his hands more conscious than usual of the feel of her, of the trim waist beneath the cloak and the fabric of her dress. 'What a growing concern Hemsford is these days. Our little Christmas market has turned into quite the attraction.' He guided her out into the street, a hand at the small of her back, careful to manoeuvre her around a pile of horse droppings.

'I remember my mother telling us the story of how the Christmas market got started.' She smiled at him, her blue eyes bright. 'She liked to say it all began when Squire Lytton came back from his travels and all he could talk about was the German Christmas markets. Then Reverend Thompson and his wife—they were newlyweds back then—decided they should do something like that here.'

Tristan laughed. 'I don't think I knew any of that until today. The market was well established by the time the Lennoxes arrived, although it has certainly grown since then. It didn't occur to me to question its origins.' He gave a contented sigh. 'I think that's one of the beautiful things about living here. The roots go deep. People keep each other's history.' The battle in him between tradition and the discovery of travel began to stir once more. Hemsford was at its best during Christmas, projecting the comfort and security that came with being home and being known. To be here with Elanora on his arm made the images of potential all that more potent.

This could be a wonderful life not just for him but for his children. There was no better place for them to be raised. The fantasy of staying whispered loud in his mind. All it would take would be a small concession on his part: to give up travelling, to work alongside his brother in investing, spend his days behind a desk with ledgers. But in return, he'd potentially receive so much more.

She slanted him a coy look. 'And yet you keep wanting to leave.'

'But I always come back.' He made the argument

for himself as much as for her. Perhaps this was the realisation he needed. He *did* always come back. When
he was away, he thought of Hemsford, his family and
friends. Wherever he went, this was the place that an-
chored him. Perhaps that would be enough to stay. 'This
place is my home. It's the only place I remember living. It does a man good to know that no matter where
he goes in the world, India, Barbados, Belize, or Canada, there is a place where he will always be welcomed
back. A place where he will belong in a way he'll not
belong anywhere else. Hemsford is that place for me.'
Because his family was here, because *she* was here, his
memories were here.

They came to the High Street and he took her arm,
threading it through his, wanting the debate to leave
him alone for a moment. It was not a question that could
be easily resolved. 'The day is ours. We can do as we
like. Shall we start with the shops?'

They took their time, pausing to appreciate each window display, talking about how clever the arrangement
was or how attractively shown some items were. The
bakery window made her laugh with its iced gingerbread men standing upright encircling a twelfth night
cake that looked like a work of art. The fruitcake was
covered in a gold marzipan and trimmed at the base in
white icing that looked like lace while the top of the
cake sported a white sugar crown. 'That is too pretty
to eat,' Elanora exclaimed. 'Even Cook would have to
admit it is spectacular.'

'My mother is ordering a cake for our Christmas
party from Manning's this year. Several of them, in

fact, because the cakes are decorations themselves,'
Tristan shared. 'I think the Lennox Christmas party is
all anyone at the house has talked about all week, and
the party is still two weeks off.'

Elanora smiled. 'I forget you've been away. The party
has become quite the fixture of the Christmas season
around here. Baron Babcock and his family came last
year.'

'Yes, I think Mother wrote something about that in
one of her letters,' Tristan said, remembering now. 'I
had not understood the scope, though. Hemsford has
quite the slate of events—the tableau at church, the
Grisham panto, the Lennox Christmas party, the Advent
concert at the church the Sunday before Christmas, and
the midnight service on Christmas Eve. Coupled with
this market, Hemsford will make a name for itself yet.'

Elanora smiled, but for a fleeting moment Tristan
would have wagered there was a hint of sudden sadness
in her eyes. Was she remembering Christmases past?
Being with her family? Perhaps that was one of the reasons she didn't want to leave Hemsford—her family
was here in a different way than his was. To leave their
graves, to leave the house where they'd all last been together, would be asking too much. But today was not
for such considerations. It was for fun and merriment.
'Manning's is even better inside,' he said when she'd
looked her fill at the delicious window. Let's go in and
get a gingerbread man to eat while we window shop.
My treat, I insist.'

Inside, the bakery was crowded with people ordering twelfth night cakes in advance, and gingerbread

men seemed to be flying off the trays. 'We can't fill the cases fast enough,' the pretty, dark-haired girl behind the counter said, smiling his way. Susannah? he thought, the baker's daughter. She came over to personally take their order. 'What will you have, Captain Lennox?'

'Miss Grisham and I will take two of the very popular gingerbread men.' The girl's smile fell a little at that, her gaze sliding in Elanora's direction as she handed the biscuits over.

Outside, they moved down the street, taking a first bite of their gingerbread men. 'Oh, no!' Elanora suddenly exclaimed, a look of horror on her face as she stared at him. 'Do you always eat the head first? You did out at the house, too, only I didn't think much of it then. But now…'

Tristan chuckled. 'What do *you* eat first?'

'The feet, of course.' Elanora's answer was immediate and sure as if there was definitely a right way to eat a gingerbread man.

'The feet?' Tristan furrowed his brow in playful debate. 'But that's not very efficient. The head is right here, closer to my mouth. I have to turn it around to get to the feet.'

'The feet are more humane,' Elanora insisted and Tristan laughed out loud.

'More humane?'

'Yes, it lets them live longer.' Elanora was laughing now, too, and he was thoroughly enjoying himself.

'But to what end? To be aware they're being devoured whole? I, for one, think if *humaneness* is a consideration for nonsentient beings, eating the head first puts them out of their misery and offers them a soldier's death of honour.' He slanted her a teasing glance. 'Feet first, eh, barbarian. I think we shall have to agree to disagree on this point.' Just then he spotted a crowd gathered around a window. 'There's the dressmaker's. Let's set aside our gingerbread quarrel and I will show you the dress I was telling you about.'

She stared at it for a long while, and he stared at her, watching her eyes widen, noting the soft, almost inaudible 'oh' that escaped her lips. He noted, too, the involuntary caressing motion her fingers made at her sides as if they could feel the fabric beneath their tips. 'You're right, it's stunning.'

'You should have it. It would be divine on you.' The words were out of his mouth before he could think better of them. They were, in truth, wildly inappropriate even if they were his thoughts in that moment.

'Me?' She laughed and shook her head. 'Such a dress would be wasted on me these days. It would end up wrapped in tissue paper in a box under a bed. That dress deserves better. It deserves a ball, a chance to be seen.' He wondered for a moment if she was talking about more than the dress.

'There's always the Lennox Christmas party,' he suggested, half teasing. 'I hear it's got quite the guest list.'

She wrinkled her nose and gave another shake of her head. 'I hadn't planned to go.'

'And miss my mother's cake display?' he joked and then sobered as they moved towards the commons where the market was set up. 'Why wouldn't you come? The Grishams always come.'

'It's too much this year, too many memories with Teddy gone.'

That sounded like a very vague, not entirely truthful, reason to Tristan but he did not press her on it. He had some time yet until the party. He would change her mind. She would be there, on his arm, wearing that red dress and be the belle of the ball as she should have been years ago, even if it was only for a night. 'Do you smell that?' He grinned, steering her down a market aisle to their left, following the nutty aroma. 'Smells like chestnuts.' They found the vendor and he bought them a cone of roasted chestnuts to share as they wandered. He liked the chestnuts, but he liked even more how sharing the cone kept her close, their hands occasionally brushing as they reached for a chestnut.

They stopped at a woodcarver's booth to marvel over cunning little box puzzles and carved blocks that sported alphabet letters on each side. There was a wood boat with a real linen sail that caught Tristan's eye. 'The fountain at Heartsease might need a boat. Every good fountain does.' But he set it aside. Such a purchase would be frivolous. If there were money problems at Heartsease, Elanora would not be spending funds on a toy boat and she'd not allow him to.

He'd noticed her today, wistfully looking at items and doing mental math in her head. She was window shopping only. Yet, she'd afforded the Stir-Up Sunday feast. But not a headstone for her brother. She eschewed company at the estate to keep others from guessing the truth behind the stage she'd so carefully erected. Stir-Up Sunday had been limited to tenants with the exception of Reverend Thompson, but even then, he'd been kept in the kitchen. She was putting on a brave show and he sensed he needed to get to the bottom of the Heartsease finances soon before the curtain came down irrevocably.

As they turned to leave the woodcarver's stall, they were stopped by the vicar and his wife. 'Captain Lennox, Miss Grisham, how wonderful to see you, together,' Mrs Thompson enthused, and Tristan didn't miss the spark of interest in her eye. 'Miss Grisham, it is good to see you out. Your flowers were lovely last Sunday for Advent, but we'd hoped you would accompany them as well.' Mrs Thompson got a polite remark in about Elanora missing the first Sunday in Advent. 'Perhaps you will come for Shepherd's Sunday *with* the fresh flowers, my dear.' She paused with a kindly smile. 'Of course, we'll see you at the panto planning meeting. After all, we should come out to Heartsease for that. It might be easier if we did so we could see the space.'

Tristan felt Elanora tense beside him at the unsubtle request for an invitation to Heartsease. The stir up had been one thing, with everyone settled in the kitchen. A ladies' meeting would require more of the house to be on display, provide more opportunity to expose the hardships there. 'It's the same space we use every year, so there's no need to come out. It's much more convenient for everyone to meet in town and I don't mind the ride. Let me come to you.' Elanora made the offer sound gracious. Tristan thought it was a rather indirect negotiation. Tenacious Mrs Thompson had made it clear she was going to get Elanora involved one way or another. If

Elanora wouldn't come to town, Mrs Thompson would bring town to her. Tristan thought it was rather skilfully done on Mrs Thompson's part.

Tristan intervened before Mrs Thompson could argue the point and made their farewells, but it was only the first of several brief meetings as they wandered the market. There were people who'd not yet had a chance to welcome him back, and there were people who were pleased to see Elanora. There were those, too, who didn't bother to hide the speculation in their eyes at the sight of them together. Tristan didn't mind. It was how small villages were, a consequence of everyone knowing everyone. Perhaps it did not come as a surprise to them. Maybe it even made perfect sense to them. Tristan supposed at the distance of a third party looking on, he and Elanora together seemed a natural evolution of things given how close their families had been.

In truth, their speculations were a mirror of his own. Wasn't he also trying out this idea of what it would be like to stay in Hemsford? To be with Elanora? That last part was the most crucial. *If* he stayed it would be for her. There'd be no other reason. Two weeks ago such thoughts had not even been on his mind, and now he was contemplating a very different future than the one he'd anticipated.

'People are talking,' Elanora said under her breath as the Misses Simpsons, two gossipy old spinster sisters, passed them with sly looks as they stopped at a booth selling milled French soaps.

'It's what people always think when a man has a

beautiful woman on his arm.' Tristan was tempted to
laugh the idea off, but something about the stiffness in
Elanora's posture cautioned him against a breezy brush
off. He'd been so wrapped up these past days in examin-
ing his own feelings and responses that he'd not stopped
to consider hers. *Did* she want him to stay? It seemed
like it from what she'd said on the picnic blanket. But
did she want him to stay for her, *with* her? Did she share
his same interest in growing this relationship? That was
where he was unsure. She was attracted to him; there'd
been too many moments in the past two weeks to deny
that, that hug yesterday not being the least of them. But
to what end? Where did she see this relationship going?
Where did she want it to go? Or did she assume it could
go nowhere because he'd not given her reason to believe
it could? He'd talked only of leaving, of his job with the
army. If he was unclear on what she wanted, perhaps
he needed to be clearer with her about his position. He
would stay for her. Soldier though he was, the thought
of putting that position to Elanora came with some trep-
idation. What if she rejected him? Would their friendship survive it? She'd already rejected so many other
suitors. But none of them had been her friend and all
of them had wanted something for themselves. Tristan
liked to think he was different and that he could offer
her something far better.

He gave Elanora a conspiratorial smile as another
couple passed, sending curious glances their way. 'Does
it bother you that people will talk? What do you think
they'll say?' He meant it as a joke, but the look on Elanora's face bordered on horrified. He paused in front

of a ribbon vendor, another idea, less pleasing, coming to him. He was starting to realise how much he'd assumed and taken for granted. 'Elanora, do you not want to be seen with me?'

Usually, she appreciated Tristan's directness. But not today. She felt like a fox flushed from cover, forced out into the open. 'Those are two very different questions,' she scolded. 'You are the handsomest, most interesting fellow in the village, and you know it. Any woman would be thrilled to be seen with you, so stop fishing for compliments.' She started walking again but Tristan tugged at her arm and pulled her aside from the crowd, his voice low.

'That's not what I am asking. I do not give a fig about any other woman. What I am asking is, are *you* embarrassed to be seen with me?' His dark eyes glinted with a new intensity, an intensity meant exclusively for her.

She met his gaze, although it took courage to do so. 'It is what people will say that embarrasses me, not you. Never you, Tristan.'

'What will they say?' His voice was a fierce growl and she could imagine him striding out into the crowd and daring them to say anything at all. 'Will they say "How nice that Miss Grisham is getting out again"? "What a lovely friendship it is between those two families, how they look after one another in good times and bad"?'

She gave a dry laugh. 'They *might* say that. But they will mean more. They will say you've taken pity on me.' That was the least of what they might say. They might also say crueller things, that she was looking to get her claws into him, desperate for a last chance at marriage. If anyone guessed there were financial problems, it would only affirm her desperation in their eyes. But she could say none of that to Tristan without alerting him to more.

'A woman must always be careful when there's talk, Tristan. You know that. You will simply leave Hemsford, but I will still be here.'

Tristan gave her a cryptic smile. 'What if I didn't leave?'

The very thought made her stomach flip for good reasons and for bad. *He'd stay for her.* The thought had all the warmth of every fairy tale she'd ever read. But he couldn't stay. That was not part of the middle ground she'd allowed herself. This discussion was getting too close to things she did not want to discuss with him. She flashed him a wide smile. 'If you didn't leave, you'd be crazy within a month.' She laughed but Tristan didn't laugh with her. In fact, she'd never seen him look more grave, more intent, more handsome.

'I'm serious, El. What if I said there was no place I'd rather be? No one I'd rather be with? That perhaps everything I'd been searching for in my wanderlust was right here, with you.' At those words, words she'd longed to hear, everything within her ached for him, for what might have been if circumstances had been different. But she could absolutely not lean in to this greatest of temptations. She would not have him give up his career, his aspirations, in order to take on her debt, her problems. She'd begun this affair thinking of the need to protect herself from hurt. She'd not imagined she'd also have to protect him—from her, from his inherent generosity and goodness.

'I'd say I feel the same, in this moment. One day at a time, Tristan, I think that is all we can promise.' All she could ever promise.

Tristan gave her a soft smile. 'Then come enjoy the fair with me and let them talk if they must. Do not let it steal our happiness tonight.'

She nodded, making a private pledge to herself. She would take Tristan's advice and not allow her worries to ruin the outing. Her mind was abuzz with the import of his words and a hundred images of today that she would treasure always. She'd not enjoyed a day like this for some time and that he'd divined her need and given her this day touched her all the more. She would let nothing taint the magic of that.

Chapter Eleven

With the arrival of dusk the Christmas market had become magical with fairy lights and lanterns. Not even Mrs Thompson's prying questions or the Misses Simpsons' overt speculation could dim that.

Music began at one corner of the village green. She tugged at Tristan's coat sleeve. 'Do you hear that? There's singing.' She loved carols, loved the old tunes and the old words. Tristan found them a place at the back of the crowd that had gathered. 'This is one of my favourites.' She smiled up at him even as she shivered. The evening had turned cold but she wasn't ready to give it up yet.

'You're shivering.' Tristan moved behind her, draping his big greatcoat about her and wrapping her in his arms, lending her his warmth and his strength. Those about them could not fail to notice his gentle possessiveness or their closeness. For once, Elanora didn't care as they stood there, listening to the carollers while the stars came out and the fairy lights twinkled, the moment so beautiful to her she didn't want it to end. But it did. The carollers finished their songs; the crowd wandered off to the inn and the tavern to warm themselves. Merchants boarded up their stalls for the night, leaving them alone in this little corner of the green.

'I suppose that's our cue to go home,' Elanora laughed. 'The carols were lovely. I didn't want them to end.' She turned in his arms to face him, aware of his chocolate gaze on her, his earlier words still hot in her ears. 'Today was perfect, Tristan. I haven't had a day like this in so long.'

'Me, too.' Tristan's hands were at her waist, and she was aware of his reluctance to let her go, of the little trill of excitement that seemed to leap between them, the way his eyes darkened.

'I don't have any words to express what today meant.' It had been like coming alive again, if even only for a short while. It was a wondrous feeling but she couldn't trust it.

'Maybe this will do instead.' Tristan's voice had become a gentle rasp that made her pulse leap with ridiculous hope and fantasy as his gaze dropped to her lips. It was all the warning she had before his mouth captured hers.

It was a kiss long in the making, a kiss of sweetness and desire newly acknowledged, and Elanora thrilled to it, to all of it; the questing of his mouth, the nutty flavour of chestnuts on his lips, the soft press of her breasts against the hardness of his chest, the feel of his hands at her hips, and the scent of him, his soap a spicy mixture of nutmeg and cinnamon on the sharp, wintry air. And yet, for all its tenderness, the kiss was underlaid with a sense of desperation, of a hunger firmly leashed but still present. Did that hunger belong to her or to him? In this moment of oneness it was hard to tell. Perhaps it didn't matter. There was only the complete bliss, the complete joy of being in his arms, the one place where she could set aside the trials of the past years.

Tristan gently released her mouth but not her, his eyes dark with something she'd never seen in them before, and they shone like polished onyx. 'Elanora.' He breathed her name like a lover's hymn, and the very depths of her soul trembled with the knowledge of it.

'Shh. Say nothing.' She pressed a finger to the lips that had kissed hers. She wanted nothing to ruin this moment, no words that would undermine what had just happened. He nodded and tucked her arm through his, holding her close to his side as they walked slowly back to the livery and prepared for the drive home, a chance to extend the evening a little while longer.

They drove home in silence, communing instead with hands interlaced beneath the warmth of the red plaid blanket spread over their laps, her head against his shoulder as the light of a new December moon shone down on them, and the horses' harnesses jingled in the night. Out here there was no one to see. Out here it was just the two of them.

And the memory of that kiss.

Her lips could still feel the echo of his on them, and when he slid a look in her direction as he drove, one hand on the reins, the other holding hers beneath the blanket, her blood warmed again. Was this how Cinderella had felt with her prince? Warm and happy, complete and safe at last? Had she grappled, too, with the implicit knowledge that joy such as this would not last? Cinderella had known from the start that when the clock struck midnight it would all be over.

And you know it, too. You know you will leave Heartsease at the end of Christmas, and Tristan will leave as well, off to collect his horses. You told yourself it would be better that way, that you could live with the middle ground of happiness for now, knowing you would have to give it up.

But that was a deal she'd made with herself before that kiss, before she'd experienced something she wanted to hold on to forever. Now she was wondering if the middle ground would ever be enough. If there was some way in which that middle ground might be expanded if not in time then in experience. What experiences might she allow herself?

Now, her own 'midnight' was approaching as they turned in to the drive at Heartsease. She could almost count the clock strokes in her head as the horses trotted down the oak-lined lane.

One, two, three...

When they reached the fountain, silent for the night, the evening would be over. What would it be like between them when they saw each other next? Would this desire, this exquisite warmth, remain between them or would there be the awkwardness of regret? Would they never speak of this again? Would they relegate it to being a beautiful moment out of time? That would, perhaps, be the safest option, the one that could pre-serve their friendship.

Rebellion rose swift and hot within her. She didn't want to be safe. Safety was an illusion. She'd lived on illusions too long and to her detriment. They had not prepared her for reality in a world where beauty and pleasure and joy and happiness were fleeting things, and the only person you could or should rely on was yourself. Everyone else would fail you given enough time to do so.

Ask for what you want, take what you want, the voice of her mind whispered. *While there is still time, before you must go, before he leaves, before he fails you. It is inevitable that he will. The men you loved most failed you: your brother, your father. All men fail. There are no exceptions to the rule. There is only you now. There will be no husband, no family, there will only be you forever.*

'El, did you fall asleep?' Tristan's voice was soft, solicitous, in the darkness as the team came to a halt.

She lifted her head from his shoulder and he jumped down off the bench. 'No, I was just thinking.'

He reached up for her. 'So was I.' His dark eyes lingered meaningfully on her, his mouth curving in a smile, his voice low as the warmth flooded her once more, and something fluttered low in her belly. 'I was thinking how much I'd like to kiss you again.'

His hands were still at her waist and it was easy to reach her arms up and entwine them about his neck. How easy this was, to touch him, to be with him. 'Funny, I was thinking that exact thing, too,' she murmured, his mouth taking her words as soon as they were spoken. But this kiss was different, there was a new heat to it, a new intensity. She could not get enough of him, the feel of him, the taste of him, and neither, she thought, could he. This kiss carried a ragged edge to it that said this kiss alone would not bring satisfaction. She was breathless when they parted, her hands fisted about the lapels of his greatcoat, her words a hoarse plea, 'Tristan, stay tonight. I don't want to be alone.'

'Do you think that's wise?' His own voice was rasped with jagged desire.

She held his gaze, letting him see the determination in her own. 'I do not wish to be wise tonight. I will save wisdom for the morning. For now, I wish to be with you. Will you stay?'

'Do you know what you're asking?'

'Yes, I absolutely do,' Elanora answered solemnly. Perhaps she knew even better than he. She was asking for one night, with no promises, no strings. Just him. Just her. Together.

'Yes, I will stay.' He nodded soberly even as desire and want thrummed through every pore he possessed until it was a fire in his veins. 'Give me a moment to put the horses away.' And to get his head together.

'I'll help. It will go faster with two,' Elanora immediately volunteered. So much for getting his head together. But then again, maybe he didn't want to think too much. To its credit, logic did try to assert itself as he unharnessed the team, reminding him that to stay was to disregard the core teachings of gentlemanly behaviour, to abandon all sense of proper conduct. Yet, those reminders were no match for the desire he felt coupled with an awareness that a great Rubicon was being crossed from which there would be no going back. Elanora smiled at him over the back of a horse and logic lost its battle.

He did not want to leave her and yet all the rationale left to him screamed that he should. But how could he abandon her? To leave her to face a dark house full of memories—memories that would undo all the good, all the joy, that had been achieved. Today she'd remembered herself. It had been there in her smile, her laughter as they'd eaten the biscuits debating if it was better to eat the feet or heads of the gingerbread men first. He would never eat a gingerbread man again without thinking of that. Nor would he ever taste chestnuts without also remembering the taste of her lips on his.

Today had been magical for them both. It had shown him a different trajectory for his life. He could stay here, work with his brother. Perhaps in time he would come to love investments and real estate as much as he loved travelling and horses. He could give Elanora the life she deserved, help her put her sorrows behind her. He watched her hang up the jingle bells on a spare peg and stop to pet Marian's nose when the mare swung her head over the stall door.

With Elanora, there will always be horses. She loves to ride as much as you do.

Temptation was whispering loudly in his ear or was it simply an attempt to justify what he wanted, what they both wanted in this moment?

Elanora came to stand beside him as he finished putting the blankets on. She smiled at him and arousal rode him hard. 'Shall we go in?' She slipped her hand into his and led him through the dark, up the stairs to the point of no return.

'El, are you sure you want this?' Tristan asked even as he shut the door behind them.

She turned up the wick on her lamp and faced him, an angel in the light. He'd never seen anything more lovely, more heartrending. 'Tristan, this is the first thing I've been able to want for me and it may be the only thing I get to decide for myself. I am more than sure.' She moved towards him, her hands resting on the lapels of his greatcoat. 'Are you? Do you want this? I won't have pity from you. Are you sure?'

He took her hand in his, lacing his fingers through hers, and raised it to his lips. Surely, she had some idea how she affected him, how his body screamed for her. He pressed her hand against his heart. 'Do you feel that? How my heart is racing for you?' He journeyed her hand lower, moving it over the rigid hardness of him. 'Do you feel that? I assure you pity is somewhat softer.' He leaned towards her, his mouth at her ear as he nipped at her lobe. 'I am burning for you, El. If you mean to stop this, it must be now or I shall be beyond the point of restraint.'

'I do not mean to stop.' Her voice was a sensual rasp in the dimness and his world faded to her, only her. This room. This woman who was the sum of his reality now.

'Neither do I.' Tristan stepped back, shrugging out

of his greatcoat. 'Shall I undress for you or would you like to do it?'

In answer, her hands worked the buttons of his waist-coat open and pulled the tails of his shirt free from the waistband of his trousers. He tossed the waistcoat aside and drew the shirt over his head, taking pride and en-joyment in hearing her breath catch at the sight of him, chest bare in the lamplight.

'Touch me, El. It's all right.' He could see hesitation mixed with awe in her eyes. He reached for her hand and pressed it to his chest. 'I want you to touch me,' he whispered, his lips finding hers in a long, slow kiss that brought her up against him. A soft moan escaped from low in her throat. Lord, how he loved kissing her, feel-ing her come alive in his arms. 'And I want to touch you. May I?' He kissed her lips, her ear, her neck, until he ran into the fabric of her gown. His fingers worked the buttons that ran the length of her bodice, thankful that she'd not worn a dress that laced up the back. He didn't think his coordination skills could have managed it.

She stepped out of the dress and he made short but gentle work of her undergarments, his own breath hitch-ing as the loss of each garment revealed her: the long, willowy legs, the narrow waist, the high breasts with their rosy tips. He'd not guessed such loveliness lay beneath those plain clothes. Perhaps because it had not mattered. She was still El.

She took a step back as the final piece fell and Tristan sat down hard on the bed. 'You are a goddess, El,' he breathed. An untouched goddess, he reminded himself.

He would worship her fully but carefully, he cautioned his body. He would give her no reason to regret this.

'And *you* are still clothed,' she remarked with a coy smile, approaching the bed. 'Perhaps I might do something about that.' She knelt before him and worked the fastenings of his trousers loose. Did she have any idea how provocative the act was? How it made his blood roar and his heart sing? He lifted his hips and let her pull his trousers off, his gaze watching her as she took in the whole of him naked before her. His cock was showing to advantage tonight, ruddy and strong, as upright as a cock could be, desire's dewdrop glistening at its head. And he took a certain amount of manly pride in knowing he was the first man she'd seen nude.

She stared for a long while at him, at *it*. Tristan would have given a small fortune to know what was going through her head. Intimidation? Fright? Ought he say something to ease her concerns? How much had her mother explained to her about the act? How did he delicately ask such a thing? He opted for lightness. 'Do I pass muster?'

Her blue eyes looked at him from his thighs, twinkling with a mischief to match his own. 'What is there to pass muster on? It's not as large as a horse's pizzle, but what can one expect from someone who eats their gingerbread men head first.' That was a rather erotic image, but one for another time perhaps.

'Minx!' Tristan laughed, mentally tabling the gingerbread fantasy. He reached for her and pulled her on top of him as he fell back on the bed. He'd not expected *that*; hadn't expected the teasing, the fun. 'I see

I shall have to teach you how to handle a man's pride more delicately.'

'A man's pride? Is that what it's called?' she replied, a wicked smile on her lips before it softened. 'Yes, you must teach me, Tristan. Teach me all of it, show me all of it.'

He bussed her lips with a gentle kiss, whispering his pledge. 'I will, I promise.'

He began the tutorial at her earlobe, trailing gentle nips and kisses down her jaw; her neck arched, offering the long column of her throat to him. He kissed the pulse at its base. 'You want me, as I want you,' he whispered, his hands, his mouth, moving to worship at her breasts, slowly, intently. There was no need to rush other than the mounting desire of his own body. But he would not rush this for her. She deserved to know what her body could feel, what it should demand from a lover as its due.

She gave a pleased sigh as he took a nipple into his mouth and licked it with his tongue. 'Lovely.' She managed to breathe the one word. That was probably one word more than what he could manage at present.

He framed her hips with his hands, his mouth at her navel with a sweet kiss. She gave a gentle arch of her back, pushing herself towards him, hips raised in invitation. His cock responded like a magnet summoned to magnetic north; immediate and without question of where it belonged.

He lifted his body, repositioning himself over her. Looking down at her, her hair spread on the pillow like Rapunzel's, her blue eyes shining with the awe of discovery and awakening, was like looking at Venus come down from Olympus with all the innocent passion of Psyche. It was an irresistible combination. His desire ratcheted, threatening the leash on which he held his control. 'I'll be gentle, El,' he whispered at her ear, his cock testing the feminine portal between her thighs.

Ingress was tight, progress was slow, the ultimate paradox of delighting in the journey while desperately wanting to reach one's destination. The pleasure in feeling her body learn him, take him in, stretch around him, fit itself to him, and only him. He shuddered as he reached full sheathing, aware that she shuddered, too, a little cry of amazement escaping her. 'Wait, there's more. We're just getting started,' he promised with a smile, although in some ways it was enough to be here like this with her, joined, together.

Her arms went about his neck; her legs wrapped about his hips. 'Show me,' she urged, and he began to move within her, joy and pleasure mounting with each stroke. Her hips rocked against him, her breathing coming in increasingly rapid gasps, pleasure riding her as hard as it was riding him. He stayed with her long enough for her to fall apart in his arms, to watch her pleasure sweep through her before he took a gentleman's finish in the sheets, although it had taken all his willpower not to stay until the very end because it occurred to him as his cock gasped into the sheets, that being with her had been about more than physical pleasure; it had felt like coming home. That she was home. His home. It was a pleasant thought to fall asleep on, with Elanora tucked against him, but it would be a complicated thought to wake up to. Perhaps, Tristan thought dreamily, they could stay like this, inside this room where the rest of the world didn't matter, where mornings wouldn't come, where it would always be night and pleasure would be simple.

Chapter Twelve

Elanora had not been prepared for the simple pleasure of waking up beside someone she cared for, or the peace that came from lying in their arms, half-awake and knowing that all was well. For the first time since Teddy had left, Elanora's first waking thoughts were not filled with worry for the estate, for all those who counted on her, or for herself. Her thoughts this morning were focused on more immediate things, like the rise and fall of Tristan's chest at her back, the feel of his arm draped across her hip, warm in its reassurance that last night had been real. There were other reminders it had been real as well. Her body bore the echoes of it in the not unpleasant soreness between her legs.

Tristan shifted, his body tucking in around hers, his phallus nudging at her bottom, his voice low at her ear, hoarse with a morning rasp that she found utterly seductive. 'Are you awake, El?'

'A little,' she murmured. 'Would you like to wake me up further?' She wiggled against his phallus—a lovely Latin word she'd learned for cock—and he groaned.

'How shall I wake you, minx?' Tristan nipped at her ear. 'Lazily, from behind, or on top?'

Both sounded promising, but she could probably only choose one.

'On top, please. I like to see your face when you come apart,' she instructed, adjusting her own position. She'd learned a lot about what she liked, about what she wanted, last night. She'd learned the pleasure of lovemaking was not only physical but emotional, that watching a lover find his pleasure was as intoxicating as achieving one's own. Watching Tristan climax—another new word from last night to add to her vocabulary—was an extraordinary, private, intimate experience; to see his eyes go dark, to see the muscles go taut at his neck and in his arms, to feel his body gather and to know that pleasure was near, was akin to seeing someone totally revealed, completely undone, at their most vulnerable, most exposed.

'On top it is, my Aphrodite.' Tristan lifted himself over her and their bodies began the exquisite, slow process of joining, of hands interlocking, fingers interlacing, legs wrapped about hips until at last he was within her, the intimate connection complete. She liked morning lovemaking, Elanora decided. There was a slow serenity to it, an openness and honesty, surrounded as it was by daylight. There could be no secrets here, no shadows in which to hide. She gave a soft moan as pleasure lapped at her, building languorously like small waves against a shore, claiming her softly.

They lay abed a long while after that, neither in a

hurry to leave this wondrous cocoon they'd woven. Until at last, Tristan stretched. 'We have to get up sometime.'

Elanora gave a moan that had nothing to do with pleasure. Getting up meant a return to reality. The servants would know something was up. There was no disguising that Tristan had spent the night. His horses were in the stable as was his curricle, and it wouldn't take an enormous amount of intelligence to puzzle out that he hadn't occupied one of the guest rooms, especially given how late they were rising. Of course, they wouldn't say anything, but they would know.

Tristan levered himself out of bed with a groan of regret and began gathering up his clothes. At least as a consolation prize, she could watch him get dressed. He was even more beautiful in daylight than he had been by lamplight. His skin still bore the tan of the Caribbean sun in places, and his chest was a smooth atlas of muscle, all ridges and planes her eyes could spend a day exploring—and not just her eyes; her fingers wouldn't mind an expedition of their own. He turned from her, reaching down for his trousers on the floor and treating her to a glimpse of the firm rounds of his buttocks. *Divine* was a word that came to mind. It seemed to her there was no part of his body where fat lingered or that muscle faltered.

He turned and caught her staring, his eyes holding hers but not scolding as he fastened his garments, the simple act sending warmth to pool in her belly so soon again for the man who'd just left her bed. But it wasn't just the sheer nakedness of him that had warmth pooling already; it was the intimate nuance of watching him dress, of watching his fingers work the buttons of his trousers, of his shirt and waistcoat, and knowing what else those fingers were capable of, of what they felt like on her skin, what they could do to that skin, to her. He offered her a knowing smile that said he guessed the trajectory of her thoughts. 'I shall go downstairs and have some coffee while you dress, then we'll take breakfast, and maybe talk a bit.'

'We don't have to talk, Tristan.' She liked the sound of breakfast, but not the rest.

'I think we do,' he said with quiet firmness. 'I'll see you downstairs.'

She lay back against the pillows after he left the room, dull reality intruding a little further. The night was over. She'd gotten what she wanted and more. But it was done with now. Talk could change nothing, although Tristan would try. She already anticipated that his deeply embedded sense of chivalry would no doubt lead to a very predictable conversation about what he thought he owed her after last night. She would have to be stalwart. She could not allow herself to be persuaded otherwise for both their sakes. She did not fool herself that such resistance would be easy.

Elanora got out of bed and padded to her wardrobe to select her armour. She chose a dark blue dress with a high neck trimmed with a bit of white cotton lace at the collar and wrists. It was a sensible gown. Ideal for sensible discussion. She needed him to see that it was she who owed him and that what she owed him was his freedom.

She would not use their friendship, their intimacy

or her circumstances to trap him into a situation he ultimately did not want. In fact, up until yesterday, he'd had no plans to settle down, or to stay permanently in Hemsford until he'd breathed the idea into life: *What if I stayed?* Spontaneous words were the product of being caught in the joy of homecoming and Christmas. She couldn't let him mean it. He meant to travel for the army, procuring them horses. Such things could not, *should* not, change overnight or because of one night.

She reached for a cameo and fastened it at the top of her high collar. She took a final look in the mirror, pleased. She looked sensible and in charge. Excellent. Someone needed to be. Tristan was used to protecting but sometimes it was the protectors who needed to be protected—mainly from themselves and their good intentions. Today she would be his and eventually he would thank her for it.

Tristan looked up from his coffee at the sound of Elanora's shoes on the hardwoods—half boots if he had to guess. She looked neat and presentable, as she always did. The blue dress brought out her eyes and the cream of her skin. She'd taken time to put her hair into a chignon at her neck, and to attach a small brooch to her dress, but she'd not made him wait long and for that he was glad. There was much to be explained and much to be settled and he was eager to get on with it. He rose and held out her chair. 'May I fix you a plate? Cook has eggs in the chafing dish and sausages in the other.'

'Yes, eggs would be rather nice, and sausages, two

links, please. Thank you.' She smiled. 'I find I'm quite famished this morning.'

'Outdoor air and…activity will do that to a person.' He was rewarded with a blush staining that silky skin, what he could see of it anyway. He was resentful of that blue dress covering up so much of her even as his fingers itched in anticipation of defeating the buttons that ran the length of her bodice.

He fixed his own plate and returned to his seat at the round breakfast table, struck by the domesticity of the moment, of this room, his mind wandering to contemplate what it would be like to take breakfast with her every morning, to sit together and plan their day: When would they ride? Did they need to go into the village? What projects at Heartsease required their attention next? What plans might they make for the fields and the horses? He *could* do it. He could give up his wandering for this, for her and a lifetime of mornings like these. But that was setting those horses before the carts. They hadn't even talked of a future and here he was already living in it. She would resist, of course. That was a given. He would have to help her see that this was the best way to move forward. But there were things he needed to understand first.

When she finished her plate, he rose and held out his hand. 'Shall we walk in the garden?' The garden was her place, a place where she ought to feel safe, safe enough to discuss things she'd so far been reluctant to share. It was also private. They'd be away from the sharp ears of Mrs Thornton and Cook. She nodded and took his hand.

He let her take him about the garden, showing him the rose bushes, which had just been mere twigs when he'd left, the little square knot garden of herbs, and last, the little glass house in the corner where she grew her year-round blooms, the special ones she generously displayed at Christmas at the church. When they finished the circle tour of the garden he put the statement to her. 'We have to talk about last night, El.' He spied a stone bench set amid bare trellises and led them to it.

'Do we, though?' She shook her head as she sat. 'I think you make too much out of it. We made each other no promises and asked for no promises in return. I asked you to stay, that was all.'

He interlaced his fingers through hers, patient. He'd expected this. 'We are to pretend last night never happened? I cannot do that, El.' He held their joined hands up between them. 'We are intertwined now, in new ways than before.'

'No, not to pretend it never happened, but it doesn't have to define us or our future. Surely, there is some middle ground between the two.'

He arched a brow at that. She wanted to relegate last night to a moment out of time so that it needn't be explained or perhaps repeated. Neither option was satisfactory to him but such a strategy did make him wonder why she'd choose that option especially when she could have more. Surely, she understood implicitly that he *would* offer for her if she wanted that. 'If we are not to repeat last night, El, which, by the way, I think would be a shame, why start it at all? Why me? Why now? I do find myself mystified by your choice given your reticence this morning.'

She gave him a long-suffering look as if he'd missed a key element. 'Why so? You have plans, Tristan. I will not have you give them up for me.'

He chuckled with a sense of relief. Ah, so that was it. It was so simple, he should have seen it sooner. How like Elanora to think of others before herself. 'The army has not sent word officially yet. They may not want me after all.' He did think it odd he hadn't heard yet. 'Even so, I can't believe you truly thought I could take you to bed and leave it a single night. You know me better than that. At least I hope you do.' He dropped his voice although there was no one to hear. 'I do not need you to protect me from my decisions. I knew full well what I was doing last night when I agreed to stay with you. I took your virtue, something that society has decreed should only be given to one's husband.'

'I am not looking for a husband, Tristan. Last night was not about coercing a proposal. Far from it. Last night was because I shall *never* have a husband, Tristan. Last night was because I simply wanted to know what such intimacy might be like and I wanted it to be with someone I trusted.'

He wondered if she'd *wanted* it to be with someone who was leaving, who wouldn't be around to coerce her into changing her mind. Why was she so certain she wouldn't marry? That bore thinking about. But those thoughts had to be set aside as she fixed him with a hard stare that demanded all of his attention, a warning that he would not like what she said next. 'I wanted someone who I could trust not only with my body but who also could be trusted to keep my wishes. Primarily the wish that last night compels nothing on your behalf, changes nothing for you.' There was censure in that for him, that somehow by trying to do the honourable thing by her he was betraying her.

'Why do you think you'll never marry, El? There is time.'

She shook her head. 'It's too late, too much has happened, too much has changed.' He made to protest. She was being ridiculous. She was young and beautiful. But she pressed a finger to his lips as she'd done last night. 'No, listen to me, Tristan. I know what you're thinking, that twenty-five is not too old, that I come from a respected family, that I should have the same opportunities I might have had when I was eighteen. But you cannot make up for lost time. Mother died, so I did not come out that year, or the next. Father simply couldn't face it and I could not ask it of him to go up to London and make merry when his heart was here in Sussex with Mother.

'Then he died, and I was twenty, nearly twenty-one, and the walls Teddy and I thought were secure came crumbling down. There was so much to do, there was no question of a London Season, and Teddy was not as discreet as he should have been about our finances. Word got out that the Grisham wealth was on shaky ground. We had to shore up loose ends as quickly as possible to put those rumours to bed before they could do real damage.'

Grim realisation began to dawn. 'Your dowry. That's

how you and Teddy put everyone off the scent, in hunt parlance.'

'It was a good decision and it worked,' she replied defensively.

'In part,' Tristan argued. 'It may have shored up your defences, allowed you to keep up a certain front for society, but the damage was already done, wasn't it? The right kind of suitor wasn't keen on allying himself with a family that had proven to be ridden by tragedy and riddled with financial concerns. Even if there was someone, there was no way to hide there was no dowry if or when they met with Teddy to discuss marriage settlements.' That explained why neither her father nor Teddy had taken pains to see her cared for, why a husband had not been found. Tristan sighed. 'I am sorry about your dowry.' Sorry, too, that he'd not been here to talk sense into Teddy. One more way in which he'd failed his friend.

She leaned forward in earnestness. 'Don't be sorry, Tristan. No one took anything from me that I did not freely give. Teddy and I agreed on it together. It was my decision as much as it was his. It bought us time and it gave us a chance.'

Tristan ran his thumb over the backs of her knuckles. How like her to give so selflessly all she had. Of course she'd given up her dowry for her family. 'I remember once that you gave up a sweet bun from Manning's when we found that mangy cur in an alley in the village. We'd saved up for those buns, you and me and Teddy. You longer than either of us because Teddy and I had a chance to earn a few coins by haying for Mr Bradford and you didn't have the luxury of work. We'd just got the buns when you heard the dog whine. You spent a half hour in the alley trying to coax it to your hand.'

'And I succeeded,' she interrupted. 'It followed us home, and became the most loyal dog we've ever had. You do recall how he saved the whole barn when it could have burned down a few years later. He was the one who woke Old Mackey in time. Old Mackey gives him all the credit. So your point is…?'

Tristan chuckled. 'You gave up your precious sweet roll for a mangy dog no one else wanted. Of course you gave up your dowry, only it's not the same thing.' He let his gaze linger on her. 'When you gave up your dowry, you gave away your chance for the life you wanted— a home, a family, children to spend your love on, your life on.'

She put her hand over his, her blue eyes sad, sincere. 'I think you're not looking at it the right way. When I gave up that sweet bun, I was giving that dog a chance at a life. When I gave up my dowry, I was giving my home, my family, a chance, too.'

'But the ending was very different,' Tristan protested.

'We can't always know the endings. That doesn't mean we don't embark on the journey.'

'I would write a better ending for you,' Tristan insisted, seeing an opening. He had his answers now; most of them, at least.

'I think I should write my own ending, one that doesn't include upsetting your own plans,' she said meaningfully. She rose and brushed her skirt. 'Thank you for last night, for being my friend, for making it possible, all of it. But it's over now. If you could excuse me, I need to make the flower arrangements ready for church tomorrow.'

'You don't believe that. Your eyes give you away. You don't want this to end.' The conversation had not gone in the direction he'd intended. Somehow, she'd managed to outflank him.

She rested a hand on his sleeve. 'What I want is of no consequence. It was never my intention to trap you. You needn't feel obligated to do more, to offer more.'

'But what if I want to?'

'Then you should go home and ask yourself the same question once the fire in your blood has cooled.' Her eyes shuttered as if the gates had been pulled down on a castle. The conversation was over. He'd gain no more ground today but he might be able to leave himself some rope with which to scale the castle walls tomorrow.

'I will look forward to seeing you in church tomorrow, and your flowers as well. I'll call for you early so you have plenty of time to have them in place before the service begins and you will sit with us in the Lennox pew.' He offered his terms with a stern look and she nodded, as if she understood that these were the conditions of his retreat, temporary though it might be.

As he drove the curricle down the drive at Heartsease and headed home, he thought perhaps she hadn't dismissed him or what had passed between them as much as she'd simply tried to protect herself. Maybe she also needed some of the space and time she suggested he take to think things over. Much had happened since he'd departed Brentham Woods just twenty-four hours ago. He'd left intending to restore Elanora's Christmas spirit with a visit to the Christmas market, and he thought he'd been relatively successful there. But the market and Christmas had worked their collective magic on him as well.

Last night had been exquisite beyond imagining, had him wanting things he'd not thought to want. No, not things. *Someone.* He wanted Elanora. Just the thought of wanting her made his heart soar, made him smile at nothing in particular. He wanted a life with her, but how to make that happen? And how to convince her of it? Those were not inconsiderable obstacles, but his step was still light as he arrived home at Brentham Woods.

His brother was in the stables when he pulled in. 'There you are…home at last,' Julien called out over a stall door, having just put his own horse away.

'I have big news, brother.' Tristan jumped down from the curricle, feeling a smile plastered across his face.

'Then you've already seen the letter? What did it say?' Julien grinned. 'I hope it doesn't mean I'm losing my business partner before I've even got him up to speed.'

'Letter?' This past week he'd given up hope that it would show up, and by the mid part of the week he'd started to hope it actually wouldn't.

'Yes, it came yesterday after you left for the market.' Julien stepped out of the stall and clapped him on the shoulder. 'It's just us tonight. Mother and Father are dining elsewhere. So we're on our own for supper. Let's go in. Joe will take care of the team. You and I will read your mystery letter and open some of the good stuff to celebrate.' Tristan felt some of his ebullience deflate. So much had happened in twenty-four hours and it seemed that change wasn't done with him yet.

Chapter Thirteen

'I was wondering if you were ever coming home.' Julien passed him a snifter. 'It's cognac from a new importer I'm hoping to contract with. Tell me what you think.'

Tristan swirled the amber liquid and held it to the light before taking an experimental sip. 'It's good. It's heavy on the nuttiness, though.' It reminded him too much of the nutty flavours on Elanora's tongue when he kissed her at the market, of chestnuts eaten as they strolled the booths.

'And you're gone again.' Julien sighed and slouched in the club chair set before the fire in the study. 'You are one distracted man. While I agree with your assessment of the cognac, I find I'm curious about what was happening in your head just now and does it have anything to do with that letter you opened but have barely glanced at.' He gestured to his desk, where the letter lay.

'It's complicated, Jules.' Tristan rubbed a hand over his eyes and took the chair opposite. 'I wouldn't know where to start.'

Julien held up the decanted cognac. 'I've got all night and a case of this stuff. Start where you like, or maybe, start where I like. What's in the letter?'

Well, that was easy. 'The army would like to contract me, as a private citizen, to procure and train horses for the cavalry. It would require some travel around Europe and spending time in London at Horseguards.' Up until earlier this week it had been a position he coveted, the perfect post-military career.

Julien raised an eyebrow, looking impressed. 'Celebrations are in order indeed. Congratulations, brother. Although, I assume this means I will be losing my active business partner.' He started to raise his glass in a toast and then stopped. 'Why so glum, then? I sense this letter doesn't meet with your approval? Although I can't fathom why not.' Julien slid him a sly look. 'Does it have anything to do with where you've been since yesterday or even all week, for that matter? You've hardly been around here.' There was censorious scold in his tone, and Tristan felt a twinge of guilt. 'You were going to help me with my business venture. But you're up early and gone before I've even been out of bed.'

'Elanora needed my help more than you did. I've been at Heartsease,' Tristan confessed, knowing Julien would hardly hold that against him.

Julien nodded. 'I'm glad to hear she's permitting a little help.' He sat back in his chair. 'You always could persuade even the hardest-headed people to see things your way.' If only that were true, Tristan thought. The only hard head he wanted to persuade these days was Elanora's and the going was slow.

Tristan shrugged. 'It was nothing, just some lawn work, some whitewashing, and a few nails for loose shutters, cutting a little ivy. Oh, and I got the fountain to work. The place looks better and it's all ready for hosting the Christmas panto.'

'Impressive.' Julien swirled his cognac. 'That doesn't sound like *nothing* to me.' He swallowed, his gaze fixed on Tristan in a way that made Tristan want to squirm. 'I was in the village this morning to handle some papers at the bank. Mr Thompson was in as well. He said he saw you at the Christmas market yesterday with Elanora.'

'Yes.' There was no reason to deny it. Tristan leaned forward. 'She needed cheering up. She'd lost her Christmas spirit and I thought seeing the shop windows and the market would restore it. You were right. She's too much alone out there, and consequently, too lonely.'

'And were you successful?' Julien persisted.

'I like to think so. Julien, how do you eat your gingerbread men? Head first or feet?'

'Head first of course, why?' Julien gave him a perplexed stare.

'Me, too. I was just wondering.' Tristan reached for the decanter, wanting to redirect Julien's questions. 'May I pour you another? Tell me about this new cognac supplier.'

'No, I think we should talk more about the Christmas market or perhaps what happened after the market? You didn't come home last night. Will you tell me or should I tell you what I suspect? You can tell me, you know. We're brothers after all, and if it's part of what is plaguing you, perhaps it's best to talk it out.'

It was clear Julien wasn't going to stop until he knew everything and perhaps talking it out *would* help. Tristan met his brother's gaze with stern directness. 'I made love with Elanora.' He chose his words carefully, deliberately, to convey what the night had meant to him and to be sure his brother understood this was no fleeting one-night whim. He was rewarded for his forthrightness with Julien's spewed cognac staining his breeches while Julien choked so hard, Tristan had to get up and slap his brother on the back.

'Good God, man, she's like our sister!' Julien rasped out hoarsely when the coughing had passed. 'Our *little* sister.'

'I do not see her that way.'

'Obviously not,' Julien said wryly, then he sobered. 'All joking aside, what are your plans?'

'I would marry her.' Saying the words out loud felt new and strange and right. He wished he knew what that looked like; a vision of a life with Elanora was a happy one if also an incomplete one, especially given that he wasn't sure that was what she wanted; nor was he sure how he would support her if he gave up the army's offer.

'But?' Julien prodded gently.

'She will take some convincing,' Tristan admitted.

'Seems like she's already convinced if things went as far as they did,' Julien argued.

'It wasn't like that. She's given up on marriage because she doesn't see herself as marriageable. Julien, you were right. There are money problems at Heartsease. Teddy spent her dowry to keep them afloat.' He gave Julien a moment to digest the news. Julien was a money man. To raze a woman's dowry, her one key to finding a mate who could continue her security, would be, in Julien's eyes, tantamount to money lenders in the temple: a crime of egregious import.

'Teddy should have known better. He should have secured her a match.' Julien swore under his breath. 'I knew we should have pushed harder to come alongside him when his father died. If I had known such chicanery was afoot over there...'

Tristan sighed. 'My thoughts exactly.' Hearing Julien voice those regrets only intensified his own guilt. Teddy had been his friend. 'She thinks she's beyond marriage. Of course, I don't care about the dowry. I sense from what she's shared that there were men after Teddy died who did care quite a lot about her dowry and the rumours about the financial health of the estate.' He looked at his brother. 'Do you think they were just rumours or was there any teeth to them?'

Julien shrugged. 'I couldn't say. I know there was talk after her father died and then it faded away. Now I understand why. Her dowry was shoring up the loose ends. When people expect you to have money, that's all they see. I didn't think to question where the funds came from. The first time I thought they were truly in trouble was when Teddy died and that was because of the lost cargo.'

Tristan nodded. 'I only ask because I wonder if there's something more behind her reticence besides not having a dowry. It's enough that she'd bring Heartsease into any marriage. That would more than compensate for any lack of dowry.'

'But a man has to be able to support an estate that size. For some men it would be a millstone.' What Julien meant was the kind of man she'd most likely attract: a merchant or a banker, a man of decent means but not a man who knew about running an estate so that it could pay for itself without digging too deeply into his pockets. Julien's fingers drummed idly on the tabletop beside his chair. 'Is that what you're worried about? Supporting Heartsease? You have your money from your investments, quite a tidy sum, as I've shown you, and there will be more returns. You'll have your work with me as well. You will not be a poor man.' He paused. 'Ah, that's it, isn't it? You would prefer the army's offer.'

'It pays plenty and I'd still have the investments with you.' Tristan sighed. His brother had divined correctly. 'I'd be gone a great deal and Elanora is not one for travel. She can't bear to be away from Heartsease and her gardens for long.' Nor did he think he could bear to be away from her for months on end. What would that do to their relationship, their marriage? He feared they would grow apart before they ever had a chance to grow together. Too much disparity led to separate lives. 'It is easy to fall in love, Julien. The difficulty is what comes afterwards.'

Julien laughed. 'Having never been in love, I will take your word for it. But surely, there must be a solution. We shall both think on it, if marriage is what you want.'

Tristan furrowed his brow. 'I'm not sure I follow.'

Julien looked distinctly uncomfortable. 'This is difficult to say because I care for you and for Elanora. I want your happiness. This has been rather fast, don't you think? You've been home for two weeks and suddenly you're talking marriage with someone you haven't seen for ten years.'

'I've known her most of my life. I've known her family. I was Teddy's best friend,' Tristan protested. Julien was making it sound like he'd gone out and picked a complete stranger off the streets to marry. 'This is Elanora we are talking about.'

'That's what worries me. Are you doing this because of your loyalty to Teddy? Or because of fond memories of a childhood that has long since passed? Or because you feel compelled to save her from whatever she's running from? When all that is taken away, what is left? Is it enough for two people to make their own life together, a life that belongs to them now, not to the shadows of the past? Can you even have a fresh start amid the ghosts of Heartsease?' That was quite a speech coming from Julien, who preferred to communicate with ledger totals and tally sheets.

'I'm starting to see why you've not fallen in love,' Tristan muttered wryly. 'Not everything can be costs and benefits and profits.'

Julien quirked a dark brow. 'Maybe people would be happier if they were. I think it's important to consider in a relationship what you're investing in, why you're making that investment, and what you hope your return will be. I don't want you mistaking love for pity.'

'This is not pity,' Tristan retorted hotly. 'I did *not* take her to bed out of *pity*, for heaven's sake.'

'Please, don't be angry, Tristan. Just tell me you'll think about it, and that you'll be honest with yourself.' Julien picked up his glass again. 'Now, I've said my piece, and you've said yours. We can set that aside and move on to our other items of business, the cognac importer. What do you think?'

'I think I need another glass.' Tristan gave a congenial sigh. It had been a difficult conversation but he was grateful for his brother's insight even if it was hard to hear. There was much that he needed to sort out, starting with his heart and with hers, then he would move on from there.

Elanora moved back from the worktable in her glasshouse and studied the arrangements of red and white cyclamen amid sprays of evergreens. Cyclamen was a hardy flower, meant for cold British winters with their preference for moisture and their ability to thrive in cold weather. The Americans were pushing the warm weather poinsettia as a Christmas flower these days. Tristan's mother made a presentation on them at the flower club last December, but Elanora preferred the cyclamen. The poinsettia were beautiful but too fragile for cold British climes, and the cyclamen had always been Britain's Christmas flower.

She stepped forward and retied one of the wide red ribbons about one of the white bone-china vases. There, that was better. Her mother had provided the arrangements ever since she'd first come to Heartsease as a young bride. It wouldn't be Christmas without the Grisham Cyclamen. It was a tradition Elanora was proud to continue.

Well, what do you think, Mother? Will they do?

She felt closest to her mother when she worked with the flowers and she was sure this time of year her mother was standing over her shoulder.

Tristan Lennox is coming tomorrow to help me carry them down to the church before the service, Mother. I think I am falling for him. I know I shouldn't. I know it can never be. What do you think of that?

More to the point, what would her mother have thought about last night? Had she been too reckless? Too selfish in wanting this one thing of her own after a lifetime of giving? But of course, there was no answer except the clamour of her own thoughts. How nice it would have been to have someone to talk it over with. But her family was gone and her one friend was the one she was falling for. If she told him, he would do the right thing and marry her; he'd feel compelled.

She could not allow it, not as long as there was the mortgage and the Grisham debt looming. She could not wish that on him. Not as long as he would feel he had to give up his ambitions. He'd been excited about the prospect of being a horse procurer and trainer for the cavalry. The Lennoxes were a family with money, but they worked for it. Tristan would have to work in order to have wealth. There would be no time left for Heartsease, or for her. She could not possibly follow him on his travels and expect Heartsease to survive intact.

You're assuming he'd save Heartsease for you, go to his father and beg for money to pay the loan.

Which the Lennoxes probably would do out of their long-standing friendship. But she would be in *their* debt forever, never able to equal the playing pitch between them. Cameron Lennox had already done enough by buying her father's horses. Then again, if Tristan had to travel for work, he might not choose to save Heartsease at all, realising he had no need of such a place.

Why does it matter? You're going to lose Heartsease in a few weeks anyway.

It was the first time in twenty-four hours that horrible reminder had intruded. Hadn't she just been thinking about how she loved carrying on the tradition of the cyclamen? That it wasn't Christmas without the Grisham flowers? What silliness. The tradition ended this year. Unless... Unless she was able to take some cuttings with her and raise enough in the garden at the cottage.

This is what came of being with Tristan. She'd given him a day and he'd coaxed her spirit back to life with gingerbread men and carollers and roasted chestnuts, stolen kisses in the dark of the market and secretly held hands beneath an old plaid blanket.

You gave him more than a day. You gave him a week. He fixed up the outside of the house, he repaired your fountain, he raked your leaves and you created a potent fantasy out of his goodwill.

And then she'd begged that fantasy to take her to bed and he had. What had happened in that bed, though, had been very real for them both, and now she very much feared the consequences of what she'd set in motion.

Tristan was coming to take her and her flowers to church, to sit her beside him in the Lennox pew for the second Sunday in Advent, Bethlehem Sunday, because he thought he could save her. But that was only because he didn't know better. He thought there was still hope. But she did know better. She knew there was none.

Chapter Fourteen

'Today we light the Bethlehem Candle as a sign of love and remembrance of Mary and Joseph's journey to Bethlehem…'

Reverend Thompson intoned with his usual reverence the words that had opened every Second Sunday of Advent that Elanora could remember. She did not think it was by accident that Tristan chose that moment to send a surreptitious smiling glance her way and to close his hand secretly around hers where it rested between them on the pew, hidden by the folds of her skirt. His thumb made a slow caress over her knuckles and a heat inappropriate for church started low in her belly, his caress a reminder of other caresses, of other touches.

'You're wicked,' she whispered, keeping her eyes fixed on the prayer book in her lap, careful to give nothing away. He was also playing a dangerous game. Did he *want* people to comment on them? Had he forgotten how things worked in Hemsford? No one was allowed their secrets unless they retreated entirely, which she had done successfully up until now. People had left her alone to grieve Teddy—well, most people. That list did *not* include Mr Atwater or his nephew, Elias Bathurst. Nor, technically, did it include Tristan.

She managed a sideways look at Tristan's handsome profile, the straight nose, the strong jaw; there was a man's strength and a soldier's hardness in that profile, but there was kindness, too. A kindness she knew intimately. She knew how those dark eyes warmed to the consistency of melting chocolate, how a smile transformed his face, how laughter lit him up from within. She knew, too, how a single touch, a single look, could transfer that warmth to another, could make that other feel safe, cared for, protected.

Illusions all. Be careful. Your father, your brother, didn't they, too, have those characteristics? They failed. The securities they promised were not real.

But with Tristan those promises felt real, that this time it might be different. That was the real danger: that she might believe in them against her better judgement.

They rose for the final hymn and to receive Reverend Thompson's benediction. Tristan's hand was at her elbow, his eyes twinkling like dark stars as if to say, 'Are you ready?' It might be light fun to him, but it was not to her. She braced herself for what she knew would come as they filed out of the church.

'Miss Grisham, it's good to see you in church again. The flowers are lovely,' Reverend Thompson greeted her as she and Tristan passed out into the churchyard. 'Thank you for bringing her, Captain.' Reverend Thompson turned his attention to Tristan. 'It is good to have you both back. Christmas is a time for homecoming and families, people returning home, not unlike Joseph answering his own call to Bethlehem.' Reverend Thompson smiled. 'I will look forward to seeing you both, I hope, at all the festivities we have planned between now and Christmas Eve.'

Tristan offered the vicar a wide grin. 'Just give me a list and we'll be there. I am looking forward to this Christmas especially. Nothing is better than a Sussex Christmas.'

The vicar's gaze took on a knowing cast as he split it between them. 'I imagine so, Captain.'

They moved on and Elanora hissed a scold. 'Do not encourage him, Tristan. He thinks we are *together*.'

Tristan slid her hand through the crook of his arm, his eyes merry as he whispered at her ear, just for her to hear, 'We *are* together, Elanora.'

There was no time to argue this. Outside in the cold morning air, people lingered for conversation, wrapped in their cloaks and coats, hands tucked into muffs, throats swathed in mufflers, breaths coming in puffs on the cold air of their conversations. There was always news to share and introductions to make this time of year. Relatives were indeed arriving for Christmas. Several families had proudly been sporting an extra cousin or two in the pews this morning, including Mr Atwater.

Elanora had not been pleased to see Elias Bathurst sitting next to his uncle three rows behind the Lennoxes. She was even less pleased to see them standing outside talking with a few other businessmen, Elias catching sight of her as she exited. She thought perhaps he'd been watching the door especially for that reason, his icy gaze narrowing on her. She did not avert her gaze fast enough and Tristan followed it.

'Elias is in town for Christmas, I see,' he commented drily, his own gaze shifting to her. 'Has Elias been making a nuisance of himself, El? I can't tell if it's you he's pleased to see or me he's disappointed to see.'

She stiffened at that. 'Why would you think he's been making a nuisance of himself?' Had Tristan heard something? If Mr Atwater had been indiscreet again about her personal situation... Then what? She could do nothing about it.

Tristan chuckled. 'Because Elias Bathurst is always a nuisance and he's never forgiven me or Teddy for the incident at the swimming hole.'

Elanora frowned. 'He started it.' In truth, the swimming hole had been one of many incidents in which Teddy and Tristan had squared off against Elias, who'd been something of a bully, a trend that had continued up until impending adulthood had sent Tristan to the army and Elias to university.

Tristan's gaze narrowed, too astute for her liking. 'He makes you nervous, El. What is it? Has something happened?'

She smiled and deflected. 'Would you excuse me for a moment? I need to discuss some things about the panto with Mrs Phelps and the ladies.' As she moved to join the women, she noticed how quickly the men absorbed Tristan now that he was free of escort duty. The men were eager to talk with Tristan and Julien and of course there were plenty of men who wanted to talk horses with Cameron Lennox. The hunt club was never truly on hiatus, she knew from experience. She'd have liked to listen to the horse talk, but Helen Lennox and the other ladies wanted to discuss the cyclamen.

'The flowers were gorgeous. You get the best colour on your blooms,' Mrs Harris commented. 'You must tell me your secret.'

'It's the—' she began but was interrupted by Mrs Phelps.

'She gets the best men, too.' The gregarious Mrs Phelps winked. 'Here she's been hiding away at Hearts-ease and emerges with the handsome Captain Lennox on her arm. I say she's got more than one secret to share.' Mrs Phelps looked to Helen Lennox. 'Perhaps you will get a daughter in the New Year, after all.'

This was exactly the kind of talk Elanora had wanted to avoid but it was the price for leaving the protection of being on Tristan's arm. Elanora flushed and was only somewhat grateful when Tristan joined the group to retrieve her a few short minutes later, leading to Mrs Phelps fixing the group with a smug 'I told you so' smile.

'You looked like you were in need of a rescue.' Tristan helped her up into the curricle and tucked the blanket about her before taking his seat.

'I'm not sure the rescue helped or made it worse,' she said in all seriousness as he set the team in motion. 'Mrs Phelps has us married by spring.'

'So what if she does?' Tristan was unfazed and his lack of chagrin irritated her.

'I think it's principle I object to. Sitting with the family at church and going to the Christmas market should not be enough to conclude marriage is in the offing. Might I not simply spend time with my friend?'

'Your friend? Is that all?' Tristan made a frown that was only playful in part. 'I rather thought I might have been…promoted after the other night.'

She furrowed her brow. 'I did not think promotion was expected. I thought we were clear on that in the garden yesterday.' She felt the tone of the conversation change, moving away from a discussion of village busy-bodies, and moving towards something more difficult, something she did not want to discuss any more today than she had yesterday. But today she was a captive audience in the curricle if he chose to push his cause. She could not dismiss him now.

'You were clear and I disagreed.' He slid her a strong sideways look. 'I *want* to talk about marriage, Elanora. I did go home and do as you instructed. I thought about us away from the attractions of our bed.' Oh, Lord, she wished he wouldn't say things like *our bed*. It made her want to forget all her caution. Two Sundays ago they'd been stirring up pudding. This Sunday they were stirring up trouble.

'Don't you feel it's too soon?' she prompted, trying to ignore the contradiction in her own argument. If it was too soon for marriage, then it was definitely too soon to have taken him to her bed. And yet, she felt she'd lived a lifetime in this week. Tristan was changing her, changing her life without her permission, in ways she'd not intended. He was bringing back hope, and that was dangerous for its ability to disappoint.

'No, I don't. A gentleman does not take a woman to bed without understanding where that path leads.'

'So you've said, even though that woman did the inviting and made it clear she had no expectations, and she knew you had commitments elsewhere.' She was losing control of this argument; letting him forget about his plans to leave. 'Our night was not meant to lead anywhere.'

'Not even to another night?' Tristan queried, his eyes dark, more onyx than chocolate now. 'Are we to have discovered perfect passion and not revisit it?' He turned the team around the final corner leading to Heartsease. 'It is your decision, Elanora. I am offering you a lifetime of passion, of friendship, a family to stand instead of your own. I can give you a good life, Elanora. It has always been your decision. I just don't understand why you're making the one you are. I don't care about your dowry being gone. If that's your reason it's no good.' Her heart wept at his words, at all she was giving up.

It wasn't the only reason. She hadn't been truthful with him. She needed to protect him from all he didn't know. But she was used to it. She'd been sacrificing things for years. She would not sacrifice him, not Tristan, who was strong and good and too kind for his own benefit. In some ways, it was too late to tell him about the mortgage even if she wanted to. He would feel that he couldn't retract his offer. Perhaps she ought to have told him from the beginning; perhaps it would have kept him from walking this path, kept him from thinking things were possible that weren't. Or perhaps, knowing would only have redoubled his efforts, provoked his pity. Either way, it seemed she could not win.

'Will you do something for me, El?' He tooled into the long drive.

'You know I would, anything.' Anything that would keep him safe; anything that would let him pursue his own ambitions.

'You think it is too soon to plan a future. So give us two weeks, until Christmas. Give me these weeks to show you what our life could be like, to show you that this can work, to convince you that my offer is not out of pity for your circumstances or out of obligation to your brother's memory. Let me prove myself to you. Let me prove *us* to you. At the end of those two weeks, if you still feel that it's too soon, or that it will always be too soon, then I won't press the matter.'

She wondered if it was wrong to make a deal with the devil on Bethlehem Sunday, also called Love Sunday, or if perhaps it really was the magic of the season tugging at her heart, freeing it from the chains that usually shackled her. Two weeks with Tristan would be a temporary freedom. It could not last. It would be only an extension on the freedom that she'd briefly allowed herself on Stir-Up Sunday, at the Christmas market, and the other night. But freedom, she discovered, was addicting. The more she had of it, the more she craved it. Or was it the man she craved? The more she had of Tristan Lennox, the more she wanted of him.

What did she have to lose in two weeks that wasn't already lost? What did denying him and herself gain her? It wouldn't stop the talk in the village; it wouldn't stop the mortgage; it wouldn't stop Mr Atwater from foreclosing on Heartsease Christmas Eve. But it might stop Tristan from being too curious if he had what he wanted.

She curled her hand around his, her decision made. Two weeks to throw herself into Christmas; two weeks to throw herself into Tristan's waiting arms. Two weeks to hold against a lifetime of loneliness. 'Did you know Cook and Mrs Thornton have this Sunday off, to make up for the extra work last Sunday?'

Tristan's gaze settled on her with a slow smile. 'Does that mean what I think it does?'

'It means you have your two weeks. Starting today.'

'No,' he corrected. 'It means *we* have our two weeks.' He cast a sharp eye at the house. 'Everyone is gone, you say? Have you ever had lunch in bed?'

'No, as you well know,' she teased, her spirits lifting at knowing a decision had been made, that she had two weeks before her of happiness renewed, rediscovered. In this moment those weeks felt like an eternity. She slid him a coy look, joy welling up. 'Is it as good as breakfast in bed?'

'It's better,' he flirted, pulling the team to a halt at the fountain. 'I will go help Old Mackey put up the team, while you fix a tray to take upstairs. Take plenty up because you never know when lunch in bed might become dinner in bed.'

'You are pleasantly optimistic.' But so was she. She laughed as he swung her down, stealing a kiss that flustered and ignited her. She was all thumbs in the kitchen on account of that kiss, nearly dropping the silverware and forgetting to put glasses on the tray, but she still managed to make it to the bedroom before Tristan.

Breathe, Elanora. Just breathe.

It was a good thing she'd breathed when she had a chance.

One look at Tristan stepping into her bedroom was all it took to steal that breath, and the next one. His eyes burned like two dark, hot coals as he crossed the room, his intention clear, and then she was in his arms, her hands in his hair, his mouth on hers, her body pressed as close to his as humanly possible with clothes on— clothes she was fast coming to resent. 'I want to be naked with you.' She managed the breathless words.

'I thought you'd never ask.' Tristan was equally breathless as he stepped back, yanking his cravat from his neck. That neckcloth would be the first casualty in their race to nakedness, each of them undressing themselves in hurried chaos, gazes riveted on one another, fingers flying and fumbling all at once in their need.

Intuition told her this would be a fast and furious coupling, the result of a night spent apart, of bodies burning with the recent knowledge of knowing what was possible if they could just lay claim to it, and perhaps, too, the energy that comes with overflowing joy. 'Hurry, Tristan.' She was beneath him, her body inviting him in all the ways it could, her thighs open and ready, her hips arching into his. She gasped aloud when the first thrust came, hard and swift, going straight to the depths of her. 'Yes.' The word was a ragged cry on her lips.

Tristan wasted no time setting a pace that pushed

them rapidly to where she wanted to be—on that sea of pleasure, adrift with him, only him. But before drifting, there was storming. Pleasure came like a lightning bolt, sudden and sharp, jolting her senses so that all she was capable of was a series of gasps and moans as the squall of pleasure rolled over her, leaving her exhausted and sated in its wake.

Tristan let out an exhausted sigh beside her, one hand thrown over his head as he drew deep breaths. 'I thought I would explode.' He turned his head towards her. 'May I make a confession? I thought of nothing else throughout church but making love to you. There was the vicar up at his pulpit in his robes with his purple stole and the beautiful flowers in the niches, the candles on the altar, everything looking so neat and perfect. Then there was you, also so neat and perfect with your hair done up and all those tiny buttons tidily fastened on that dark green dress. All I wanted to do was wreck you, to rip those buttons open, to take down your hair, to plunge into you and be welcomed home.' He gave a chuckle. 'Have I shocked you? Are you appalled that I thought such things in church?'

'In truth, I find it strangely arousing.' She bit her lip and turned on her side to face him better. She drew a circle on his chest. 'I wonder what Reverend Thompson would think if he knew how inspiring you found his sermon,' she teased.

'Make no mistake, you were the inspiration.' Tristan kissed her, a long, slow kiss, very different from the heated rush that had just taken them.

She sighed beneath his lips. 'How is it possible that I want you again already?'

'Because we were made for one another. Let me show you.' Tristan's mouth moved down the familiar trail it had taken once before to breasts, to belly, and this time lower to the damp curls at her thighs. He blew softly there and she sighed at the gentle warmth. 'Certain parts of my body may need a bit more recovery time than you allow, but other parts are happy to serve in their stead.' He looked up at her with a wicked stare, sending a delicious tremor of warning through her.

'Such as?' she queried with cool playfulness although her body was already hot with guessing.

'My mouth, my tongue, my lips, pressed in service to your most hidden treasure.' He gave a growl, fierce with desire. She wished he wouldn't say things like that; it only made the wanting worse, the waiting worse, but it also made the release so much better when it came. But it was his thumb that slid into the depths of her folds and found the nub within already sensitive and raw with want. She gasped at the exquisite tremolo of pleasure that shot through her and that was only the beginning, but with the first lave of his tongue, her body could tell the end would not be long in coming.

Chapter Fifteen

One week later

She did not want this to end, this exquisite existence lived in Tristan's arms, wrapped in his presence in all the ways a woman could be wrapped in a man: emotionally, physically, mentally. She wanted to live in this delicious limbo of a paradise forever, this place that inhabited the space between Bethlehem Sunday and Christmas Eve.

It was Elanora's first thought upon waking and her last thought upon sleeping, followed by the strange assurance that it would go on for a while at least and each day that it did was sufficient unto itself, replete with its own joy, its own happiness and satisfactions. Each day mirrored the extraordinary delight and the extreme danger of falling in love, both of which she'd underestimated in their power. The danger was in the temptation to believe in things again—she was forgetting the harsh lessons she'd learned and that had been her constant these past six months—the notion of believing in things she'd wisely set aside to protect herself from things that had already proven to be false once. But the real devil was in the delight loving Tristan brought. It was far more difficult to resist that which brought her pleasure.

There were moments when she forgot entirely why she had to resist; moments when he looked at her as if she were the sum of his world, moments when he took her hand and raised it to his lips, moments when his hand rested gently at her back, guiding her through a crowd. Those moments happened at any time: in bed, in a crowd, across the table, at church, walking the grounds of Heartsease, or galloping across a meadow. One would think their sheer quantity would diminish them but by some equation unique only to love, the amount of those moments only added to their value. Against her better judgement, against all the cautions she'd issued herself, she'd fallen in love with Tristan Lennox.

Of course, there was always the reasoning that she'd never had that far to fall. She'd always been halfway there. That only made the act explainable. It didn't make it acceptable. It was no more acceptable this morning as she snuggled close to him in the grey light of dawn than it had been the day he'd stood beside her in the Grisham graveyard. Her problems still persisted. His dreams to travel still existed. Beyond this precious limbo, they were not made for one another.

She shivered and nestled closer still, his body a delectable contrast of warmth against the cold of a winter bedroom. She closed her eyes, wanting to go back to sleep in the hopes of prolonging the morning. Tristan was going away briefly with Julien on business today. He would leave after breakfast. It would just be for one night and two days. Goodness knew she had plenty to keep her busy with Christmas and the panto quickly approaching, and there were flowers to arrange for Sunday service. Still, the idea of being alone in her bed for even one of their fourteen nights made her feel low.

You will have to get used to it.

The negative thought intruded on the edge of sleep, startling her back to wakefulness like a moth who could not resist the lure of the light even if it killed him. Her bed would be empty soon enough and on a much more permanent basis than a single night. It was the first time since Bethlehem Sunday she'd allowed such a thought to creep in. More importantly, it was the first time in eight days. Yesterday had been Shepherd's Sunday, a celebration of joy, particularly the joy of searching and finding. It was a most apt message, she'd thought at the time. But the sharp edge to joy was sadness. On this grey Monday morning as she faced the prospect of Tristan leaving and the realisation that even though he'd be back in less than forty-eight hours, there was only one more candle to light—the Angel Candle. From there, the distance to Christmas Eve was short.

Tristan stirred in his sleep, his body waking, sleepy eyes meeting hers, his voice a drowsy murmur. 'How long have you been awake?' He pushed a tangled strand of hair back behind her ear with a gentle gesture.

'Long enough to know I don't want you to go.'

His smile said he thought they were only the words of a lover loath to leave bed. 'It's just one night. I'll be back before you know it.'

She shook her head. 'I'm afraid something bad will happen if we're apart.' For a wild moment she thought about asking to go with him, but too many people were counting on her here. She could not rearrange her plans.

He pressed a finger to her lips. 'Nothing bad will happen. It's just a business trip, with Julien, nonetheless. Julien is the antithesis of living dangerously.' He thought this was about Teddy, not her. Perhaps that was best. There was too much explaining to do otherwise. He would want to know what she had to fear in Hemsford of all places.

'Tell me again why Julien needs you to go with him.' She slid a hand beneath the covers to find him already in a state of partial arousal. She curled her hand about him and he sighed.

'I forget when you touch me like that.' He gave a sharp moan as she raked her fingernails gently down the hardening length of him. 'Something about introducing me to a new partner in a cognac venture.'

She smiled wickedly and pulled him atop her. 'Come make me forget, too. Make me forget you're leaving.'

Three hours later she saw him off in a more public goodbye. He'd ridden with her as far as town and seen her to her meeting before setting off on horseback with Julien by his side. She stood on the porch at the church, watching until the brothers were out of sight. Five minutes down, forty-seven hours, fifty-five minutes to go, she thought, as Mrs Phelps called her inside.

She threw herself into the planning meeting and volunteered to take on extra responsibilities with the costumes for the pantomime, all with a smile and a laugh. They'd decided at the last meeting that the panto would be Cinderella this year. The women talked her into asking Tristan to play Prince Charming, and Mr Manning's daughter, Susannah, would play Cinderella. Mrs Phelps would donate one of her grandmother's old-fashioned gowns for the ball scene, and Mrs Truesdale offered the use of her heirloom tiara, much to Susannah's delight. 'Perhaps Captain Lennox can wear his uniform. That would be very princely,' Mrs Manning suggested. 'It would save us from having to make another costume.'

To which, Elanora said, 'I'll see what I can do.' The response earned her a knowing look from the ladies, who clearly thought she'd have no trouble at all talking Tristan into just about anything.

After the planning meeting she strolled the High Street with the ladies. She was in no hurry to return to Heartsease knowing Tristan wouldn't be there. They stopped to look in store windows, an exclamation going up from the group as they passed the dressmaker's.

'The window has changed,' Mrs Phelps gasped and the ladies stared.

There was a pretty display of Christmas accessories, dark green leather gloves and a white fur muff set against a backdrop of evergreen swags, but the red velvet dress was gone.

'I wonder who bought it,' Mrs Harris said in almost reverent tones.

'Perhaps Mr Atwater for Mrs Atwater?' came one quiet speculation. That would be a waste, Elanora thought. But only a person of means would be able to afford it and that did limit the pool of prospective buyers.

'I suppose we'll find out at the Lennox Christmas party.' Mrs Phelps sighed wistfully. 'Whoever bought the dress will surely wear it there and she'll be the belle of the ball.' She chuckled. 'Makes me wish I was thirty years younger and a few stone lighter. I don't think my waistline would do a dress like that justice these days,' she laughed and the group laughed with her as they said their goodbyes, preparing for the rest of their day. Elanora lingered at the window after the ladies had left. She hoped it had gone to a good place where it would be worn, where it would be part of celebrations for years to come.

'Such fancy things, Miss Grisham.' Mr Atwater's words startled her out of her contemplations. She'd not been aware of his approach and she immediately regretted letting her guard slip. Dear Lord, but she had so much to guard against these days. Appearing to be happy so no one expected the sorrow and turmoil beneath the surface took an enormous amount of energy. Mr Atwater's approach was proof that one could not lay down their burdens for even a moment. If they did, that would be the moment their troubles chose to pounce.

'We are lucky to have such a talented dressmaker among us,' she replied noncommittally. Surely, Mr Atwater didn't think she'd been contemplating a purchase?

Of all people, he knew her circumstances wouldn't allow even a small luxury purchase.

He cleared his throat. 'I am glad to have caught you. You are so seldom alone these days and I have something to discuss with you that is best done in private.' He was fishing for information. She heard the subtle probe: Where was Captain Lennox? Would she prefer that he be part of this conversation because there was an understanding between them? Or was she alone? There was a certain avaricious undertone to that concept. If she was alone, she was vulnerable and he wanted to know how vulnerable she was, and how he might exploit that advantage. 'Perhaps we might walk to the bank and discuss.' He smiled but it was a crocodile's smile, all teeth and anticipation.

At the bank he took his seat behind his desk and spread his hands wide on its surface. She assumed her usual position, perched on the edge of the hard chair reserved for clients, her hands gripping her reticule for support although there was nothing in there that could help her now. Butterflies stirred in her stomach. 'It gives me no pleasure to say this,' Mr Atwater began. Ah, so it was to be 'opposite day,' where everything one said was really just the reverse of what they meant. She wanted to shout 'liar.' Whatever he was going to say, she was sure he *did* take some pleasure in it.

He steepled his hands. 'As you know your lien against Heartsease comes due in a few days.'

'Not a few days, Mr Atwater, in five days,' she corrected. She would take every last one of them.

'Yes, very well, five days.' He said it as if he was

granting her a lavish boon. 'If the loan is not paid the house is forfeit to the bank. Just the house, mind you, which is why we now need to insist that you vacate the premises on the twenty-fourth. You are welcome to visit the house during the day to arrange for the auction of the contents that are not attached to the arrangement with the bank, but you cannot *stay* there. You cannot give any impression of living there once the house is no longer yours. I do not think that detail was made clear in our prior meetings.'

'No, it was not.' She drew a breath to steady herself. 'I had been led to believe I might stay for two weeks beyond that in order to prepare for the contents auction after the first of the year.'

He dusted his hands together, his usual gesture that suggested they were done with the conversation. 'Well, I'm glad we're clear on that now. You will need to be off the premises by the twenty-fourth.'

Elanora leaned forward, anger getting the better of her. 'You mean Christmas Eve, or can you not say it? It is bad enough that you are dispossessing a woman alone of her family home, a home that has been in her family for five generations, on the holiest night of the year, a night that stands for love and compassion and the very best humans have to give, and you are doing it knowing full well that she moves to gravely reduced circumstances.'

'How dare you make me the villain when you're the one who owes money. I am only asking for what is mine by rights.' Mr Atwater stiffened at her rebuke. 'It is only a date. It is simply when the money is due and it just so happens to be Christmas Eve, which would not be a concern if *your* brother had paid the mortgage on time.'

'My brother *died* trying to pay that mortgage,' Elanora snapped.

'These are the rules, Miss Grisham.'

'And who are *you*, Mr Atwater? Are you not a cofounder of this bank? The bank's most important person? Are you not the person who makes those very rules you cite as if they have birthed themselves and impelled *you* to follow *them* instead of the other way around?' She clenched her reticule so hard her knuckles were likely as white as the heat of her anger. 'You do not have to enforce those rules. You are choosing to. You are doing this to me on purpose.' She hissed the last.

'Now, see here, Miss Grisham, you are out of line.' Mr Atwater's eyes were two hard black beads in his face. 'Atwater and Schofield have been generous with you, giving you plenty of time and applying no pressure even when it became obvious you were not going to be able to pay. We were happy to give you a few extra months out of respect for your father, respect for your brother.'

'No. Nothing that has been done has been done out of respect.' She cut him off. It was all becoming clear now, clearer than it had ever been. Why had she not seen it before? 'It is not respectful to badger a woman into a marriage proposal a week after her brother's death.' *Badger* was a tame word for what Elias had done. 'I refuse to be patronised, Mr Atwater, and I refuse to be lied to. It wasn't me who was generously given time. It was your nephew, Elias.'

'I don't see how my nephew has anything to do with this,' Mr Atwater began but she was having none of it. Men who valued money didn't do anything without it or for nothing. They'd given her time, a whole half a year since Teddy's death and their finances had fallen apart. Bankers would not do it unless it was worth something to them.

'He has everything to do with it. He proposed to me at what he thought was an opportune time a week after Teddy's death, a week in which you disregarded my confidentiality as a client of this bank, and told him about the mortgage.'

'Client? You are a woman—you are a proxy client at best,' Mr Atwater scoffed. 'What you needed and still need is a husband. This emotional, irrational outburst of yours is proof of that. You are forgetting yourself and in a public place.'

She was not put off. 'A husband *you* thought to provide by pushing your nephew on me. When I refused him, you offered me time to pay the lien on Heartsease because you saw it not as time for me to succeed but time for me to fail, to recognise that in order to keep my home, I'd need to trade myself in marriage for the right to stay at Heartsease. When I recognised that and came to my senses, your nephew would be there to court me again, to generously reinitiate his offer.' Articulating the words out loud made the malevolence real. It had been easy to pretend that her bad luck was simply the cards fate had dealt her, and in part it was, she knew that much, but that deck *had* been stacked with other people's intentions in mind, intentions that were designed to see her fail so that they could have what they wanted.

'The Bathursts have always been jealous of the Grishams,' she challenged. And the Lennoxes, who'd managed to achieve in a much shorter time what the Bathursts had always coveted but never achieved— belonging. The realisation gave her pause. How it must gall Elias to know that Tristan was back, to see her on Tristan's arm and to think that Tristan was about to steal away his chance once more. The only weapon Elias had left was his knowledge of the mortgage and the hope that perhaps she hadn't told Tristan about it, and that if Tristan did know, that it would be enough to send him packing. She swallowed against the realisation that followed: Elias had only the one weapon left and it was one she'd unintentionally given him by choosing not to fully disclose her situation to Tristan. She'd never meant to be on Elias's side.

Mr Atwater gave a cool smile. 'Women always think it's about social drama. Men know better. My nephew is doing you a favour. He needn't offer you marriage to possess Heartsease. This is about money and time, Miss Grisham, both of which you have run out of. Unless you change your mind, find a fortune in buried treasure, or have some other fortuitous event occur, please be prepared to vacate Heartsease on the twenty-fourth. I appreciate your time. Good day.'

It was all Elanora could do not to run out of the bank and all the way to the churchyard where she'd tied Marian. She felt hunted and she was filled with dread that Elias Bathurst might be lurking nearby, waiting to strike now that his uncle had wounded his prey. No, not wounded, she corrected, reaching the churchyard and swiftly mounting Marian. She'd been flushed, perhaps, but nothing more. She was not a wounded doe whom the hunter would stalk until she fell down dead. She *would* go to ground, however, at Heartsease and regroup but she would not, she promised herself, be intimidated by this latest development. She turned her mare out of town.

She should not be upset, she reasoned once she reached the safety of her home. In truth, Mr Atwater's mean-spirited behaviour changed nothing but the timeline. The malevolence had always been there; she'd just allowed herself to obscure it, allowed herself to believe that a solid knee to Elias's manly assets and a scold to reproach Clifford Atwater's indiscreet conversation had taken care of the problem. In reality, it had fuelled a sense of revenge, and Tristan's reappearance had further ignited that flame. Perhaps, too, the jarring encounter with Mr Atwater was what she needed to recall the truth of her circumstances, to strengthen her resolve when it came to Tristan. Today was the reminder as to why she could not let Tristan sway her to think there was a future beyond the one that had been charted well before he'd come home.

It was going to be messier now, though. He wouldn't be gone by Christmas Eve. He would be here to see her shame instead of hearing about it in a letter once he was far away—too far away to do anything about it. He would be angry with her for hiding it from him until it was too late. She'd not intended for that to happen, not in that way, at least.

Unless you let him go now. Let him go sooner rather than later. A lover would be angry, but if he isn't your lover...

The thought nearly broke her. There had to be another away. After a lifetime of sacrifice, she didn't want to give him up, not before she had to. What did love demand of her? To trust him with her secrets? Or to set him free to pursue his own dreams?

Chapter Sixteen

Elanora did not let her thoughts wander any further. She'd learned years ago in the throes of loss over her mother that busyness was the antidote for the unsolvable. There was much to be busy about given the speed at which the panto was approaching. She spent time discussing plans with Mrs Thornton. The house had to look immaculate for the big night and there must be plenty of food. She would give the people of Hemsford a panto to remember, a party that would bring Christmas cheer to everyone.

She tried not to think about the lessening weight of her purse as she gave Mrs Thornton money for Christmas foodstuffs and ingredients for delicacies, but the purse was definitely lighter, the pound notes wrested from the bank diminishing like sands in an hourglass. When the money was gone…

No. She would not think on it, would not add this to the clouds on her horizon. This money was *meant* to be spent. She'd decided this weeks ago. *Before* Tristan was home. Nothing had changed except for the return of her Christmas spirit, and that was for the better. She had Tristan to thank for that. It was a gift of unimaginable value. He had no idea how much it meant to her to have these weeks of joy—weeks that she'd been dreading, where she'd expected she would just go through the motions in order to bring pleasure to others. Instead, the making of the efforts brought a personal joy to her she'd not anticipated.

Because love changes everything. It finds joy even in hard times.

Her love for him would have to sustain her in the days to come in the knowledge that when the time came, she'd make the right decision for him.

'Are you all right, miss?' Mrs Thornton peered at her curiously and then smiled. 'You are missing Captain Lennox. He'll be back tonight.' She tucked the money into her apron pocket. 'Captain Lennox is a fine man and he cares a great deal for you. Perhaps we'll have something more to celebrate at Christmas.'

It was Mrs Thornton's way of asking if a proposal was imminent. Elanora looked down at her hands. She didn't want to disappoint the woman. There would be more disappointment soon enough. She'd hoped to put off that disappointment until after Christmas but with Mr Atwater's latest pronouncement, that would no longer be possible. She would at least wait until after the panto. 'I think Captain Lennox has not been home very long. To assume too much would be reckless,' she offered vaguely, her ears pricking at the sound of hooves on the drive. It was early afternoon, but perhaps not too early to hope...

'Mrs Thornton, if you might excuse me?' She was up and moving towards the door in anticipation, her pulse pounding with the litany *Tristan is home. Tristan is home.*

She heard Mrs Thornton chuckle as she headed down the hall, her footsteps clicking a rapid tattoo on the hardwoods. She was hungry for the sight of him, her heart, her body, starving for the feel of his arms about her as if being in them would somehow hold the world at bay a little longer. She ran a little faster.

She was a sight for sore eyes, breathless and flushed as she paused for a moment, framed in the doorway of Heartsease at the top of the steps, and Tristan's own breath caught as he swung off Vitalis. His eyes may have been deprived of her for two days but she'd been on his mind nonstop. He'd no doubt worn Julien out with all of his talk. But decisions had been made, proof of those decisions, his commitment, and his love, packed safe in the deep pocket of his greatcoat until the right time. He took the front steps by twos and gathered her into his arms, stealing a robust kiss as he whispered against her lips, 'I missed you.'

'I missed you more,' she whispered back, and at her words, Tristan knew he was home. *Home.* What a concept that was, what a *feeling* that was, for a man who'd thought he didn't need it, who'd thought up until last month that he needed to spend his life wandering the world in order to be happy, or had he simply been wandering because he'd been *searching* for happiness, as opposed to actually *being* happy?

He took her hand, his excitement and elation threatening to overwhelm him now that he was actually here with her. The sooner he could lay out his plans, the sooner they could move forward. Once he told her all that was in his heart, she would not doubt his intentions, would no longer fear his feelings were impetuous or born of pity. 'Come walk with me.' He cast a quick eye to the skies. 'We have time before the rain begins, I think.' He grinned, tucking her arm through his. 'Tell me what you've been up to. How was the panto meeting?' As much as he wanted to spill all of his news, he knew better than to move too fast. She would feel ambushed and she would retreat. He had to go slowly, gradually.

She slanted him a look that had him laughing. 'Why am I afraid to have asked?' He chuckled.

'The ladies would like you to play Prince Charming. I told them I would ask.' She made a cute grimace. 'Don't be too mad?'

He was in too good of a mood to mind. He raised her hand to his lips but he couldn't help a little teasing. 'It is lucky for you that I have a bit of acting experience in my background. In my regiment, I did perform a few roles whenever we put on theatricals.'

She blushed. 'Thank you, Tristan,' she said a bit more seriously. 'It is much appreciated, truly.'

'It is. By me, as much as the ladies, believe it or not.' A wave of nostalgia swept him as a smile passed between them full of warmth and togetherness. The feeling of belonging, of being connected to her, to Hemsford, was wondrous. This was new territory for a man who'd spent his first decade of adulthood roaming the world on the army's shilling. 'Of course I would do it, El. Do you remember when we thought it was a privilege, an honour, to have a part in the panto? Growing up, all of us wanted to be the lead in the panto and if not that, to be Joseph in the nativity tableau.'

She rewarded him with a laugh. 'You and Teddy were always shepherds. Although, there was one year after you left, that Teddy got to be Joseph and Elizabeth Cates was Mary.' She laughed.

'Teddy must have been in heaven. He was infatuated with Elizabeth Cates for years.' Tristan laughed with her and the memory felt good. It reinforced his decision that staying here, to be with her, was indeed the right choice, a choice he could happily live with. 'Were you ever Mary? I think every girl must dream of playing Mary.'

She shook her head. 'No, I was too much of a tomboy in those days. When my mother took ill, it didn't seem right, and then...' She shrugged. Then everything had fallen apart. He nodded, understanding. It had probably been easier for her to appreciate such things from behind the scenes. 'After that, there'd come a time when Teddy and I were too old for such things. Twenty-something girls don't play Mary.' She fabricated a smile but Tristan hadn't missed the sadness that smile was intended to hide before she took refuge behind a tease. 'In a couple of years you'll be eligible to play one of the three wise men.' The three wise men were roles usually reserved for the older men, the town businessmen like Clifford Atwater, or Richard Grisham.

'You mean "men of a certain age"?' Tristan teased back, but there was a certain new sense of peace in the realisation that he'd be here in a few years, that he would grow into middle age here. 'Are you suggesting I'm old?'

'You're getting there,' Elanora laughed and then squealed as the first raindrops fell, thin and cold on their faces. 'We'd better go back. It's going to be a deluge.'

They made it as far as the stable before the skies opened up. 'We'll be soaked before we reach the house!' Elanora laughed breathlessly, peering out from under the stable eaves.

'Let's stay here until it lets up,' Tristan suggested, taking her hand. 'I think my news is best shared here anyway. Shall we stroll?' This would be the perfect place to lay out his plans, his wants, his heart.

'There's nothing to see,' she protested as he led her down the dark, empty aisles that used to be filled with the Grisham string. He could feel her anxiety over his news despite his promise that it was good.

'Not yet.' Tristan grinned, his eyes crinkling. 'But maybe soon. El, the army has written. My position as a procurer of horses has been approved.'

He could hear the excitement in his own voice, the happiness. He watched her features, looking for signs that she was happy, too, but her response was restrained.

She slipped her arm out of his. 'Tristan, I am so pleased for you. When will you leave?' If her happiness was less than his, he understood why. She was thinking he'd leave her when their two weeks were up. If so, that was his fault. In his excitement, he was not laying this out clearly.

Tristan reached for her hand, his thumb drawing circles on the back of it, his eyes watching her. 'They've left it to me to decide when I report. I can decide if that's immediately after Christmas or at the end of January if I prefer, but I was thinking, El, that perhaps London might come to me instead of me going to it.'

She shook her head. 'I don't understand.'

He raised her hand and kissed her knuckles. 'It's my job to find horses and train them. Right now I am slated to train them at Horseguards because there's a facility for that. There's the parade grounds and stalls. But what if I had another facility? What if we brought the horses here and trained them before they went to London to take up their duties? You have plenty of stalls, and paddocks, and space here at Heartsease. This place was meant to be a horse farm and I need one, one that is preferably empty. I know I'd still have to travel occasionally to collect horses but I'd be here for the months of training. We can make a life here, together, the best of both of our worlds.' He paused, confused. Why wasn't she saying anything? Why wasn't she celebrating? This silence was not the response he'd been anticipating. This solution should have allayed all of her concerns. Why hadn't it? It was perfect. Was that the problem? Perfection? Perhaps she was overwhelmed. For a woman who'd lost everything maybe it was too much to believe she could have happiness again, love again. He would spend his life making up to her all that she'd lost.

He squeezed her hand. 'Just say you'll think on it,

El. We don't have to decide anything today.' He nodded towards the hayloft as hard rain pelted the roof in a dull thud. 'But perhaps I can sweeten the deal in the hayloft?'

That won him a cryptic smile. 'Perhaps you can.' And perhaps a bout of lovemaking was exactly what was needed to help her see the potential of what he offered.

Chapter Seventeen

What Tristan wanted was impossible. She couldn't give him what wouldn't be hers to give, and her heart broke as they climbed the ladder to the hayloft. She didn't have Heartsease to offer him. His perfect plan hinged on that. Atwater's eviction echoed in her mind. The thought sprang afresh that she needed to let Tristan go sooner rather than later. This latest plan of his proved it. While she'd spent their time apart thinking of endings, he'd spent it thinking of beginnings. She couldn't let him do that any more than she should have allowed herself to believe that things could somehow be different for her, that the pattern of her life—finding something, someone, to care about only to lose them—could be changed.

She reached the top rung and breathed in the warm, sweet scent of hay, letting it steady her as she made her decision. She should do it now, today. She should not let him leave here thinking they were going to build a life together. It wouldn't be fair to let him think the impossible, to care for her more than he ought.

Tristan stood in the middle of the loft and turned to her, eyes dark with a desire that tore at her resolve. 'What do you think of our bower for the afternoon, El? Will it do?'

They were closer to the rain up here, its hard thud on the roof a loud and insistent drum. She went to him, allowing herself the comfort of his arms one last time. The loft would do fine for one last fantasy and then farewell.

She reached up and kissed him softly on the mouth, the words *I love you, Tristan* whispering in the safety of her mind where the only one they could hurt was she.

She undressed him slowly, deliberately, wanting to remember the feel of him, the scent of him mixed with the scents of nature: hay and horses, winter wind and rain. It was a process that was equal parts treasure and torture as she stored up her memories. Haylofts weren't made for complete nakedness, though, and she had to settle for an incomplete effort on that front. But there was something admittedly erotic about a man in partial dress, the fall of his breeches open in provocative invitation, the billows of his shirt untucked, making it easy to slide one's hands beneath the loose fabric and run them up the warm ridges of his torso.

'You're a wicked tease, El,' Tristan growled against her neck as they lay in the hay.

'Me?' She gave a husky laugh. 'It is you who is tantalising me, with your breeches open, promising but not delivering.' She tugged at him, drawing him over her. If she had him inside her, passion could obliterate the pain of losing him, assuage her guilt, and, oh, there was so much guilt. She couldn't escape it: the guilt of pushing him away knowing it would hurt him, the guilt of not having pushed him away already, of letting their hearts get too far ahead of them. Any way she turned, there was guilt, because she'd not told him the truth; because in her heart, in her own way, she'd been unfaithful to him.

'Greedy minx,' Tristan laughed down at her, letting her tug him into service. She gave a luxurious sigh as his warm hands ran up her legs, pushing back skirts until she felt the erotic sensation of air on bare thighs.

She looped an arm about his neck, reaching up for a kiss. 'There's something undeniably wild about making love with clothes on.'

'Maybe it's you.' Tristan moved against her, the indication of his hardness, his desire, evident through the fabric of his breeches. 'You drive me wild. Clothed or unclothed, awake or asleep. I cannot imagine a scenario where you do not drive me wild.'

She pushed at his breeches, shifting them down over his hips. 'Then you'd best get busy reciprocating.' She licked her lips and stared up at him. 'Drive me wild, Tristan.' In that moment she wanted to be as wild as the horses below, as wet as the rain above.

Tristan did his best. He came into her hard, taking swift possession of all she offered. She revelled in the roughness that followed, the sharp nip of his teeth at her neck, the ragged kisses that left her breathless, the vigorous thrusts of his phallus that had her hips rising to meet him and her back arching. And it was almost enough. Almost enough to obliterate for a time the things that must come next. Almost enough to make her forget that she was losing him, losing her home. Almost. But try as she might, it was not quite enough.

She felt Tristan's body tense in his telltale gathering before climax, and desperation swamped her. She wasn't going to make it, wasn't going to be there with him when he came. In the crucial moment she closed her eyes and let him go. Alone. Almost, but not quite. The story of her life. Like all the other fronts she'd put up over the years since her parents' deaths, she put up one last, brief pretence, that she was indeed there with him, that they had reached love's pinnacle together. This was one more thing she could pretend for the sake of another so that they could lie in the hay in peace, with the rain overhead, and think for a little while longer that everything was all right.

'El, is everything all right?' Tristan whispered the question in the quiet aftermath of passion. She'd made love with her body but not her mind, something Tristan had become acutely aware of too late, much to his chagrin. He was not generally a selfish lover.

He pressed a kiss to her hair and tucked her close against him, his own body satisfied but not entirely, because the woman he loved had not been with him completely in the moment. Although she'd done a fairly good impression of it from the pleasure purling up the column of her throat in exquisite moans, to the fierce lock of her legs wrapped tight about his hips—almost too tight—it had been difficult to disengage in time. He almost hadn't. But he'd not solve whatever demons plagued her in that way by taking the choice from her if there should be consequences.

She'd been with him, at least he'd thought so, right up until she'd closed her eyes. That had been when he'd lost her. El never closed her eyes, never hid her own pleasure from him, but today she had and now she was refusing to answer his question. *Was* everything all right?

'El, are you upset about the horses? Should I not have mentioned it?' It was all he could think of that would have caused her to withdraw. They'd promised themselves two weeks with no talk of money and the future. Perhaps the horses had crossed one of those lines. He'd just been so damned excited. He should have handled her better. He sighed and breathed in the soft rose-scented rinse of her. Even in winter, she smelled like her beloved flowers, the promise of spring. 'I thought you'd be excited about the horses, about the prospect of bringing them here.' He meant for it to be an apology but it sounded wrong.

Her fingers drew circles on his chest through his shirt and he wished they were naked, lying skin to skin in her bed upstairs at the house. Nakedness was not for haylofts. She looked up at him, her eyes sharp, too sharp for having just made love in the hay during a downpour. Her gaze was further proof that while her body had been enjoying the activity, her mind had been busy elsewhere.

'I think it's too big of an undertaking. There's no staff. Old Mackey can't possibly look after so many horses on his own. The amount of hay and oats would be staggering and that takes men to unload and store. Then there's the issue of tack. There's the issue of exercising them, too.'

Practicalities? Something rang false. Was that all she was worried about? That seemed a bit short-sighted. She wasn't thinking straight. 'Grooms can be hired. I don't expect the three of us to do it all alone. Everything else is already here—the turn-out paddocks, the arena.' He shifted to roll to his side even though it meant dislodging her. Perhaps he should take it as a good sign she was at least thinking about the horses. He propped himself up on one arm. 'Don't tell me you haven't thought about seeing the stable restored to its full glory once your current situation improves.' That earned him a soft smile although it didn't come without a hint of sadness.

'You really are an optimist, aren't you, Tristan?' She reached a hand up to pluck straw from his hair, resignation in her eyes. 'My current situation will not improve. I can't possibly think of supporting horses here or hiring help. Not today, not tomorrow, not three months from now.'

'I know it doesn't seem that way at the moment, but losing one cargo is not insurmountable, and it won't be your money spent on the hiring. It will be the army's. You needn't worry,' Tristan consoled.

It was as he and Julien suspected, then, that the cargo had perhaps not been insured and that made the loss all the more dear. But surely, it was not as crippling as she made it out to be. And surely, his father's purchase of the Grisham string had provided a tidy sum to off-set those losses.

And yet, she was still economising.

'That would be true if it was just one cargo, Tristan.' Her eyes held his solemnly, intent with warning as if they were preparing him for something he didn't want to hear and he braced. A curtain came down behind her eyes, something in her seemed to harden and she looked more like the woman he'd met in the street that first day in Hemsford, less like the woman who'd warmed to him and let him into her heart. Where was her heart now? It was not in her eyes where she usually wore it for him these days. 'Tristan, I have not been honest with you. Nor have I been faithful to you and the trust between us.'

The very core of his being froze. When he'd come up to the hayloft he'd had every intention of telling her he loved her, of proposing marriage as a way to begin their life together, to show her the two items in his coat pocket acquired for them on his trip with Julien. But this didn't feel like a beginning; it felt like an end. She was talking about infidelity, about breaking trust, the last two things he'd ever have thought possible from her.

'Listen to me, Tristan. I have not told you the truth about Heartsease. It's not just one cargo that plagues me. It's thirty years of more losses than gains. This cargo was just the latest.' She rose from the hay and held out her hand. 'Come with me. You once asked for a look at the ledgers. Now you can have one. I think it is the only way you will believe me when I say that all is lost, including us.'

Foreboding gripped him. He did not want to take her

hand. He did not want to leave this hayloft. Something deep in his gut said that if he left this quiet, warm place, nothing would ever be the same because El did indeed intend to leave him.

One should be careful what one wished for, Tristan thought a while later. He had wished to see the Grisham ledgers but not at the expense of losing El. He sat behind what had once been Richard Grisham's desk, the official seat of power at Heartsease, its surface covered in open ledgers and the truth El had obscured from him and Hemsford: the Grishams were broke. Not just broke, but also in debt. Heavy debt.

The debt had existed before Teddy's failed cargo, before his father's failed investments. The failures went back to 1815 and a large purchase of shares in an ammunitions factory that had come too late in the war to turn much profit. From what he could see, that was the beginning. Tristan ran his finger down the columns, watching a pattern emerge. Always, though, there was something that bailed them out: an investment that finally went right, or a few not so insignificant inheritances from relatives who had passed. Most recently the bailout had come from Elanora's dowry. The Grishams had lived lucky for a long time or else they would have felt the pinch much sooner than now.

Tristan's finger stopped at the large deposit made in May of this year to her from his father. 'Where did the money go from selling the Grisham string?' He'd expected it to have gone into the cargo debt but now he wasn't so sure. If she had used it against the debt, that debt would have been resolved.

To her credit, Elanora had sat patiently in a chair by the fire, reading, or pretending to read. He didn't think he'd actually heard or seen a page move as she'd allowed him time to study the ledgers on his own. He appreciated that she'd not tried to tell him what to notice but instead let him come to his own conclusions and ask his own questions. She looked up now at his question and set aside the book, meeting his gaze firmly. 'I used it to pay off the staff.'

Tristan hid his frustration behind a sigh. Of course she had. It made sense—though not in the financial way, as Julien would be quick to point out. Tristan could almost hear his brother choking at the words. But it made sense in the Elanora Grisham way. If one understood Elanora, and he *did* understand her, the decision made perfect sense. 'Once I realised I didn't need so many gardeners, grooms and maids for just one person, I let them go,' she explained. 'I couldn't afford to keep them for long at any rate.' But she wouldn't have just turned them out, although many other employers would have, seeking their own self-preservation rather than considering what lost jobs would mean to their workers, Tristan thought as he patiently let her continue.

'Many were older and close to retirement, so I paid their pensions,' Elanora said. 'Those who wanted or needed to keep working, I paid a severance to, enough to see them through until they had a position they liked, and gave them letters of reference. Some I was able to help place in homes.' Like her strays. Tristan couldn't help but smile at the image her words conjured up, and his heart filled to bursting with love for this woman who could have saved herself with that money but had chosen to save multiple others instead.

'There wasn't already a pension fund?' Tristan flipped back through the pages.

'Not by that point.' The tone of her voice drew his gaze back to her and he waited for the revelation. 'Grandfather Edgar had used it decades ago for improvements to the estate, thinking that he'd replenish it over time with dividends from an East India venture. But the dividends never seemed to find their way back into the pension fund. There is a little left for pensions, but it's meant for Mrs Thornton, Old Mackey, and Cook when the time comes.'

Tristan chuckled. 'I don't think any of them are going anywhere soon. Old Mackey insists he'll have to be carried out in a coffin. Have you thought of investing those funds and letting them grow over time until they are needed? Even if they could be invested for five years, you'd make a little, enough to hire more staff when they do retire. Julien could help you,' Tristan offered.

Her blue eyes hardened and he felt he'd misstepped again. This afternoon had been full of missteps. 'Isn't that what got my grandfather into trouble in the first place?' she snapped.

'Your grandfather didn't have Julien advising him. My brother's a wizard with the Exchange. The money would be safe enough,' Tristan assured her. He stretched and sat back from the desk. He wanted Julien to take a closer look at the ledgers. At least he had answers now as to where the money had gone, what had happened to the staff, and why the estate had looked as it did when he'd arrived. But he didn't have all the answers. The ledgers didn't explain why she didn't feel she'd crawl out of this hole.

'So, El, how much do you owe on the cargo? You might as well tell me or I will figure it out myself. It would be quicker, though, if you told me.'

'Two thousand pounds.' There was a touch of defiance to her tone as she threw out the numbers. The voice in his head warned himself to be careful. This was a touchy subject with her. She didn't have two thousand pounds. She had only the rents from the tenant farms, which was enough to run the estate on a bare-bones budget, but not enough to pay off debts or to build up any substantial savings quickly. Or, his mind thought rapidly, to afford the largesse of a usual Grisham Christmas. And yet, she had, and she had shouldered the expense of hosting the Christmas pantomime, even though he'd watched her think carefully about the coins she'd placed in the collection plate at church, and how she'd not bought anything at the Christmas market, not even a length of ribbon. Yet, he'd bet his last coin there would be lavish food baskets going out to the tenants and those in need on Christmas Eve as per usual, and that there'd be the Boxing Day bonus for the staff that remained.

He fixed her with a stern stare that said he'd brook no refusal as he asked quietly, 'El, tell me. How are you paying for Christmas?'

The question was the straw that broke the camel's back—perhaps an apt metaphor, given the season. Her blue eyes filled with tears she was trying not to shed. 'I used the money meant for Teddy's gravestone.' She managed the words before she was overcome with sobs.

Her sobs nearly undid him. What an idiot he'd been for pushing too hard! He'd not meant to make her cry, only to help. He was around the desk and beside her in an instant, an irrational anger rising in him: anger at the ledgers, inanimate though they were, anger at Teddy, at her father, at her grandfather, whom he'd never even met, anger at all of them for leaving her to bear this burden alone. He was angry at his father, too, for not having done more, for not having tried harder to intervene when trouble had been evident. Most of all he was angry at himself. He should have come home when he'd had the chance. This was yet something else he could have prevented. If he'd come home, Teddy might still be alive. Teddy would have shown him the ledgers, and together, they would have solved the financial problems, perhaps even restored her dowry and seen her married.

But not to you. Do you really want that? All that has happened has allowed you to find love, to find El. How could you wish to undo that?

And yet, in these moments of seeing her despair, Tristan would have done anything to make her world right again.

Chapter Eighteen

Tristan held her close, aware of her head against his chest. 'Oh, my dear girl, you've been brave for so long. You've helped so many when you might have made it easy on yourself instead.' Would that he could take her pain and her loss as easily as his shirt took her tears. This was love's jagged edge, he thought, the pain that tore at you when the one you loved suffered. 'You've carried so much on your own. But I am here now,' he murmured against her hair. Perhaps if he could just show her this didn't need to be the end. That there could be a phoenix from these ashes. 'We can sort it all out together. I'll pay the debts, wipe the slate clean and we can start afresh. You will be free from worry.'

She lifted her head from his chest. Tristan looked down at her, expecting to see a smile of relief, a smile of love and perhaps appreciation that they were in this together. It took a moment to readjust his thoughts. Reddened blue eyes looked at him in horror, perhaps even a hint of anger as she moved away from his arms. 'You most certainly will *not* pay those debts.'

Perhaps it was because he was shocked by her response, or perhaps it was because he was supremely disappointed by her response, he said the first thing that came to mind. 'Whyever not? It's very clear you cannot pay them.'

Blue eyes blazed. 'Because *I* am not the Thomsfords. You can't simply throw money at me and expect that to fix everything.'

'But, El…' He softened his tone, not wanting this discussion to turn into a row. 'It *would* fix everything. That's the part I don't understand.' He didn't understand any of this. One moment she was sobbing in his arms and the next she'd become a virago with more pride than was good for her. 'El, I came out here today to tell you I loved you, to ask you to marry me so that we could run the horses here for the army and add income to the estate through that. I came to show you I could provide for you and that we could make a good life here.' He'd used those words to little effect in the stable earlier. Perhaps they'd mean more to her now since she knew he wasn't going to run at the sign of debt.

He was making it too hard and fracturing her heart in the process. The ledgers had not done the dirty work for her, although she supposed that had always been something of a gamble. She was going to have to say the hard things herself. From where he stood, he couldn't see the one remaining obstacle, the thing she had to protect him from, and she was running out of reasons to put him off without it. But she refused to tell him about the mortgage, that Heartsease would no longer be hers on Christmas Eve. Every honourable bone in his body would want to leap to her rescue even at the expense of his own financial ruin. His reaction to this small debt proved it. He'd not flinched, had not run like she'd hoped. She'd wanted the debt to scare him off, to make him see reason, but it had not, and it wasn't even the largest debt she had.

She could not possibly tell him now. The two thousand shown in the ledgers was just what she owed locally. It didn't account for the mortgage. He'd want to pay that, too, although she doubted he could afford it, not without trading her debt for his. A woman's finances, for better or worse, became her husband's upon marriage. The way he'd so quickly offered to pay her debts affirmed she'd made the right choice to hold back on this. He would willingly let himself be dragged down with her. She would not plunge him into debt, too. Heartsease was a losing proposition at present.

She tried an appeal to his honour. 'You promised me if I gave you two weeks you wouldn't bring up money.' She adopted the most defensive tone she owned.

'I didn't. You did. I never agreed to not discuss it, just not to start the discussion.' He hitched a hip on the corner of the desk and folded his arms. 'Stop being stubborn, El. Let me pay the bills for you so that you can start to grow this place again, and you can start to *live* again.'

'I could never pay you back. I would always be in *your* debt,' she argued. 'It would come between us eventually. Money always comes between people when there's an imbalance.'

Tristan seemed to think about that for a moment, his hand at his chin. 'Not if we married. Then, everything is ours. There is no scorekeeping. Besides, you'd bring Heartsease to the marriage. That is no small consideration if you insist on scorekeeping. Perhaps I am the poor catch, bringing no property of my own,' he tried to tease but she didn't laugh. 'Still, El, it's a good match— my money, your property.'

'My debt,' she reminded him without mentioning that she'd not have property to bring. 'You'd pay the debts and people would say I sold myself for the money.' She drew herself up. She knew what she had to do, to protect him and to protect what might be left of her heart. The moment had come when she had to cut her happiness free, had to cut him free. She wouldn't survive until Christmas Eve if she didn't. 'I don't think this is going to work, Tristan. Money is already getting in the way. We can see it already. I think it might be best if we end things here since we are at an impasse and that will not change in a few days.' They were without a doubt the hardest words she'd ever spoken. She was throwing away happiness with both hands, but happiness was just another illusion, wasn't it?

She would remember forever the stricken look on Tristan's face, but over the years Tristan had become a soldier through and through. Stricken or not, wounded or not, he was not prepared to surrender. She'd misjudged that. 'This is not over, El. Take some time. You're upset.' He moved towards her, wanting to offer comfort, but she stepped back.

'It *is* over, Tristan.' Saying the words made it too

real. She needed him to leave before she broke down, before he saw through the facade of her strength. *Over* meant so much. *Over* meant more loss. No more Sunday lunch in bed, no more haylofts in the rain, no more racing rides across frosty meadows, no more sitting beside him in church as if she belonged somewhere again, no more days waking up and feeling alive instead of defeated. 'It was always going to be over, sooner or later. I am just choosing for it to be over sooner, that's all.'

Tristan's dark eyes registered his disagreement. Why did he have to persist in making this hard on them both? 'I do not believe it, El. This is not what you want. This is not a choice you have to make.' His voice was a growl. 'You cannot deny it. You are happy with me. I make you happy, and you make me happy.'

'I've lied to you. I've been financially unfaithful to you. You should not love me.' She shook her head. 'Happiness is fleeting. Happiness will not last. It cannot last, not in this world. Something will come along that destroys it. I would rather remember this idyll the way it is and not for what wrecks it. Please, Tristan. I would like you to go.'

'Because you ask it, I *will* go, but it does *not* suit me. It is not my choice. If you call for me, El, I will come. I will leave but I still stand at the ready for you. You can banish me, but you cannot banish our friendship.' He held her gaze for the longest of seconds, perhaps hoping she'd relent. She almost did. Everything in her was breaking. She'd hoped the ledgers would do the work for her, convince him that he had to step away from her, but they'd done what she'd feared most—they'd encouraged him to step *towards* her, towards trouble, towards burdens he would shoulder but come to hate her for later when he realised those ledgers were just the tip of the proverbial iceberg.

She found enough strength in her waning reserves to wait in stoic, unmoving silence until he left the room and the sound of his boots faded from the house. For good this time. He wouldn't be back, the pantomime evening being the exception. But that wouldn't count. The house would be crowded with people and she would be too busy behind the scenes making sure the show went off well, that everyone had enough to eat and drink, to run into Tristan. Besides, while she would be behind the scenes, he would be out in front of them, a literal and figurative Prince Charming.

And Susannah Manning would be thrilled to note that he was unattached.

That last galled. Susannah had made her interest in Tristan quite obvious the day they'd stopped in for gingerbread men.

Well, at least she wouldn't be around to watch that flirtation in progress. She'd be out at the cottage trying to make it habitable, trying to figure out how to move on from here. She wouldn't be in town much. That was another reason she knew Tristan wouldn't be back here, not for her. In a week, she wouldn't be here. Heartsease would default to the bank and from there go to auction.

It was time to face it, time to prepare. She should begin to discreetly pack up things, move the things she needed to the cottage, start sweeping it out, run the numbers one more time. The bank would get the house but she had the contents. Most would go to auction and those funds would go to pay the debts outside the mortgage. She would make her start on the remainder, slim as it would likely be.

Don't worry, you have ideas. You'll grow flowers to sell at markets, and how much money can it really take to keep you and Marian? Not that much. You can grow vegetables and you know how to make economies.

The encouragement she usually found in those words was absent in the wake of Tristan's words. She didn't have to choose the cottage with its leaky roof and a life that was best described as ignominious. She could choose Tristan. But he was only choosing her because she'd not told him everything. And she could not tell him everything because she would not set him up for failure. A real friend would set him free and that was what she'd done, at great cost to herself. She'd not wanted to let him go. She'd *needed* to. And so, like her dowry, like this house, like the Grisham string, she'd let him go.

Elanora put a brave face on when she rode into town the next morning for a church meeting to discuss the tableau that would be part of the Christmas concert on Angel Sunday. She'd rather have stayed home, hiding beneath the covers of her lonely bed, but it had occurred to her that she had to keep a facade in place, of enjoying the Christmas festivities. Otherwise, people would suspect something had happened. Otherwise, Tristan would put in an appearance and demand she explain herself. She was out of explanations. Even the ones she'd offered him that last day at Heartsease were flimsy at best. If he stopped to think about them too long, he'd know she'd left something out and he would not give up until he had her last secret. She just had to stay strong a little longer.

The end, sad as it was, was almost here and there was an odd sense of relief in that. There was certainly busyness in it. Now that eviction was only three days away, there was much to be done, especially given that she was fighting a two-fronted battle. On one front, the facade of providing a wondrous Grisham Christmas, and on the other, the gloom of closing down the house and moving to the cottage. All this must be done while keeping the vultures away, primarily Elias and his uncle.

Elias Bathurst had managed to corner her today after a ladies' meeting long enough to make an awkward suggestion of resuming their nonexistent courtship. He'd gone so far as to explicitly state marriage would keep her from being homeless. But she'd reminded him just who was doing whom a favour. What a coup it would be for a Bathurst to marry a Grisham. He'd all but spat in her face after that, his parting rejoinder cruel if honest. 'I'll just buy the house at auction. You can't stop me entirely.' No, she thought. But he can't buy *me*. That was something, at least. He might take the house but he would not take her family name and make it his own by connection.

In these final days, she would not let the Atwaters and Bathursts see her beaten. She was going to give Heartsease a final Christmas send-off and for that and more she'd need an ally who could no longer be Tristan, especially now. If he knew the depths of her troubles and that Elias Bathurst was involved, he would not rest and it would cost him dearly, a price she did not want to see him pay. Friends did not ask friends to beggar themselves.

She gave Marian to Old Mackey and strode into the house, calling for Mrs Thornton. She would tell the housekeeper the bad news first. It was time, particularly now that she could not wait until *after* Christmas Eve. Atwater's eviction just meant that Christmas would come a little earlier. There were still baskets to deliver, gifts to give, a pantomime to put on, and most of all, there was celebrating to be done. They would go out in a blaze of glory, starting with the Yule log.

Mrs Thornton sat in the housekeeper's chair and dabbed at her eyes with a handkerchief from her apron pocket. 'What are we to do, miss? Have you asked Captain Lennox for help? Perhaps he could offer assistance?' she asked hopefully. The news had taken her hard even with Elanora's assurances that she'd have a good reference and be financially taken care of.

Elanora gave an emphatic shake of her head. 'No, this is not something Captain Lennox knows about. I have not discussed the mortgage with him.'

Mrs Thornton brightened. 'Perhaps if you did…if he understood…'

'No, I will not have him dragged into this mess, not when it would mean dragging him down, too. He hasn't the funds. He's an army captain and one who has mustered out at that.'

'But I thought the two of you…' Mrs Thornton persisted and Elanora had to give her credit for tenacity. Few would dare to gainsay their employer.

'You thought wrong,' Elanora said firmly. 'My situation is not his concern.'

Mrs Thornton straightened at the stern reprimand and resumed her usual professionalism. 'What are we to do, then, miss?'

Elanora gave her a broad smile. 'We are going to celebrate. Tomorrow we are going to decorate. Invite the farmers and their families. We will go greening and come back with boughs for the mantels and banister, and holly sprigs for vases, perhaps even some mistletoe. I have more cyclamen in the garden. We can get the boxes of red bows down from the attic and we'll put up every decoration we have. Mother's nativity—we'll put it out where everyone can see it when they come for the panto in the drawing room, and we'll use the good china for the food.' Even as she said the words, visions leapt to life in her mind—lovely visions, happy visions. 'Do we have enough money left for candles, Mrs Thornton? I want candles, lots of them.'

Mrs Thornton smiled. 'Yes, my dear, I think we have just enough. I'll have Cook add it to her list when she goes to town tomorrow. I'll tell Old Mackey to send word to the farmers that this afternoon and tomorrow are an unofficial holiday of sorts.'

Elanora smiled, unable to contain the happiness that bubbled up within her. 'I'll get my cloak and some baskets ready. We'll have to hurry…there's only a few hours of daylight left this afternoon.' They would be up late tonight, too. There were deliveries to prepare and a party to plan. There was much to do and very little time. She stepped into the foyer and took an experimental twirl in the entry, looking up at the banister and the chandelier that hung in front of an enormous thirty-two-paned window above the front doors of Heartsease, imagining it already lit and waiting for guests, and she was happy. It was almost Christmas! She let the joy of that fill her heart even though it let in an errant, contrary thought.

If only Tristan was here to see it, then you'd be truly happy. This was what he'd wanted for you: to enjoy Christmas.

And he would be here to see it. He'd come to the panto, he'd see the house lit up and decorated and full of life the way he remembered it one last time. In its way it would be her gift to him, an apology for what could not be and a thank-you for all that had been, for all he'd given her, and that would have to be happiness enough because she loved him. She just couldn't have him.

It was the solstice today, the longest night of the year. Elanora had nearly forgotten. It came to her randomly as she cut greenery alongside the Heartsease tenants. She would need every minute of that night if she was going to have everything ready for tomorrow and beyond. Her ancient Celtic ancestors would stay up all night on the solstice to protect themselves against the darkness. She would stay up all night to prepare herself for Christmas. Elanora snipped sprigs of holly from a bush, careful not to cut herself on the holly's prickly edges.

The holly is the crown worn by Christ on the cross.

The old Sunday lesson came to mind, creeping soft and unexpected amid her thoughts as she set the sprigs in her basket. Other thoughts came, too, of other lessons, of Tristan with the children in her kitchen teaching the lessons of Stir-Up Sunday. How time had passed! They were the adults now, the keepers of tradition and the teachers of it. They'd grown up here, tracking time by the parts they could play in the nativity or the Christmas panto. How wondrous and yet how odd it had been to see Lissa Phelps as Mary in the tableau last night. It seemed she'd been a small girl just last year but she'd been a radiant, golden-haired Mary last night, standing next to Thomas Manning as if she were announcing to the community that she was ready to take her place among them. Based on the way Lissa and Thomas had looked at one another, Elanora did wonder if there might be a tableau of another sort that will take place in the next couple years, this one at an altar exchanging vows.

Childhood, marriage, children… This was how time was marked, events punctuated by tradition and love in Hemsford, Sussex, a village that was perhaps of no note to anyone but its occupants. For Elanora, all she'd ever wanted was to live her life as part of that, contributing to that. For a man like Tristan, a man who had travelled the world, would such things ever truly be enough?

Tristan. All her thoughts seemed to lead back to him against her wishes. She couldn't escape him. She'd acquired another ghost, it seemed. His presence marked her house; he was in her bedroom, the memory of him in her bed, in her kitchen, on her stairs. On her body. Perhaps that was the hardest part—she could close her eyes and with little effort summon the feel of his hands against her skin, his lips on her. She cut a strand of ivy.

Ivy needs to cling to grow. Her mother's voice was soft in her head. *We are the ivy, Ellie. We must cling to hope, to love, in order to grow, to live.*

Yes, Mother. I am trying.

Her basket was nearly full when the shadows began to fall, Mother Nature giving the signal it was time to return to the house. The little troop gathered at a flat-bed wagon someone had driven out so that evergreen boughs could be piled on it along with a Yule log the men had cut. A lantern hung from a pole on the wagon, lighting their way. It was a happy, content party that made their way in the falling dusk back to Heartsease; mothers walked beside the wagon holding children's hands; husbands put arms about wives' shoulders.

Wanting and missing rippled through Elanora. If Tristan were here, it would be his arm about her, his body warm against hers. She would belong to this intimate little club of people in love. But she'd sent him away and her heart ached with regret. It probably would for a long time, maybe forever. A familiar tune started up ahead of her in the cold evening air, a clear, pure feminine voice.

'The holly and the ivy when they are both full grown, of all the trees that are in the wood the holly bears the crown.'

Others picked up the song, joining in as a round, the men singing one part and the women the other. This, too, was another, wondrous tradition long sustained, everyone raised to their part. There was something indescribably beautiful and comforting about a song sung in the falling dark, and in comfort there was power, the certainty that somehow all would be well. She would learn to live with the aloneness. Without Tristan, she was starting to realise she would always be alone whether she was at Heartsease or at the cottage. But she would cope with it, endure it, with the knowledge that he was free to have the life he wanted, the life he was meant for, and she would find comfort in that, just as she found comfort in the song. Elanora let that comfort fill her as they walked towards Heartsease, where Mrs Thornton would be waiting with warm drinks, and she felt a little less alone.

Chapter Nineteen

Tristan put on his uniform, his buttons carefully polished in preparation for the pantomime tonight. Tonight he'd play the soldier and the prince, but he felt like neither. He should not have left her alone. A good soldier never willingly ceded ground once he gained it and yet that was what he'd done. He was paying for that choice. These past few days without Elanora had been torment because he hadn't exactly been 'without her.' She was in his sphere of influence, at the same events he was at, and he would have to get used to this concept of being with her but not being *with* her. It was a small village; everyone knew everyone.

She'd not spared a look for him Sunday at church when she'd sat across the aisle, alone in the empty Grisham pew. She'd been conspicuously busy with other things when he'd come by the church to practice lines with Susannah Manning for the pantomime. There'd been no chance to speak with her, to get her alone.

She had *looked* happy, though, and he *did* take some

consolation in that. He tied a bright yellow sash about his waist. It wasn't an official part of his uniform, but Mrs Phelps, who was playing the stepmother tonight, had thought it added a bit of dash. He'd set out to restore Elanora's Christmas spirit and perhaps in that he'd been successful. Elanora Grisham with her giving heart, her love for others, her care for those less fortunate, was made for Christmas. He never wanted her to lose that, even if he had lost her.

There was a knock at his door and Julien poked his head in. 'Prince Charming, it's time to go,' he joked and then sobered. 'You're going to have to look happier than that, brother.'

Julien stepped inside and shut the door behind him. 'You've not said anything but I am surmising things have gone poorly with Elanora.' Tristan winced. One didn't need to be a genius to conclude that. The whole village had probably come to that conclusion on Sunday when she'd elected to sit alone and he'd done nothing about it. He'd honoured her wishes instead of crossing the aisle to invite her to join them, or if he was refused, to stubbornly put his backside down in the pew and sit beside her. That had been the second mistake. Leaving her at Heartsease the night she'd told him about the debt and refused his help had been his first.

'She's in trouble, Julien, the exact trouble we guessed she was in. She owes money. The family has been in debt for ages.' He could not lay the entire fault at Teddy's feet, only the most recent. 'She spent the money Father paid for the Grisham string in pensioning off the servants when she let them go this summer. She saved nothing for herself.'

Julien nodded, unsurprised. It was, after all, merely confirmation of his suspicions, and Julien was seldom wrong about money. 'How much?'

'Two thousand pounds. I do not know how she intends to pay it. She showed me the ledgers. The farms keep the estate running but extra is hard to come by. And yes, before you ask, I offered to pay the debt.' He'd done more than that. He'd laid out a beautiful life for them training horses, doing what they loved in a place they both loved, together. He'd laid out happiness for her and she'd said no.

'So there's something else afoot.' Julien spoke Tristan's own suppositions aloud.

'But what? She cares for me, Julien. That's not ego talking. I know she loves me as I love her.' He reached for his ceremonial sword and added it to his costume. 'That is the one thing I am sure of. Yet, she has turned me away. Doesn't she understand I would do anything for her?'

Julien looked out the window and thought for a long moment. 'Perhaps that's it, then. You *would* do anything for her. If she loves you the same, you must acknowledge that she would do *anything* for you as well. Even give you up if she thought it was in your best interests.'

'Are you suggesting she is protecting me?' For a man who'd never been in love, Julien had some fairly good insights on the subject. 'What is there to protect me from?' He was a soldier; the thought of protection sat poorly with him. *He* protected others. Others need not protect him. More than that was what that protection required—a sacrifice. Elanora had made enough of those. He was not going to be another sacrifice on her list.

'That is for you to find out. I can't help you there.' Julien turned from the window. 'Joe has brought the horses round. We must go down.' He smiled. 'You make a fine Prince Charming. All the ladies will be a-swoon tonight.'

Tristan offered a wry smile. There was only one lady he wanted swooning tonight and that was Elanora. Perhaps, though, there was something to be learned from Prince Charming. He'd not given up when it came to finding the woman he loved. He'd bent his resources to turning his kingdom upside down until he'd found her. Cinderella had run from the prince after refusing to share her situation with him even though her esteem for him was evident, not unlike Elanora with her kind heart for animals and strays, her stubbornness in not taking help for herself while offering it abundantly to others.

'You're smiling, brother,' Julien teased as they made their way downstairs. 'You must be thinking of how you're going to win Elanora back.'

Tristan chuckled. 'I am. It seems I have a lot in common with the prince, after all.'

Turning onto the drive at Heartsease was like riding into a fairy tale. 'Sweet heavens, what magic has been wrought here?' Julien intoned low under his breath beside him. 'Is this your doing, brother? Look at these oaks.'

The oaks did look magnificent with lanterns hanging from their branches, the flames twinkling in the night like low-hung stars. 'I trimmed the branches, but I cannot take more credit than that,' Tristan laughed, looking about as neighbours and villagers flowed around him on foot, on horseback, or in wagons and gigs. There was merriment in the air as people called greetings to one another and children ran on ahead despite being dressed in their Sunday best for the occasion.

Ahead of him, Heartsease glowed like a glitter diamond at the end of the drive, and candles floated in the fountain as it bubbled, a quiet burble in the night. Julien leaned across his saddle. 'It's as if the whole place is a set piece for the pantomime. It's wondrous. We're all guests at the ball. Look, there's even grooms in livery.' Julien nodded to where Old Mackey and three young men Tristan didn't know stood at attention in blue-and-silver coats and dark breeches.

'Wherever did they come up with those?' Tristan asked.

'Mother said something about borrowing some spares from Baron Babcock. He'll be at the ball tomorrow so they're easy to return.' Julien laughed. 'You would know all the gossip if you hadn't spent the last couple days moping about.'

The two *grooms* came forward to take their horses, and Tristan took his time wandering outside, admiring the fountain, the lanterns in the trees, and the riveting sight of the Grisham chandelier illuminating the paned window over the doors. He'd only ever seen it lit up a handful of times. Lighting it was reserved for special occasions, usually ones that involved the whole community. Richard Grisham had soundly believed that beautiful things should be enjoyed by the community. The treat of his chandelier, of his house, was as much for the village of Hemsford as it was for him.

A lovely wish but perhaps a foolhardy one as well, one that had him spending too much and saving too little. Some would say he'd been reckless in his giving, given current circumstances. Tristan wondered if Richard would agree in hindsight or if he would say that it had all been worth it to see the pleasure on children's faces, to know that his money had supported local businesses with his patronage. Tristan listened to the conversations around him, the people oohing and ahhing, and most of all remembering and telling the story.

They light that chandelier every year...

It's got eighty candles on it. I counted it once when I was twelve and the old Mr Grisham hired me to clean it...

I remember the first Christmas I came to Heartsease. I was five...

He had memories, too, and they soared to the fore as he exchanged a look with Julien; memories of him and Teddy and occasionally Julien, filching endless amounts of shortbread biscuits from the buffet table on Pantomime Night and eating sweets until they were very nearly sick before the show even started. He remembered the first year he and Teddy had small parts in the panto, playing characters in *Jack and the Beanstalk*. He and Teddy had green caps with feathers in them and two lines apiece. He'd been thrilled.

'I wonder if they still have the shortbread biscuits.' Julien nudged him. 'Why don't we go in and see?'

Inside was like another stage. Heartsease had a unique layout on account of it being old, older even than the Grishams. Heartsease had been built in the days of great halls and that was what the front foyer was—a medieval hall with an enormous fireplace to the left with the entrance to what in the modern era acted as both the drawing room and the ballroom. In that fireplace tonight a Yule log crackled splendidly. To the right was the ancient oak staircase. 'Like old times,' Tristan breathed, his eye drawn to the swags of greenery on the oak banister caught up in red velvet ribbons with long tails. Below the stairs, on its own table set against the stair wall, was Anne Grisham's nativity, all thirty-one pieces of it, hand carved and brought from Italy with the fountain.

'I see shortbread,' Julien teased as they wound their way towards the long buffet table set against the far wall. There were people to greet and toasts to share as they found mugs of cider and filled their plates with honey-braised ham that was Heartsease's specialty, and sweets: little petit fours iced in Christmas colours, gingerbread men, the requisite shortbread, minced meat pies, and Christmas puddings. He recognised those, although it seemed odd she'd include the puddings instead of saving them for Christmas Day. There was laughter and exclamations distracting his thoughts as someone nearby discovered a charm in theirs.

'Did you know she was planning this?' Julien asked,

his mouth full of a gingerbread man's head, bitten off *first*, Tristan noted.

'No,' Tristan said absently, still staring at the puddings, a few thoughts coalescing in his mind. Perhaps Elanora had planned this. But when he'd thought of her hosting the annual pantomime he'd not thought of it on this grand of a scale. Of course, he recognised the biscuits and cakes as being heavily supplied by Manning's. Cook had done some but not all the baking. It wouldn't have been possible. This kind of baking had to be done days in advance and nothing of that sort had been underway the last time he'd been here. The planning committee would have come out this morning to decorate and put up the set in the drawing room, but the decorations in the great hall cum foyer were not the committee's work. She would try and pass all of this off as things others had done: the food, the decorating; but he knew better. This—the foyer with its evergreens and holly sprigs, the trees with their lanterns, the chandelier, the Yule log—was Elanora's work. How had she done it? How had she afforded it? Well, he knew that in part. This was Teddy's tombstone money and Teddy would find it well spent on this grand party.

He drifted into the drawing room, where chairs were set up and the red stage curtains the Grishams had used for years for the panto draped the stage. They were old but in good shape, spending most of the year in a carefully packed box in the attic. Despite a ten-year absence, Tristan noticed the stage looked as it had always looked, slightly raised from the ground so that everyone could see. The best thing about a pantomime was the audience participation. He'd always liked listening to the audience tease the characters and call out suggestions.

Elanora's touch was evident even in the drawing room. Garlands of holly and ivy festooned the walls, and the mantel over the fireplace contained pretty vases of cyclamen. Tristan looked for her, his eye always on the alert. He wanted to speak to her, to tell her she'd done well, to ask his questions because beneath the beauty of the night, something else lurked. He just hadn't put his finger on it and he was worried. Julien was not wrong. What was she protecting him from?

He did not find her before Susannah pulled him away from the party, tugging him behind the set in the drawing room where the other actors were gathering in preparation for the play to start. As always, Reverend Thompson was the master of ceremonies, calling everyone to their seats, and the room began to quiet in anticipation of the show.

The answer came to him halfway through. An audience member was giving parenting advice to Mrs Phelps as the wicked stepmother, and her response had the audience laughing uproariously. Everyone was part of this, playing their parts; even the audience had a role. Even the house had a role. For the night, a world had been created and when one turned down the drive, one was stepping into that world, crossing a boundary.

It struck Tristan that there was a play within a play. Elanora had created a fairy tale within a fairy tale for everyone to enjoy, to participate in. But plays were just that: fantasies. They weren't real. What people saw out front on stage was all glitter and illusion. Backstage was all chaos and honesty, the reminders that the set was just paint and wood, that up close, the costumes weren't nearly as elegant as they appeared from a distance in the audience. This was all just an elaborate facade for whatever it was Elanora was hiding. Someone gave him a push and fiercely whispered instruction from Mrs Thompson, who was quite credible as a stage manager. 'You're on, Captain. You have to tell the king you want to marry the girl that fits the glass slipper… her and no one else.'

He did his part, enjoying every moment of it, but his mind held on to one phrase: *her and no one else.*

There was a moment where he thought he'd spied her in the back of the audience. By the time the curtain came down and he'd taken his bows along with Susannah Manning, who had been truly a wonderful Cinderella in a blue ball gown and a borrowed tiara, he was desperate to find Elanora.

He found her in the kitchens. She was at the worktables, directing trays. He stood out of the way for a few long moments, watching her with the others, her hair tied back, an apron about the waist of her green dress, her cheeks flushed from the work of keeping the buffet table full. But he knew the moment she became aware of him. He saw her stiffen and look up, meeting his gaze. He gave her a smile and began the careful journey of winding his way through bustling committee members and Cook's makeshift crew for the evening to reach her.

'Hello, El.' He kept his voice low, his words for her

alone despite the crowd around them. She smelled of cinnamon and shortbread, like Christmas itself.

Only one thought went through his mind. *I cannot lose her.*

'What a splendid night you've put on. Your parents, Teddy, all of them, would be so proud.'

'Thank you,' she managed, her eyes glittering with tears when she looked at him and he could see how much his words had touched her.

'Will you come with me, El? Just for a few moments? I know you're busy, but we must talk.'

She nodded and took off her apron. 'Just for a moment, Tristan, truly. There is much to do.' He led her out into the hall past guests gathered for a second round of the buffet table, laughing and talking, to the table with the crèche. Children were looking on it with awe, taking in all the animals. But Tristan didn't mind. The children wouldn't bother them.

'I liked seeing your mother's nativity set,' Tristan began. 'I'm glad you put it out. It's the first time since she died, isn't it? Mrs Phelps may have mentioned that.'

'Yes…' Elanora fingered a lamb figurine. 'Father couldn't manage having it out. Emotionally, it was too much for him. After he died, Teddy and I put some of it out in the private family area as a way to remember her, and him.' She gave a smile. 'But I thought it should be out tonight, all of it, for everyone to enjoy. Father felt it was important to share what one had.'

'I think your father would have loved tonight best of all, everyone together, laughing, having a good time.' Tristan ran his thumb over her knuckles, his gaze on her. 'You've put on quite a play within a play, creating this immersive fantasy for everyone. We've all come to the palace whether we're in the pantomime or not. When I turned down the drive, I was dazzled, El.' He smiled at her and then sobered. 'But then I wondered why would you do that? What is behind this marvellous effort to convince everyone, to convince *me*, that all is well at Heartsease when I know it is not?'

'Teddy would have wanted me to give everyone a good Christmas. Christmas was as important to him as it was to all of us.' It was a true answer. He could not argue with that. But was it the reason she'd done this? 'You were splendid as the prince tonight, Tristan. Thank you. Now, I must get back to the kitchen.'

'El, wait. How did you—'

She shook her head and he knew he'd gone a step too far. 'I do not want to talk about anything as sordid as money tonight, Tristan.'

'Please, El. I don't want to quarrel, either.' He could give her peace. He had time. He didn't need to be anywhere until January. He captured her hand and raised it to his lips. 'I've missed you, El. I've been miserable these days without you. All I want is to be with you.'

Another shake of her head. 'I don't know if that is possible, Tristan. We will just keep heading down the same road and it will keep ending in the same way.'

'Then let's not go down roads. Let's just worry about tomorrow. I want to dance with my real Cinderella tomorrow at the Lennox Christmas ball. Say you'll be there. Say you'll dance with me? We will not talk about money or the future.'

Something flickered in her eyes. 'Promise?'

'I promise.'

'Then I will come.' She smiled and hurried back to the kitchens. Tristan helped himself to more short-bread, too happy to wonder why it was that the usually stubborn Elanora had agreed so quickly and without argument, too happy to solve the puzzle of the pud-dings and why they were out early. All that mattered was that Elanora would dance with him tomorrow night and he would find a way to convince her that he could protect them both, that she need not live a life of sac-rifice anymore.

Chapter Twenty

She'd done all she could to protect those in need in her care from the harsher qualities of winter, Elanora thought as she returned home after a day of delivering Christmas baskets. The baskets had been welcomed, filled with items certain families would appreciate the most: blankets for some, mufflers and mittens for others, all baskets filled with leftover breads and biscuits and cuts of ham from the party last night.

Traditionally, she and Teddy delivered the baskets on Christmas or the day after, always under the aegis of thanking tenants for a good year or under the banner of friendship, never under the assumption of charity. But she didn't have that luxury this year. It had to be today, the day before Christmas Eve. Tomorrow would be her last day at Heartsease and there was much to be done in preparation of leaving…of moving on to the next phase of her life. She tried to think on it positively. Mindset was everything.

Already, Heartsease felt hollow when she stood in

the wide foyer, dim and quiet now that the chandelier was extinguished once more and the boisterous noise of guests was gone. In fact, the whole house reminded her of how it felt when a fair or market would leave the village. There was an emptiness where all the bright excitement and colour had been. She ran a hand over a few of the nativity figurines. After Christmas had been like that for Teddy. For a few weeks after they took down the greenery and tucked the velvet bows back into their boxes, he was despondent, quicker to anger and to his darker moods. He suffered in the winters, especially on days when he couldn't ride and be outdoors.

Teddy would have loved last night, though. Last night was everything Teddy adored about entertaining. She'd loved it, too. For one brief night, everything was perfect. It had lifted her spirits greatly to light the chandelier one last time, to have Heartsease filled to bursting with laughter, to treat her neighbours and tenants to something bright and full of hope, to give them something to lift their spirits in the dark of winter.

The panto itself had gone off well. No sets had fallen over, no actors had gotten ill at the last minute, or any of the usual quirks that beset a production. Susannah had been lovely as Cinderella, too lovely, in fact, just as Tristan had been altogether too charming. She'd not liked the way the dance scene between the two of them had looked: beautiful and real, a fantasy come to life with Susannah looking up at him with undisguised admiration in her eyes.

But it is you whom he sought out; you whom he will

be dancing with tonight at a real ball, not a make-believe party.

But tonight *was* make-believe in its own way. Elanora sighed. That was the only reason she'd agreed so easily to go. It could change nothing at this point, especially not with Mr Atwater's new edict that she had to vacate the premises of Heartsease. Tonight they would dance and be merry and that would be the end. Tomorrow or the next day, or the day after, Tristan would wash his hands of her when he called at Heartsease and found she was gone. He would not know where but he would figure it out soon enough. Hemsford wasn't so large that someone could disappear. And when he did, he would be furious. He would not understand.

Footsteps announced the approach of Mrs Thornton, who'd spent the day packing and labelling. 'The house already feels as if you've gone,' she said quietly. 'I left the boughs and ribbons up, though. I couldn't bear to lose all the festivity at once.'

'That's fine, Mrs Thornton. Thank you for your help.' Elanora suddenly felt tired. The house *did* feel a bit like an empty theatre, all its sets taken down. Much of the usual furniture had been stowed away in order to make room for the party last night, and there'd been no reason to put it back out. Tomorrow she'd take the first of her boxes to the cottage.

'Miss, you'd best hurry if you're going to be ready in time for the ball,' Mrs Thornton prompted when Elanora stood there, lost in her own thoughts, unable to find her way out of them, out of the reality of what was happening around her, to her. It had been foolish to think she was going to the Christmas ball when there was so much that needed doing, when it simply wasn't feasible.

'I think I will have to decline the ball, after all. I am tired, Mrs Thornton, and I'm not as ready as I should be for tomorrow. Perhaps Old Mackey could take a note over to Brentham Woods.' Yes, of course she should stay home. It was the right decision, the sensible decision. She'd been reckless and thoughtless last night. But that had not been a practical decision. Women about to be dispossessed of their homes did not dance the night away pretending the morning would not come.

Mrs Thornton gave a stern shake of her head. 'That will not do, miss. They are expecting you. The ball is the local formal highlight of the Christmas season. You cannot disappoint them by declining and you cannot disappoint us. How will we ever hear what happened if you don't go? The Grishams always go to the Lennox ball. And don't tell me you've nothing to wear because your dress arrived this afternoon while you were out.'

Elanora knitted her brow in confusion. Did Mrs Thornton truly think with finances being as tight as they were that she would spend money on a gown? 'I've not ordered anything. It must be a mistake. Even if I had something decent, I can't possibly get there. There's no carriage and I can't very well ride Marian over in a ball gown.'

Mrs Thornton looked very smug all of a sudden. 'Captain Lennox sent word that the Lennox coach would be arriving at half past seven.' She checked the little watch she wore pinned to her bodice. 'We have very little time.'

With that, Mrs Thornton marched her, actually *marched* her, upstairs to her room, where a white box secured with a red velvet ribbon waited on her bed.

Elanora's breath caught at the sight, so lovely, so utterly 'Christmas.' And just for her. A gift just for her. When was the last time someone had given her a gift like this, one that was wrapped? Last year she and Teddy had not exchanged gifts for Christmas by mutual agreement out of consideration for their finances, deciding instead to use those funds for baskets, and Teddy had been gone for her birthday. There'd been no family left to recall her day with a small token. Instead, she'd taken flowers to church to commemorate the day for all to enjoy.

Slowly, in order to savour the thrill of a gift, she undid the ribbon and folded it carefully for saving. The length of red velvet in itself was its own treasure. She might use it next year for decorating or for gifts. She lifted the lid to layers of tissue and a card on top. The words were simple.

This was meant for you. I am always your captain.
Tristan
PS Don't argue with me over it. Put the dress on
and come to the ball. We can argue then.

The last made her laugh even as the first brought tears to her eyes. Decent women didn't accept dresses from gentlemen when even a pair of gloves were scandalous.

'The captain is a *thoughtful* man,' Mrs Thornton said firmly as if she could read her mind and thought she might balk. 'It's been some time since you've had anything new.'

But this wasn't merely something new. This was exquisite. Elanora drew back the tissue to reveal the red dress that had until earlier that week been displayed in the dressmaker's window; the red velvet that had drawn everyone's attentions and even more speculations when it was gone. 'It's lovely, but how can I ever wear it?' What had Mrs Phelps said? Whoever wore it would be the belle of the ball; no one would be able to take their eyes off her.

'No one need know the captain sent it, miss.' Mrs Thornton was already bustling about, laying out undergarments and petticoats. 'You should wear your mother's pearls and I know you have one good pair of long white gloves in one of these drawers,' she fussed.

'You should have heard all the ladies talk about who might have bought the dress. Everyone will be looking at me.'

'Maybe it's time they did. Maybe it's time you didn't hide away.' Mrs Thornton's suggestion did double duty as a scold. 'May I?' She took the dress from the box and shook it out. 'It's lovely. Let's get you into it.'

They'd just finished putting up her hair when they heard the jingle of harnesses in the drive, signalling the arrival of the Lennox coach. There was no going back, only forward to the ball, to seeing Tristan one last time as her friend. Elanora took a final look at herself in the mirror, nervously fingering her mother's pearls at her neck. Tonight she was a real Cinderella and in the morning there would be real Cinderella consequences.

* * *

Tristan was waiting for her when she stepped out of the coach at Brentham Woods, the house ablaze with lights, carriages lining the drive, and music drifting out into the night. Brentham Woods was a much more formal house than Heartsease both in architecture and appearance as much as it was in its temperament. It was decorated with precision, not an item out of place, and it was run on precision. Of course, the Lennoxes could afford it.

'You look like Christmas itself,' he whispered as he handed her out of the carriage. 'I knew you would.'

'You should not have done it,' she whispered back. He should not have bought it for her any more than she should have worn it. It would be a scandal if anyone knew. 'It is too much.' She'd thought all the way over how much the dress had cost him. He shouldn't be spending his pay foolishly.

'But do you like it?' he persisted with a grin. He looked elegant tonight in black eveningwear, a diamond stick pin in his cravat, his dark hair combed back revealing the handsome planes of his face, a true prince charming in every way. Was he counting on being irresistible?

'You know I do,' she admitted with an answering smile. 'It's so thoughtful and yet so wildly inappropriate. People cannot know you bought it for me. They will think…' She couldn't finish that sentence. They would think there was an understanding between them.

Perhaps it's not too late for there to be one? her heart whispered but she pushed the thought away.

She'd not come here to torture herself with what-ifs and what-might-bes or might-have-beens. She'd come to have one last night.

'I know what they'd think.' Tristan tucked her arm through his. 'Julien is leading out the first dance with Baron Babcock's daughter and I'll join him with you. Because it's Christmas, Mother has decided it will be a waltz.'

'Everyone will be watching,' she murmured anxiously. This would absolutely set tongues to wagging.

Tristan gave her one of his smiles. 'They'll be watching us already. Why not give them a good look? Why not enjoy it?'

Why not indeed. The next two hours might have been the grandest of her adult life. From the moment she'd stepped inside the ballroom of Brentham Woods and a not so discreet hush fell on the guests, to the thrill of taking the floor with Tristan as the orchestra struck up the first waltz, to the dances that followed, something new and wondrous coursed through her veins: life, joy, love, hope, peace. The gifts of Advent and her blood fizzed with it. And with champagne. And laughter.

Tristan was a good host and handed her off to another partner after the waltz, and then another partner, but always he was waiting for her when the dance finished, his eyes shining. This is what her life would have been like had her mother not sickened, had their finances allowed for a London Season, had her father been able to pull the family situation back together again instead of giving into grief; what she might have reclaimed if Teddy's gamble had paid off. But she could not be angry over it tonight. People had limits. They did the best they could with who they were and what they had. It felt good to admit that, like a certain weight had been lifted from her.

The only blight on the evening was the late arrival of the Atwaters and the Bathursts. Tristan grimaced when Julien brought the news, finding them catching a breath of air at the garden fountain, which had candles floating in the basin. 'Of course they show up late and expect to be greeted as if they're royalty. May I desert you for a moment, El? Unless you'd like to come with me?'

'No, thank you,' she declined. The last thing she wanted was to encounter either of them. It would be impossible to escape their notice entirely but she'd put it off as long as she could and perhaps that notice would only be at a distance. There was no need to talk to them directly. 'I think I'll stay here and appreciate the fountain until you come back.' She trailed her hand in the water, gently pushing the floating candles about. She was already thinking of the supper waltz, which Tristan had claimed. It would be her next chance to be in his arms, to waltz about the ballroom as if she were flying. Tristan was a divine dancer. The way his hand…

'Miss Grisham, I thought I might find you here. Although I did not think I'd find *that*. It's rather too exquisite of a dress for a pauper, don't you think? Then again, money management has never been your family's strong suit.'

Elias Bathurst.

She'd know those snide tones anywhere. This was

the encounter she'd hoped to avoid by staying out here. 'Aren't you supposed to be with your uncle?'

'Not particularly. He's keeping the Lennox brothers busy so that I might have a word with you. I want to offer you a final chance, although you hardly deserve one after your treatment of me the other day.' Elias's smug look making it clear the need to go and greet them had been a ploy to draw Tristan away. The hairs on the back of her neck began to prickle in warning. If he'd arranged to get her alone, what did he want? He would not have gone to the effort for nothing.

Elias sat down beside her on the fountain's edge without permission and close enough to smell. He smelled stale, lacking the inviting freshness of Tristan's scent of winter spices. He was lacking a lot of what Tristan had—a certain élan in evening clothes, an engaging manner, the ability to put someone at ease instead of on alert. But he was not lacking in size. This close, she was reminded of how large Elias Bathurst was and it made her decidedly uncomfortable. She had the sense that he was using that size in an attempt to intimidate. She could stand up, but would that be like admitting to nerves?

'I am pleased to find you here, although surprised. Given your situation, I would have thought you'd be at home tonight. It's why we're late. We stopped at Hearts-ease first.'

A finger of fear ran down her spine, leaving her with a far different sensation than Tristan's fingers. He'd gone to her home, invaded her sanctuary. No doubt, he'd made an ass of himself in front of Mrs Thornton and Old Mackey. She hoped that was all he'd done. If he'd harmed them, or threatened them she'd…what? What could she do about any of it? For the first time since she'd left Atwater's bank she felt truly powerless.

'That groom has a bit of a mouth on him. We'll have to find a new one. Can't have that kind of behaviour in a servant.'

'We'll?' The fear finger took another stroke down her back.

'You deserve fine clothes like this dress,' Elias went on. 'I've come to make sure that's possible, that you aren't evicted from your home tomorrow. I know my uncle can be strict sometimes. I would save you from that. My offer of marriage is still good. Marry me and all will be well, your house saved, *you* saved. Perhaps now that you're truly staring poverty in the face, my offer will seem more reasonable.'

She stiffened. 'I've already declined, twice now, so you know my answer.' She didn't bother to dress it up with a polite refusal. She'd tried that already. Now she did stand, wanting to put distance between them. She knew from the past that he did not do refusal well, and she had no desire to cause trouble for the Lennoxes. If she must, she could run to the house. Surreptitiously, she gathered the folds of her gown in her hand, her body tensing to make a dash for it.

'I don't understand you, Miss Grisham. You would rather lose your home, auction its contents, and live in a drippy cottage than marry a man who could prevent all that from happening? Especially when you know I will get the house anyway. That's poor business on your part. You can't stop me. Why not join me? Save yourself misery.'

'I think that should be obvious,' she snapped. Where was Tristan? Surely, he should be back by now. 'You are a bully who coerces people. And I refuse to be coerced.' She gave him a cold look. 'As for misery, it seems I'd just be trading one misery for another married to you.'

He gave her a lascivious leer that swept the length of her. 'You have no choice, Miss Grisham. Why is that so hard to see?'

'Because I do have a choice. I can simply walk away and refuse to play your game.' At great cost. He was right about all of it. No matter what, he would get Heartsease, and her own heart broke at the knowledge of it. But he would not get her. It was the best she could do.

'Is that because you think Captain Lennox will offer you something better? He's been awful slow about it.' He sneered. 'Perhaps you've been thinking of auctioning yourself off to the highest bidder? You're running out of time for Captain Lennox to take the bait. Perhaps that's part of your gamble with your red dress. You think to entice him tonight, have him panting with lust for you so that he can't see straight so when the clock strikes midnight he doesn't even care that you turn into a very expensive pumpkin.'

'You disgust me.' She turned to go into the house. The fastest way to end a conversation was to leave it, but his meaty hand reached out and grabbed her arm, the roughness of his gesture tearing the delicate, dripping lace at her sleeve.

'Perhaps I should make the *no choice* part clear to you, Miss Grisham.' Dear Lord, if he thought to use force with her she'd be out of weapons. The only real weapon she had was her wit, and it would be nothing against the bear strength of a man.

'Perhaps you should unhand the lady.' Tristan's tones were firm and commanding as he stepped forward from the darkness.

Elanora let a sense of profound relief sweep her.

Chapter Twenty-One

Profound rage swept Tristan at the sight of Bathurst's hand on Elanora; the sagging bit of lace where it had been torn from the sleeve of her dress positively inflamed him. Never mind that there were at least three maids on hand who could easily sew it back on. Hell, he could probably do it himself. Regardless, Elias Bathurst had no business treating a woman that way. That rage was augmented by the dawning realisation that this was no chance meeting, that Bathurst had engineered this with his uncle so that he could meet with her alone.

To a man of his military background, such arrangements reeked of danger and conspiracy. People alone were people cornered, people without choices. All of his senses were on alert. What business did Bathurst think he had with Elanora?

'Good evening, Captain.' Elias's contempt was apparent. 'Miss Grisham and I were just having a friendly chat.'

'It didn't look that way to me. Miss Grisham, is that

true?' He turned his gaze in her direction and held out his arm to her in suggestion that she move to his side. He'd be able to protect her better there.

'No, it is not true.' Elanora's blue eyes were sapphire hard as she took the invitation and stepped towards him. She was trembling when he put his arm about her. Whatever Elias had said to her, it had upset her. 'Perhaps we might go inside?'

'In a moment.' Tristan didn't want to go inside. He wanted to get to the bottom of this.

'Tell him what we were doing out here, Miss Grisham. Tell him how you were turning down a marriage proposal at a very opportune time.' Elias gave a cruel laugh. 'I am willing to have her debt and all. Can you say the same?' His gaze shifted between them, perhaps noting the infinitesimal tightening of Tristan's hand at her waist in protection. 'Or perhaps you are so eager to play her protector because you already have? Had her, that is. I hope it was good because she's going to cost you.' Beside him, Elanora gave a gasp of chagrin.

Instinctively, Tristan stepped in front of her, blocking her from Elias's view. 'Your remark is beyond the pale,' he growled.

'What are you going to do about it?' And suddenly they might have been twelve again, defending the swimming hole from Elias's invasion. Elias took a menacing step towards Tristan and that was a mistake. A smart man never threatened a soldier unless he meant it. Out of reflex, out of the instinct to protect, Tristan shoved him hard in the chest, sending him straight into the fountain with a loud splash.

'How dare you!' Elias spluttered, struggling to get up, his evening clothes dripping wet. 'You attack a man for speaking the truth.' His eyes blazed.

'Tristan, let's go inside.' Elanora was insistent now, almost panicky, but Tristan stood his ground and refused to budge.

'He's slandered you, El. I will not go inside and ignore that.'

'It's only slander if it's a lie.' Elias climbed out of the fountain with a knowing nod. 'Can you explain to me, Captain, why a woman who is about to be dispossessed of her home tomorrow would turn down a marriage proposal to a man who would pay her mortgage? Because she cannot, and I admit to being perplexed.' He gave a harsh laugh. 'I see you didn't know. What a little sneak she is, hiding it from you until she had you on your knee.'

'Stop!' Elanora cried, stepping from behind him. 'Stop it!'

'Stop telling the truth? Hardly. Call off your dog,' Elias growled in her direction. 'The chit is bankrupt, Lennox. I expect there's more than one reason she's hot to get into your pockets.'

It took all his willpower not to shove Elias back into the fountain because he was mad and confused, and perhaps angry at more than just Elias. But a man learned restraint; a man learned to solve his problems without violence until all other options failed. Elias might be out of line but that did not give Tristan permission to make Elias the target of his emotions. 'El, let me take you inside,' he said through gritted teeth.

They skipped the ballroom, skirting the crowd and making for the library. He had to slow his pace twice to prevent Elanora from stumbling. But it was hard to walk when he wanted to run. The faster he could get to the library, the faster he could get answers. What he'd heard couldn't possibly be true. She would have told him if it was. Elias was just shooting off his mouth because his pride was damaged.

He shut the library door behind them and turned up a lamp. 'All right, El, tell me what's going on. What is that baboon rambling on about?' She was pale and stricken, trembling with more than upset over Elias Bathurst. It occurred to him in that moment that she trembled from the fear of having been discovered, of a terrible truth having been revealed. 'Dear God, it's true. You've mortgaged Heartsease?'

'Not me. Teddy. It was the only way to pay for the cargo. And now I cannot make the payments. Atwater and Schofield have no choice but to foreclose.'

Tristan sat down hard in the chair nearest the banked fire and raked a hand through his hair. Guilt kicked him hard, again. He should have come home. He should have stopped Teddy from taking such risks. He could have given Teddy the money and not made it a loan against the estate. The pieces were coming together for him. Elias thought to use the mortgage as leverage against her to coerce an advantageous marriage. He could not imagine a worse fate for Elanora, chained to that sycophantic idiot, paying for that mortgage the rest of her life in that man's bed. He'd seen the way Elias had looked at her tonight out by the fountain and it had made his skin crawl. El belonged with him and no one else.

'How much, El?' he asked with low-voiced insistence.

'Seven thousand pounds.' Her reply was a bare whisper. He gave a low whistle. That was definitely not pocket change. But he was already running through his accounts in his head. It would put a significant dent into his funds, but it could be done.

'What happens tomorrow, El?' he asked quietly, banking his own rage. It would not help matters.

'Heartsease becomes the bank's property and will eventually be auctioned.'

'At which point Elias will purchase it anyway,' Tristan surmised. 'This is why you weren't excited about the idea of the army's horses at Heartsease. You knew it would not be yours to give.' His hand clenched around the arm of the chair, anger surfacing despite his best attempts to restrain it. She'd warned him she'd not been financially faithful in her disclosures to him. But that wasn't where his anger was directed. 'Why didn't you tell me, El? That day when you showed me the ledgers you could have told me then.' And so many other times. She could have told him that first day he'd called on her instead of tossing him out.

'Because you would have tried to fix it.' She had not moved from the door, looking beautiful and shaken. He wanted to go to her so badly he hurt with it. He wanted to take her in his arms and do exactly that: fix it. Because he could.

'Damn right I would have fixed it,' he growled. 'We

could marry and put you beyond Elias's threats forever, beyond financial insolvency forever. You can put the past seven years behind you and start fresh if you would just let me help. If you would just let yourself be happy. Why do you have to be so stubborn?'

'This is not about being stubborn. It's about being realistic,' she snapped in dark tones. 'The past seven years taught me that everything I learned growing up was wrong. The past seven years have made me strong. Now I know there is no one to count on except yourself. Now I know that nothing lasts forever. Everything falls apart sooner or later. My parents should have been more honest with me instead of letting me believe in fairy tales.'

It was personal and the realisation cut deep. His love was not enough for her. 'El, I love you. Why will you not trust my love?' He rose and moved towards her. If he could touch her, hold her, perhaps it would somehow make a difference, remind her of what they'd shared.

'Haven't you been listening? Happiness, love, those are illusions. Love is the grandest illusion of them all.'

'Let me prove you wrong.' He was nearly there, but her hand was on the doorknob and he knew intuitively he would not reach her.

She delivered her last salvo as she opened the door. 'You can't. All men fail, Tristan.' She fled then and Tristan knew she would not stop running until she was home. He leaned his head against the doorjamb. Love, her love, was supposed to be enough to keep him here. He was ready to stay for her. Why wouldn't she accept that? Why couldn't she see that? Where had he gone wrong? What had he not offered? She did not want his money, nor his love. What else did he have to give? His anger surged. Perhaps it simply wasn't meant to be. Perhaps he needed to give her up for his own sake. He'd been shot down a few times now. Perhaps it wasn't the help she didn't want, but him.

Maybe it had never been right? The thought intruded cruelly. Maybe he'd been forcing it. Perhaps he ought to continue his travels, continue his search. If he couldn't have Elanora, there wasn't anything here to stay for. But how could that be? Especially when such a conclusion made no sense. Bodies didn't lie. Passion didn't lie and yet he had no answer for how such a beautiful night had gone so wrong.

How had such a beautiful night gone so wrong? She had Elias to blame for that. He'd blurted out her secret, the biggest one of them all. And for nothing more than petty revenge. It did not make her any more inclined to reconsider her position.

But you have another position to consider. Tristan can stand between you and disaster. Maybe he's right and you're being too stubborn.

But tonight she'd gone too far. She'd thrown his love back in his face, told him that it wasn't enough, that it could *never* be enough. That was her fault. She could only blame Bathurst for so much. There'd have been nothing to blurt if she'd been truthful with Tristan from the start and yet the urge to protect him from her, from the disaster of her life, had been too strong.

Elanora managed to get out of the red dress by herself. She could not have faced Mrs Thornton's questions and excitement over the ball only to disappoint her with what had happened, although she'd be glad to note that Elias Bathurst had received a dunking in the fountain. The cad had ripped her dress, her one special gift, and even though the tear was repairable something in her had broken. Was she never to have nice things? Never to be allowed precious moments? She fingered her mother's necklace before taking it off and laying it aside. Even if she knew such moments didn't last, they could be strung together like pearls, collected on a string and taken out for special occasions.

It was all she had left. Memories, moments. She was down to her last things now. A last night in her house, in the bedroom she'd grown up in, made love with Tristan in. In the morning she'd pack up her boxes. She'd probably make a few trips to the cottage. She wanted to be out of the house before dark, before Atwater sent his men. She would not give him the pleasure of escorting her from the premises even though it would mean leaving eight hours before she had to. That was when the tears came. She'd not let herself cry the entire week, but now there seemed no point in holding back, no reason for it. There was nothing to work for, nothing to hope for. She hugged the red gown to her and sobbed. Time had run out.

'Time for bed, brother.' Julien found him at half past four, a half-empty glass at his elbow in the library where Elanora had left him hours before.

Julien's cravat was undone and his jacket was slung

over a shoulder with content, weary elegance. He offered a wry smile. 'The last of the guests have gone
home. Mother has declared the event a success and gone
up to bed herself.'

Tristan tried to rouse an answering smile. 'Go ahead,
then. I don't think I'll sleep.' His body was willing,
certainly, but his mind was a buzzing hive of thoughts
and recriminations that chased each other around and
would not quiet. But from that noise no solution, no understanding, had yet emerged.

Julien moved to the chair across from him. 'I covered for you when Mother noticed both you and Elanora hadn't danced the supper waltz or come into the
midnight supper. I assumed the two of you had sneaked
off to make…peace. She looked stunning tonight, by
the way.'

Tristan gave a dry chuckle. 'She did.'

'*You* looked supremely happy with her,' Julien said.

'I was.' Dancing with her, laughing with her, had
been a splendid dream, a fantasy come to life to feel the
way he did when he was with her. But like all dreams,
it had ended.

Julien slouched in his chair and raised a brow. 'So
much past tense, brother. Has something gone amiss?
I take it she's not here with you.'

'She left before supper, if you must know.' That had
been nearly five hours ago. For a while he'd hoped she'd
only flee as far as the ballroom and after a bit come
back, but it was a far-fetched hope.

'Before or after Elias Bathurst helped himself to a
dunking in our fountain? I suspect you had something

to do with that.' Julien chuckled. 'I should have liked to see that. Since it was Elias, I assume there was a good reason for it. He was born a pain in the backside and has not improved with age.'

'He was bothering El.'

Julien nodded. 'And what bothers El bothers you, eh? I can see you're into short sentences at the moment, but perhaps you might enlighten me about what happened since this is not the outcome for the evening you were hoping for?' Julien leaned forward and reached for the half-empty glass. 'Do you mind? If you're not going to drink that.'

Tristan made a 'help yourself' gesture. 'There's a mortgage on Heartsease that is due today. If it goes unpaid the bank will foreclose and El won't let me do anything about it.' He'd been sitting here all night trying to square with that and couldn't.

'Teddy took out the loan, I assume? How much?'

'Seven thousand.' It was a lot but not insurmountable. His account could handle it thanks to the money he'd made with Julien's investments.

'Coupled with the other debts, that's nearly ten thousand pounds, a small fortune for most men and certainly beyond the means of most women.' Julien took a thoughtful swallow of the borrowed brandy. 'That's just to start, just to clear the slate. That's not including hiring staff and finishing whatever updates the estate needs.'

'She won't let me do it, won't let me gift her the money.' His fist came down on the upholstered arm of the chair. 'Damn it, Julien. What do you give a woman who doesn't want your money and doesn't trust your love?'

Julien's eyes were steady on him although he felt in that moment his brother had slipped off somewhere else. 'You give her a second chance and a third one if you need to. But you definitely do *not* give in to her way.'

Tristan stared for a moment. He'd not really expected an answer. In the depths of his own despair he'd seen the question as unanswerable. Perhaps there was more than money that went on in his brother's head, after all. 'Sounds like there might be a story in that response somewhere.'

Julien gave a shrug. 'There is, but it's not your story and that's what we're about right now. I want yours to have a happier ender than mine.' He gave a stern look. 'We were talking about Elanora. You must remember everything she's been through. She's lost everyone she's loved, and the life she was raised to believe in was built on unsustainable foundations, none of them based in truth. The people she loved failed her. Is it any surprise she's not hasty to put her trust or love in another when she'd been repaid poorly for those investments in the past?'

No, Tristan supposed, not when put that way. What had she said tonight? That love was an illusion? It was difficult to think of El as being afraid. She was the least fearful person he knew aside from Teddy. But she feared love, feared discovering she'd believed in it and it turned out to be something else: that it was pity's masquerade, an assuage to guilt, loyalty to another but not to her, that it was the fulfilment of an obligation, to name a few. There were other, worse things. It might be professed to cover things like greed and personal gain. Hadn't that been what those suitors were after in the early days following Teddy's death? Gain for themselves through pursuing her with false sentiment when in truth they'd been more interested in what she could give them instead of what they could give her.

Love should not be a trade, a negotiation. It should be unfettered, come with no strings attached. 'I know what I'd give her, what that second chance ought to be.' Not just for her but for him, too. The buzzing hive of thought in his mind was settling now.

Julien yawned. 'Can we go to bed now?'

'How about the bank instead?' He checked the mantel clock. He and Julien had talked a good while now. 'There's time for breakfast, a shave and change, time to get my paperwork in order. I want to be at the bank when it opens.' He had no time to waste there. There was much to do before banks and businesses closed for the Christmas break. It was time to give Elanora a Christmas to remember.

The bank had barely unlocked its doors when Tristan strode in, Julien at his back, both of them sharp eyed and clean-shaven as if they'd not been up all night hosting the party of the year. Tristan spotted Clifford Atwater at his desk by the window and felt a certain smug satisfaction at seeing the man shift nervously in his seat. As well he should. The man continued to sponsor his odious nephew in underhanded ways. How else would Elias have known about the mortgage if his uncle hadn't told him?

A clerk asked if he could help him. 'I would like to speak with Mr Schofield. I have urgent business.' But it was Atwater who answered, rising from his desk.

'Mr Schofield is engaged at the moment, but I am happy to assist.'

'No, thank you. This needs to be handled by a man of integrity.' Fortunately for Mr Atwater, there were no customers in the bank, but Tristan noted the clerks exchange sly smiles. One of them hurried off to Mr Schofield's office and it wasn't long before Mr Schofield, a kind-faced, mild-mannered man with sharp eyes, came out to greet them.

'You have business, Captain Lennox?'

'Yes, I come to pay the mortgage on Heartsease. I believe it is due today.' Tristan smiled pleasantly and pulled out his chequebook from an inner coat pocket, aware that Atwater was watching him. He could feel the man's gaze trying to burn holes through him with the power of his fury.

'That is splendid news, indeed.' Mr Schofield smiled but Mr Atwater was not finished.

'It is splendid, but only if we could accept it. It's not your name on the mortgage. You're not the one who owes,' he sputtered lamely.

Tristan faced him. 'No, the name on the mortgage is that of my dear friend Theodore Grisham, who has passed. He cannot physically pay the debt. I come in his stead, as his proxy, money in hand, and with thanks—' he turned back to Mr Schofield '—for the time given to

Miss Grisham to arrange her affairs. The total please, with interest. I want her balance wiped out today. Nothing is to carry over to the New Year and haunt her. And a receipt, so that she has proof her debt is paid.' He shot a look at Mr Atwater. 'I do not want her harassed.'

'I assure you, Captain Lennox, we are not in the business of harassing our clients or sharing their personal information.' Mr Schofield looked puzzled as he wrote out the receipt.

'Perhaps you'd best remind Mr Atwater of that.' Tristan tucked the receipt into his pocket. He had other stops to make.

It took the rest of the day. Not all the businesses were keen to discuss another's account and it was quite difficult to pay Elanora's remaining debt on those grounds. But between him and Julien, the Christmas spirit, and a show of money, they were able to be persuasive. By the time they left the town, businesses were pulling their shades and locking their doors, as people prepared to head home and celebrate Christmas Eve before joining the community at church at midnight to ring the bells and hear the Christmas story.

Julien parted with him at the fork in the road to return to Brentham Woods with his excuses. His parents would understand his lateness, and with luck, he and Elanora would join the family later. He thanked Julien for his help and spurred Vitalis towards Heartsease.

The rain started as he turned down the drive and Tristan shivered despite his greatcoat. It was going to be cold and, apparently, wet tonight. Miserable weather. Heartsease looked miserable, too. It was far darker than it had been the last time he'd been here. The fountain was silent and no light shone out the windows. *Deserted* was a word that came to mind. But he rather thought Elanora would be here until the last moment, loath to give up the house until she must, and there were still several hours before midnight.

Tristan swung off Vitalis and knocked on the door. When no one answered, he rattled the handle and called up to dark windows. No one came. There was a shuffling step on the gravel behind him and he turned to find Old Mackey with a lantern standing there. 'She's gone, Captain.' There was censure in Old Mackey's tone. He never called him Captain. 'She didn't want to be here when Atwater's men came to guard the place against trespassers. We'd all thought you might be the key to avoiding such measures.'

'I'm here to change that. Those men aren't coming,' Tristan nearly stammered. He hadn't felt so severely scolded since he and Teddy had been caught smoking cigars in the garden when they were eleven. It hadn't been the scolding that had been blistering. It had been seeing the disappointment in his father's eyes. Old Mackey was disappointed in him and that cut worse than any words.

Old Mackey looked him up and down as if he were assessing his value. 'You've left it rather late, haven't you?'

'Where has she gone so that I may tell her the news and bring her back?' Tristan refused to answer the question, refused to pass the blame to Elanora by saying he'd only heard about the mortgage last night, that he'd never been intended to know.

For a moment he thought Old Mackey wouldn't tell him. Fine. He'd ride the breadth of the county if need be even in this freezing rain. Then Old Mackey relented. 'She's up at an old cottage on the north corner of the estate just beyond the estate's boundaries. She's been hauling belongings all day.'

The north corner, the corner farthest from town, farthest from life. No, that would not do at all for his Elanora. He swung up on Vitalis, thanked Old Mackey, and set off into the freezing night. So far, this was not how he'd imagined his Christmas Eve going.

This was not how she'd ever imagined spending Christmas Eve: unpacking boxes in a three-room cottage and trying to catch the drips from the roof in every bucket she possessed. Elanora placed a pan beneath the latest leak. She'd spent more time moving boxes to drier places than actually unpacking anything.

Be thankful, she told herself. *At least you will start this new chapter out well with a fresh start.*

And she was grateful. The contents of Heartsease were hers. She could take what she wanted, furnish the cottage as she liked. She'd brought drapes and dishes, and bedding and food and table linens, her clothes, utensils. She'd even brought a rug or two. She'd brought what furniture would fit. Of course, anything she brought with her was something less she could sell to offset her bills. In that regard, there was a limit and she had refrained from bringing items that would fetch good prices. Still, it was a good start. But it was hard to be thankful when she was tired and cold and hungry and there was still so much to do.

She'd been out twice to check on Marian. At least her mare was comfortable. Her first project had been to make the little shed barn warm and safe for her horse. That had taken far longer than she'd thought and the journeys between the cottage and Heartsease had also taken a considerable portion of the day.

Elanora was just about to start on another box when there was a knock at the door. That frightened her. Who could it be? She was entirely alone out here and only Mrs Thompson and Old Mackey knew where she was. She would have to get used to it. She grabbed a skillet and approached the door. 'Who is it?'

'It's me, Tristan. Let me in, I'm soaking wet.'

She pulled the door open, concern overriding her surprise and perhaps even a bit of anger. He wasn't supposed to find her here, not yet. But here he was, water streaming from his hair because of course he'd ridden without a hat, his greatcoat sodden. 'What are you doing, you silly man? You'll catch your death out there.' She pulled him inside and firmly shut the door then opened it again. 'Did you ride? Where's Vitalis?' She couldn't have the horse freezing outside. She reached for her cloak beside the door. 'I'll go put him away.'

'I already did. He's in the shed with Marian.' Tristan stood dripping on her floor, his eyes moving about the cottage, no doubt taking in the chaos and disarray.

'Let's get you out of your coat. Come sit by the fire. That's one thing that's at least working.' She cleared the one chair of a stack of linen. 'Let me help you with your boots.'

'El, you'll have me undressed in no time,' Tristan teased.

'I'd rather have you naked than have you sick,' she scolded. Staying busy, even if it was divesting him of his garments, helped avoid the reality that he was here and he hadn't come on pleasure in this weather, on this day, when he could have been at home with his family eating hot food in a warm house with a roof that didn't leak from five different places, so it must be business. Important business? Or unfinished business? She'd not left things ideally last night.

When Tristan was settled beside the fire, divested of everything but his shirt and trousers, a blanket about his shoulders to protect against the droplets from his hair, she faced him with hands on hips. 'Well? Out with it. What brings you here on a night like tonight?'

He smiled. 'A night like tonight? How do you mean that, El? The holiest night of the year? A night of true love?'

She bit her lip, feeling cut down to size. 'I meant the weather. That sleet will turn to snow by midnight. It's cold, it's wet, and its dark. Not ideal conditions. I am surprised you risked Vitalis in this weather.'

'He's seen worse. It wasn't a risk for him and this couldn't wait. Now that I've seen this place, I am doubly glad I persisted in coming.' It wasn't said meanly. His gaze went to the frying pan she'd left on the table. 'What were you going to do with that?'

'Defend myself if need be.'

He nodded. 'Out here you probably will need to at some point. Alone. Far from neighbours, far from town. Help will not be readily available. The perfect place for a stubborn person.'

'Tristan,' she began but what was there to argue about? He was right. Here, away from everyone, she could not be an object of pity. Out of sight, out of mind—everyone's mind. She would get used to it. 'You shouldn't have come, Tristan. You don't belong here.'

He reached for her hand. 'El, neither do you.' He reached for his coat. 'I came because I have a Christmas gift for you and it could not wait.' He pulled an envelope from his coat pocket, his eyes locked on hers, their dark depths soft like morning cocoa. 'Before I give this to you, though, I want you to know it is a true gift. There are no strings attached. Nothing is required of you in return.' He reverently passed her the envelope. It was thick and official-feeling, the kind of folder businesses used.

She turned it over looking for markings and found none. It was blank. Tristan nodded. 'Go on, open it.'

Gingerly she undid the flap and pulled out the papers within. Receipts. Payments. She spread them one by one on the table amid the debris of moving. 'What is this?' An idea began to form in her mind even as she spoke the words out loud.

'Your freedom. Your freedom to choose how you want to live.' She heard the catch in his voice.

She picked up one of the slips and returned to stand by the fire, emotion overwhelming her. 'You paid my debts,' she said solemnly, the enormity of it still cresting over her like an enormous wave. 'And Heartsease. You've paid the mortgage.'

She could go home.

It was all she thought she'd ever wanted. She knelt before him. 'How did you do it, Tristan?' She had to know what the price of her freedom had been to him.

'With my chequebook. It was very simple, really. I walked into the bank...' he tried to joke.

She reached for his hand. 'No jokes, Tristan. You know what I am asking. How did you afford this? Because if you have put yourself in debt for me, I cannot accept this. I will not tolerate someone making such a sacrifice for me.'

His thumb rolled over her knuckles in its customary gesture. 'That's not fair, El. Why does your love allow you to make sacrifices but mine does not? Love is meant to be unconditional. It has to work both ways.' The smile he gave her nearly melted her. How was she to resist this? 'I figured it out, El. I was mad when you left Brentham Woods. I was mad you wouldn't let me help. I didn't understand it at first. It was so obvious to me. We love one another, you needed help and I could give it. But then I realised two things. First, that you believed taking help came with strings and that made love conditional, a commodity to be traded. Second, you were protecting me from myself.' He raised her hand to his lips and kissed it. 'I don't need to be protected, but I appreciate the gesture because it is a sign of your affection—albeit an annoying one. You don't need to marry me for the debts to be paid. I'm not Elias Bathurst or any of your other suitors.'

'Tristan, I don't know what to say except that you still haven't answered my question. How did you do it?'

'I have money, El, from Julien's investments. He made me a tidy sum while I was away.' He reached for another sheet of paper. 'This is for you as well. I understand paying the debts is only a start. You need staff to keep Heartsease viable. For that you'll need funds,' he explained as she scanned the paper.

'I've written to the army asking them for an allowance to train the horses at Heartsease. That allowance will go directly to you for the maintenance of the estate. Horses cost money as do their grooms.'

Independence. That was what she held in her hand. Heartsease would have an income. It would be protected— *more* than protected. It would be self-sufficient, as would she. 'You did this for me?'

'For you, El. Not for Teddy. Not out of obligation or pity. But because I love you. That does not change. Not ever.'

'And what of us, Tristan?'

'That is for you to decide. It took me a while to understand that offering marriage was making my conditions of resolving your situation contingent on accepting my offer. I do not want you to ever feel that way. I know that my life is not perfect. I will need to travel part of the year gathering horses, at least the first few years until the programme is established. I will be a man of means but only because that man earns a substantial income. I will likely not be a gentleman in the truest sense of the word.'

'Leisure doesn't suit you anyway.' Elanora smiled

up at him, wondering: *Was* there still a chance? Was that what he was telling her? Or had he given her independence because he was done with her? After all, she'd rebuffed him twice now and her words last night had been harsh.

And then she knew. This was a test. *Her* test. Was she ready to trust love when it was laid before her in its purest form? And what better night to take that test that Christmas Eve, the night when pure love came down to earth to live among imperfect love?

Tristan was waiting for her, the embodiment of that love. Patient. Kind. Keeping no tally of what was paid or owed to him. Simply giving. There was a verse her mother used to like about that. She summoned all of her courage. She interlaced her fingers through his and looked into his dark eyes, overwhelmed by what she saw there.

Christmas Future.

'Tristan, if it's up to me then, may I ask you something?' Her voice trembled. He might say no.

Trust his love.

A small smile curved at his mouth, his eyes steady. 'You can ask me anything, El. Always.'

'Would you consider doing me the honour of being my husband?'

The smile widened. 'Are you proposing to me, Elanora Grisham?'

'Absolutely.' She smiled, joy welling up in her heart. She'd never been more certain of anything than she was right now, right here, kneeling before this man asking for his hand. 'Are you accepting?'

He covered her hand with his other one. 'Yes, I am.'

She let the joy of that moment linger a little longer, holding his gaze, wanting to remember this forever.

'Now, I have something to ask you in return. Will you marry me *tomorrow*?'

Elanora nodded solemnly, leaning forward to kiss him with all the tenderness of a woman in love. 'Yes.'

She didn't want to wait. If happiness existed in moments she wanted those moments to start as soon as possible.

Outside had grown oddly quiet, the sounds of rain absent. Elanora rose and went to the window. 'Tristan, come look.'

He padded up behind her, barefoot, and wrapped his arms about her. 'What is it, El?'

'It's snowing.' She sighed and leaned against the warmth of his chest, his body. 'We won't get home tonight.' The trip to Heartsease would have to wait until morning.

'I *am* home,' Tristan whispered against her neck. 'I have all I need right here in my arms. And there's a bed in a corner. If you have some blankets I think we'll do just fine. Maybe a Christmas Eve honeymoon.' She liked the idea of that.

She turned in his arms, her own arms twining about his neck, her gaze drifting beyond his shoulder to the little cottage. How had she not seen it before? The drippy cottage now seemed cosy, lit by firelight and lit by something else, too. *Love light*.

The Christmas she'd dreaded had been transformed

into the best, the first of many yet to come. 'Thank you, Tristan,' she whispered against his mouth as he claimed her for a kiss. 'Thank you for being the captain who saved Christmas.'

He swept her up in his arms and carried her to bed, and somewhere in the distance, the church bells began to peal. Tomorrow they would wake to a world coated in white, a world wiped clean.

Epilogue

December 25, 1849

For Elanora Grisham-Lennox, the Christmas season was, without a doubt, the most wondrous time of the year, a time when the memories of happy Christmases past mingled with the joys of Christmas present. These days she welcomed the times when those memories pressed so near she could feel them as they brushed by, hear their whispers at her ear at a time of year when nothing was more precious than family and friends and love.

She hefted the basket filled with cyclamen a little more firmly against her hip as she made her way to the stables. Such efforts were more difficult than they had been a few months ago. But a few months ago she hadn't been seven months pregnant with their second child. As she recalled, everything was difficult the last two months of a pregnancy. Not that she minded. She was besotted with her two-year-old son, Alexander Theodore Lennox.

Elanora strode down the main stable aisle, horses' heads popping over the stall doors at the sound of her approach. After three years of seeing the Heartsease stable at full capacity once more, walking the aisles still made her smile, still brought her a certain contented joy. She stopped and set down her basket long enough to pet Marian and Aramis and feed them a Christmas treat of apple slices. She made her way to the large stall at the end, the birthing box, and studied the man and boy crouched down on the hay, two dark heads together, Tristan and Alex, the two men in her life. Tristan was whispering to Alex; the boy nodded solemnly, reverently. Everything his father said entranced Alex. As soon as he could walk, Alex had toddled after Tristan, and Tristan made a point of taking the boy everywhere.

'How's the foal doing?' Elanora asked in quiet tones so as not to disturb the mother and baby. The foal was a week old, having been born on Angel Sunday. It was an odd time of year for a foal to be born but the mother had been bred inappropriately, and Tristan had found her in poor circumstances on his spring-summer tour for the army, gathering new horses for the cavalry. Tristan had brought the pregnant mare home, not for the army but for Heartsease.

'Better than expected,' Tristan answered in a whisper. He smiled at her and reached up for her hand. 'How's the mother of my child doing?' He smiled at her and she forgot her aches and pains. 'I hope the festivities haven't proved too much for you.'

'When has Christmas ever been too much?' She smiled back and made her confession. 'I did take a small nap this afternoon.' As fun as Christmas was, she *was* tired. There'd been the Lennox Christmas ball two nights ago, the panto here three nights ago, and the Christmas Eve open house at Heartsease for all the tenants last night before midnight service. This morning she and Tristan and Alex had taken the buckboard out filled with Christmas basket deliveries. Tristan's parents would be over for supper in a short while. It had indeed been a whirlwind of festivities and fun.

Tristan squeezed her hand. 'I just don't want you overdoing.' He rose and dusted the straw off his work breeches. 'Let me carry that basket. Alex, come on, son. We've got one more Christmas visit to make.'

They walked slowly towards the Grisham cemetery. Elanora wasn't sure if the slow pace was for her waddling benefit or Alex's short steps. Either way, she thought it was a lovely walk with her family on a cold, crisp winter day. There was no snow today like there had been on Christmas Day three years ago.

'Are we going to see Uncle Teddy?' Alex asked as they passed through the wrought iron cemetery gate.

'Yes, we are, my darling.' Elanora gave a bouquet of cyclamen to Alex. 'Would you like to put flowers on the headstones?' Tristan was already clearing away the flowers from last week. They'd made a ritual of laying cyclamen at the graves each Sunday in Advent and on Christmas Day, a tradition they'd started on their wedding day.

Tristan came to her and wrapped his arms about her, his hands resting on her rather prominent belly as they watched Alex move from headstone to headstone.

Even Teddy had a headstone these days. Tristan had seen to it for the anniversary of Teddy's passing. 'I've not forgotten today is also our wedding anniversary,' he whispered at her ear. 'The day I became the happiest man alive.'

She turned in his arms, a hand stroking his jaw. 'Truly, Tristan? You don't regret it? I still feel like I got the better end of the bargain.' She did not doubt Tristan loved her and she was in awe of that love every morning she woke up beside him and every night when they climbed the stairs to bed together. 'You gave up so much.'

Tristan laughed, his laughter a trail of mist in the cold air. 'What did I give up? I get to travel a few months every year, and sometimes, my wife even comes with me.' She had gone with him that first year and visited Vienna while he'd held meetings with the Viennese Riding School. She'd enjoyed it but she'd missed Hemsford. Still, it had been worth it to be with Tristan and experience part of his world. It had been amazing to watch him converse with others in German and French as easily as he conversed in English. She'd come home from the trip feeling that she knew her husband better than ever and that they were closer than ever. And of course, she'd come home pregnant with Alex. The following year she'd stayed home with their new son and she would not go with him this year on account of the new baby. But Tristan was already planning for the year after next when he'd take his whole family with him to Andalusia.

Tristan kissed her hand. 'The rest of the year, I work

horses with my wife, run the estate with my wife, ride to the hunt with my family, and play with my son. What more could a man ask for except another child to spoil, and you've already given me that.' He smiled. 'When I think of who got the better bargain, it's definitely me.'

Alex walked over. 'All the flowers are out, Mama.' He held his arms up, wanting to be picked up.

'What did you talk with Uncle Teddy about?' Tristan swung the boy up onto his shoulders for the walk back to the house.

'I told him Aramis threw a shoe this week. He likes to hear about Aramis. I told him you let me ride Aramis after his shoe got fixed.' Riding had consisted of leading Alex around with Aramis on a lead rope and Elanora walking beside him. Aramis might be an aging horse, but he still had plenty of energy. 'I think Uncle Teddy likes to know I ride Aramis,' their talkative son concluded as the house came into view.

'Grandfather and Grandmother are here! And Uncle Julie, too!' Alex squealed at the sight of the coach in the drive. Tristan let him down to run towards his grandparents.

'It's like he hasn't seen them since yesterday.' Tristan slipped an arm about her as they laughed at their son's happiness. The Lennoxes were once again a daily fixture at Heartsease. Tristan's father was here more days than not to discuss horses, and his mother enjoyed coming over to work in the glasshouse and talk flowers with Elanora and fuss over her grandson. Julien was over in the evenings to taste test cognac with Tristan, or so he said. Elanora knew it was really just an excuse to spend time with his brother. She'd made it plain Julien didn't need a business reason to visit, but Julien being Julien...

They watched Julien pick up the little boy. 'Your brother needs a child of his own, Tristan. I think this is the year we find Julien a bride.'

Tristan chuckled. 'Well, I wish you good luck with that,' he murmured under his breath.

'Wish her good luck with what?' Julien grinned as they approached.

'To see you married by Christmas, brother.' Tristan clapped him on the back.

'Why Christmas?' Julien split his gaze between the two of them.

Elanora stretched up on her tiptoes to give his cheek a sisterly kiss. But it was on Tristan that her gaze rested.

'Because, dear brother-in-law, don't you know Christmas is the most wonderful time of year?'

* * * * *

Get 3 FREE REWARDS!

We'll send you 2 FREE Books plus a FREE Mystery Gift.

FREE
Value Over
$20

Both the **Harlequin®** Historical and **Harlequin®** Romance series feature compelling novels filled with emotion and simmering romance.

Get 3 FREE REWARDS!

We'll send you 2 FREE Books plus a FREE Mystery Gift.

FREE Value Over **$20**

Both the **Harlequin® Desire** and **Harlequin Presents®** series feature compelling novels filled with passion, sensuality and intriguing scandals.

HARLEQUIN
PLUS

Try the best multimedia subscription service for romance readers like you!

Read, Watch and Play.

Experience the easiest way to get the romance content you crave.

Start your **FREE TRIAL** at
www.harlequinplus.com/freetrial.